Lorraine Mace is the critically acclaimed author of the D.I. Sterling thrillers. *Love Me Tender* is the fifth instalment in this dark and gritty series. In addition, she is the humour columnist for *Writing Magazine*, Deputy Editor of *Words with JAM* and the head judge at *Writers' Forum*. Lorraine lives in the warmer and sunnier clime of Southern Spain.

Praise for Lorraine Mace:

'Her assured and fluid writing style truly brings characters and scenes to life on the page' **Rachel Abbott**

'Gritty, topical, sometimes lacerating, but always enthralling. A truly compulsive read' **Abbie Frost**

'D.I. Paolo Sterling is instantly engaging – *Children in Chains* is a dark, gripping and unflinching read' **Louise Phillips**

'Gripping, fast-paced' **Sheila Bugler**

'Delve into the dark side. Well-constructed with unflinching plots. Satisfying enough for the most discerning crime reader' **Ruth Dugdall**

'Fast-paced and compulsive reading with tension ratcheted to the max. D.I. Paolo Sterling's humanity is tested by gut-wrenching crimes and damaged killers' **Chris Curran**

'A visceral, no-punches-pulled, gut-wrenching thriller . . . Crime Noir at its darkest' **Caroline Dunford**

'From page one the reader is parachuted into the epicentre of calculated, sinister murder. The pace is unrelenting as Mace presses on, hot ~~on the heels of the enigmatic D.I. Sterling~~' **Anna Legat**

By Lorraine Mace and available from Headline Accent

The D.I. Sterling series

Retriever of Souls
Children in Chains
Injections of Insanity
Rage and Retribution
Love Me Tender

LORRAINE MACE

LOVE ME TENDER

ACCENT

First published in 2021 by Headline Accent
An imprint of HEADLINE PUBLISHING GROUP

1

Cataloguing in Publication Data is available from the British Library

ISBN 978 1 7861 5978 6

Typeset in 10.5/13pt Bembo Std by Jouve (UK), Milton Keynes

Printed and bound in Great Britain by Clays Ltd, Elcograf S.p.A.

Headline's policy is to use papers that are natural, renewable and recyclable
products and made from wood grown in well-managed forests and other
controlled sources. The logging and manufacturing processes are expected
to conform to the environmental regulations of the country of origin.

HEADLINE PUBLISHING GROUP
An Hachette UK Company
Carmelite House
50 Victoria Embankment
London EC4Y 0DZ

www.headline.co.uk
www.hachette.co.uk

For Chris, thank you for always being there

Chapter One

Where was it? Where had Grandpa hidden it? From the moment the bastard had stopped breathing, Boy had been searching. He'd already spent hours turning Grandpa's room inside out, but he wasn't ready to give up. It would be here somewhere, he knew it. The old man would never have thrown it away. He stood in the middle of the bedroom, shifting his weight from one side to the other, the floorboards creaking in protest. A waft of sickly-sweet odours assailed his nostrils, reminding him he didn't have long before the undertakers would arrive. Funny to think the people Grandpa had employed and abused would now be responsible for sending him off. The old bastard had made their lives hell while he'd been alive. Now was their opportunity for payback and he wouldn't blame them if they took it.

Boy glared at Grandpa's corpse, lying in comfortable state on the bed.

'Where did you put the box?' he hissed. 'I know you would never have chucked it out.'

The stench made him gag; he wished he'd turned the heating off in this room, but he couldn't give up the search – not until he'd found it. The box would be in here somewhere. Maybe the wardrobe had a false back, he thought, turning towards it. As he spun, the rug caught his heel and he fell, tumbling down in a heap. Just as well the old man was dead, otherwise he would have had to listen to another of Grandpa's lectures on how fucking useless he was.

He pulled himself upright and then reached down to straighten the rug. That's when he knew he'd hit the jackpot. The floorboards didn't quite meet as they should. He put his fingers into a well-worn groove and lifted out a loose section of wood. As he'd suspected, Grandpa had been hiding money away from the taxman. A large cashbox took up most of the space and Boy knew just where to find the key to it, but money wasn't the prize he wanted.

Hands shaking, he pulled out the Tupperware sitting next to the cashbox. The plastic container was empty, but still stained with her blood. This was it – his holy grail.

Boy sat cross-legged next to the bed, no longer bothered by the smell, and hugged the container, allowing his memories to flow.

He'd just turned fourteen when Grandpa had brought Grammy's heart home in this box.

Chapter Two

Paolo's computer pinged. He glanced over and saw he'd finally received an email from his daughter. *Wow – it's about time! Well done, Dad! Very busy here. Will send more news soon. Lots and lots of love, Katy.*

He sighed for the newsy email he knew would never arrive. Since she'd left to go overseas as a volunteer, her life had revolved around the people she was there to help. That was the way it should be, he knew that, but it didn't stop him missing her.

At least she was excited for him, which was more than he was. The notification had been on his desk for days and he had yet to feel anything. He'd hoped sharing the news with Katy would stir up some emotion. For possibly the hundredth time, he picked up the official notice and read the details of his promotion. No longer Detective Inspector; the page confirmed he was, as of last Friday, Detective *Chief* Inspector Paolo Sterling. He'd never been ambitious and would have been happy to stay as a DI, but life moved on. If Dave had been around he'd have insisted on going out to celebrate. But Detective Sergeant Dave Johnson wasn't here – would never again be sitting opposite Paolo, laughing with him, often at him. Would never again suggest Paolo needed to improve his social life. He was gone for good.

Almost as if he'd conjured him into being, the person Paolo blamed most for Dave's death – other than himself – pushed his office door open and barged in without knocking. Detective Sergeant Jack Cummings had the habitual scowl plastered on his face. The man must practise in front of a mirror to have mastered that pissed-off look, Paolo thought.

3

'I sat out all night with DC Ferguson and we didn't even spot a cockroach on the move,' Jack said. 'Seems that club might be clean after all.'

'One night of surveillance with nothing happening doesn't mean it's clean. You should know that, Jack.'

'You want us watching again tonight, sir?'

The 'sir' was tinged with bitterness and sarcasm, matching Jack's sour expression.

'Yes, Jack. Tonight, tomorrow, and every night until something occurs we can act on. The information we received came from a reliable source. That club is being used as a front for drug dealing and at some point they are going to bring in new supplies. We need to be there when it happens. Any other questions?'

Jack shook his head.

'Good. Go home and get some sleep. I want you back outside before the place opens tonight.'

Jack edged out without a word. He must know I despise him, Paolo thought. If it hadn't been for his shit-stirring, Dave would still be here. How does he live with himself? But Paolo knew the answer to that. Jack didn't see anything wrong in what he'd done. In his mind, Dave had been given preferential treatment because his uncle was the Chief Constable. Reality hadn't been allowed to get in the way of perception. Dave had gone all out trying to prove his worth to Jack who would never have accepted him at face value, no matter what he did, and had died as a result.

Paolo thought back six months. He'd been determined to get rid of Jack then, but had been stymied by the Chief asking Paolo to take the bastard under his wing. Well, Paolo felt he'd bided his time for long enough. It was time to put Jack Cummings in for a transfer.

His musings were interrupted by a tap on his door. Even before he looked up, he knew it wouldn't be Jack. He never bothered to knock.

Detective Sergeant Cathy Connors looked in. For the last few months her hair had been a subdued shade of red. Paolo had much preferred it when she'd come into the office with outrageous colours standing up in spikes, but word from above had put a stop to that.

She smiled. 'Got a minute, sir?'

'For you, CC, of course. Come in. Take a seat. What can I do for you?'

'It's more what we want to do for you, sir. The lads and I feel we should do something to mark your promotion.'

Paolo shook his head, but CC ignored him.

'Sir, you've hidden yourself away since . . . since . . .' She shrugged and swallowed. 'Since we lost Dave you've been working flat out, all the hours God sends, seven days a week. Carry on at that rate and you'll wipe yourself out. If you don't want to do it for yourself, do it for us. We need a reason to go out and have a good time and we've decided your promotion is it.'

Paolo couldn't imagine a night out without Dave egging him on to relax and enjoy himself. Still, CC was right.

'Okay,' he said. 'What did you have in mind?'

She grinned. 'What I have in mind would never do for you, sir.'

He laughed. 'I'm sure about that. Take a pew and tell me what you think *would* do for me,' he said, pointing to the chair opposite his desk.

CC sat down, glancing out towards the main office as she did so. 'We need to include everyone, sir.'

Paolo grimaced. 'Have I made it that obvious?'

She shook her head. 'Only to me, but the others know what happened and have guessed how you must feel.'

'Damn,' he said. 'I should've been able to keep my feelings to myself.'

CC smiled. 'Not your strongest attribute, sir. But don't worry, most of them out there dislike Jack because he's a first-class prick. Nothing to do with you at all.'

'DS Connors, consider yourself reprimanded. That is no way to refer to a fellow officer.'

'Yes, sir. Right you are, sir.' She winked. 'Now that you've told me off, can we get back to the important topic of celebrating your promotion?'

He nodded.

'We know how much you love Italian food, so thought we'd take

5

over that restaurant near the hospital. I've spoken to the owner and he is more than happy to close the place to other customers for a night. What do you think?'

The quiet voice in his head said *I need to keep my real thoughts to myself*, but he forced out a smile.

'Sounds good to me,' he said, but the memories of the great times he'd spent there with Jessica screamed out that was the last place he would ever want to go for a celebration. After she'd taken the position in Canada their contact had gradually dwindled to an occasional email. Eventually, they'd both decided the long-distance romance wasn't working. He sighed. That relationship was now in the past. It was probably time to let go of those memories.

'I think we should set it up for the last Friday this month. It's easier to enjoy ourselves when we've just been paid.'

Paolo was relieved. That gave him just over two weeks before he needed to put on a smiley face and pretend to have a good time.

'Right, that's settled,' he said. 'I'll leave it to you to book everything. Now we need to get back to work. Okay?'

CC nodded. 'The day shift are watching The Pipe, but I doubt anything will go down in daylight, sir. Once the Chief gave that press conference and announced his intention of shutting down the clubs known to be involved in drug dealing, the people at The Pipe must have realised they were being watched. I can't help feeling it would have been better to keep quiet and let us get on with the job without alerting the dealers.'

Paolo sighed. 'Probably, but the Chief was dealing with political pressure. It's always the way, you know that. A kid dead from a drug overdose isn't news, but the daughter of an MP dead from a drug overdose makes the front page. Sally Mendip's death forced the Chief's hand. George Mendip is spouting off in the press that we aren't doing enough to protect innocent victims, so the Chief felt he had to prove we were on the job.'

CC snorted. 'Innocent victim? Is he not aware his daughter was a known user and might even have been a dealer herself?'

Paolo shook his head. 'No parent who's lost a child, no matter what

6

the circumstances, sees them in any light other than the best. We know she was dealing, but on autopsy Dr Royston wasn't able to determine if her overdose was accidental or deliberate. We can't even be sure she wasn't murdered. All we know is that The Pipe seems to be at the centre of the bad drugs flooding our streets. I understand George Mendip's need to rage and want answers, but Sally isn't our only victim. We've lost too many young people in the last few months and I can't let his grief affect the way we conduct this investigation.'

Chapter Three

The moment the undertakers took Grandpa's body away, Boy retrieved the plastic box from inside the wardrobe, where he'd hidden it when the doorbell rang.

He opened it and sniffed, but any smell that had been in there was long gone. It was funny, he thought, considering what he'd been forced to do, but the delicious aroma of hearts slowly braising for hours still gave him comfort, even now. Other than the scent of roses Grandpa bought her each week, braised hearts was the smell he associated most with Grammy. It was Grandpa's favourite meal. She'd been cooking them the day Grandpa had brought Boy home from the hospital after the accident.

Just a few days short of his eighth birthday, he'd stumbled into her kitchen, numb with grief. He'd never been in the house before, but Grammy equalled love, that he knew for sure. Whenever she'd sneaked out to visit them, his dad had always begged her to leave Grandpa and move into their home.

'You poor baby,' she'd crooned, opening her arms and drawing him into the warmest embrace he'd ever experienced. Even his mother, who'd loved him to bits, hadn't held him as tightly as Grammy did that day.

'Let the boy go,' Grandpa ordered. 'You'll make him as soft as his dim-witted father.'

She'd gripped him even harder. 'Ah, George, can't you see the boy needs comfort? He's lost both parents. We're all he has.'

'Better for him that they're dead. His father was a weakling and his mother pure trash.'

He'd pushed away from Grammy without thinking and faced Grandpa, rage filling his skinny frame. 'Don't you dare be mean about my mum and dad,' he'd yelled.

Almost before the words had left his lips, Grandpa's hands snaked out and gripped his throat, lifting him clear off the floor and shoving his back up against the cold wall tiles.

'George, please don't,' Grammy begged. 'He's just a child.'

'Shut your mouth, woman. You know better than to interfere. The boy has to learn.'

Feet dangling in mid-air and his throat on fire, he'd tried to speak, but only croaking sounds came out.

Grandpa leaned forward, pushing his face up close.

'Listen to me, boy. You are going to live here from now on. What I say is law. Your father was weak or he would never have taken up with that bitch on heat.' He grinned. 'Answer me back just one more time, boy, and you will disappear faster than you arrived here. Do you know what I do for a living?'

He couldn't have spoken even if he'd known what to say, but Grandpa hadn't waited for an answer.

'I bury people. I put them in coffins deep underground and they never come up again. Sometimes, though, I burn them. They go into a furnace so hot they come out the other side as a pile of ashes. You step out of line just once, boy, and I'll put you into one of those coffins with one of my dead customers and you'll end up six feet underground, cuddling up to a corpse until you run out of breath, or you'll burn in agony and turn into a pile of ash. Got it?'

The expression on his face must have been answer enough because Grandpa let go of his throat and he'd slid down the wall and collapsed on the kitchen floor.

'I'm going up to change. You'd better have stopped the boy from snivelling and have my tea on the table by the time I come down again.'

With every nerve in his body stretched to breaking point, he'd watched Grandpa's black-clad figure leave the room. That was the first and last time he'd spoken out during the years Grammy was alive.

For six years he'd tried not to anger Grandpa. At times he'd come close to making him mad enough to carry out his threat, but Grammy had always pleaded for Boy's life and Grandpa had given in. The only person Grandpa loved was Grammy. He'd told her every day that no one would ever love her as much as he did and if she even thought about another man, he'd know. Whenever she'd upset him, even when she'd been so stupid he'd had to strangle her and lock her in the special punishment room in the cellar, the next day he'd bring her a posy of roses to show she'd been forgiven.

Grammy smiled most of the time, but Boy sometimes heard her crying after Grandpa left for the funeral parlour. The only time he had been brave enough to ask what was wrong was when he'd found her pulling the petals off one of the roses from the last posy Grandpa had given her.

'He loves me; he loves me not.'

'Grammy, what are you doing? Why are you crying?'

She hadn't answered straight away. She put the flower down and wiped her eyes before brushing the petals from her lap onto the floor.

'Would you like one of my special sweets?' she asked.

Boy nodded and took one. It was the first time she'd ever offered him one of her love heart sweets. After a while, she smiled.

'You know how Grandpa gets cross with me?'

Boy nodded.

'It's because I'm stupid sometimes. I get things wrong, even though I try really hard to do exactly as Grandpa has taught me.'

'But he . . . he . . .' Boy stopped, unable to put into words what he thought about Grammy and Grandpa.

She pulled him close. 'You've seen how he gets angry with me and has to teach me a lesson, but what you don't see is how much he loves me. If I could only learn to be less stupid he'd never put his hands round my throat ever again. He only does it because I get things wrong. It's all my fault. You know that, don't you?'

10

Boy didn't know any such thing, but it felt so good to be held by Grammy he didn't want to say the wrong thing and get pushed away. He nodded.

Grammy sighed. 'No one is loved as much as I am. Even after I've been stupid and needed to be chastised, Grandpa still brings me flowers to show I've been forgiven.'

Boy realised he had no idea about love, but if that's what Grammy said then it had to be true. She'd never lie to him.

She let him go and stood up. 'I'd better clear up these petals before Grandpa comes for his lunch. You know how he hates an untidy home.'

Boy watched as Grammy opened the cupboard and took out an old biscuit box. She opened it and the scent of decaying roses briefly wafted from the tin. She picked up the petals and placed them gently inside.

'Don't tell Grandpa you heard me cry,' Grammy begged as she closed the tin.

No fear of that. He shuddered even at the thought of saying anything to Grandpa without being spoken to first.

He hadn't been strong enough to do that until the day after Grammy died when Grandpa arrived home early and put the Tupperware box on the kitchen table.

Boy hadn't realised at first what it was.

'I'm going back to the parlour. I want that stuffed and cooked for when I get home.'

'I've only watched Grammy cooking lamb's hearts. I've never done it myself.'

Grandpa smiled and pointed to the box. 'That isn't a lamb's heart, boy. It's Grammy's. You can cook it, but I'll be the only one eating it. She's always belonged to me and me alone.'

All the rage Boy had felt for the past six years raced to the surface.

'No! I won't do it!'

He had more to say, but never got the chance to speak. Once again Grandpa's hands circled his throat and squeezed.

'Want to go into the furnace with her, do you? There's room enough in her coffin for a scrawny little shit like you.'

Boy felt the blackness coming and fought against passing out, terrified if he did he'd wake up in Grammy's coffin. Grandpa loosened his grip and blessed air flowed back into Boy's lungs.

'You followed her around the kitchen like a baby girl enough times to know how it's done. You cook it right or you go into the flames with her.'

Grandpa released him and walked out of the kitchen. He didn't say anything else. He didn't need to. As Boy heard the front door slam, he knew he would do as Grandpa had ordered because there was no alternative.

He lifted the heart carefully from the box and placed it on the special board Grammy had kept for the lamb's hearts. She'd stressed she'd had to be gentle because the skin could so easily split.

Picking up the extra-sharp scissors she always used, Boy carefully cut away the tubes. Then he slid his fingers inside to clean it out the way he'd seen Grammy do so many times and something amazing happened. It felt like putting on the softest glove imaginable. Grammy's heart was caressing him, telling him she cared. It felt so right, he didn't want to take his hand out. He moved his fingers gently, feeling Grammy's love seep into him.

Boy wasn't alone any more. Grammy's blood flowed around his fingers. Tenderly, oh so tenderly, he slid his hand out and felt a loss greater even than when his parents had died. Tears streaming down his face, he moved his hand back into the heart. The sides closed round his fingers and held them. He wanted to stay like this for ever, safe within Grammy's love.

Eventually, the fear of Grandpa's rage overruled his needs and he removed his fingers for the final time. As he stumbled around the kitchen, gathering the ingredients for Grammy's stuffing recipe, he promised himself that one day he would find someone who loved him. Someone who loved him enough to give him her heart when she died.

★

12

Boy wiped away the tears his memories had brought and stroked the box. He glanced at the clock on the wall opposite and couldn't believe how much time had passed since he'd sat down. It was already half past five. The undertakers had left with Grandpa's body over an hour ago. Boy stood up and put the box on Grandpa's bed. There were things he needed to do before he went back to work. One of them was to bury the box in the garden in Grammy's rose bed. Grandpa had kept it because he couldn't bear to let her go – Boy was going to set her free.

'Grammy, I hope you'll understand. I hated you for dying. You'd loved me and kept me safe during those early years, but after you died, he took his pain out on me. I thought *he* was going to live for ever, like the monsters in the books you used to read to me. But he's gone now; I can finally start looking for a love of my own to bring home.'

Chapter Four

Saturday morning – two weeks later

Paolo lifted his head and felt the pounding of at least fifty construction workers all wielding jackhammers. Why, oh why, had he had so much to drink last night? Water, that would help, but that meant getting out of bed and he didn't think he was capable of standing upright just yet.

The last time he'd had as much to drink was when he'd seen Jessica off at the airport. That night he'd drunk himself into oblivion and woke up feeling so bad he'd not touched a drop since.

He wasn't really a drinker at the best of times, preferring instead to enjoy a soda or coffee while everyone else was downing alcohol. Last night, something inside had finally broken through and he'd needed to get drunk to drown out the voices in his head reminding him of the people he'd loved and lost. His mother, his eldest daughter, and Dave were all dead, never coming back; he had to find a way to accept those losses.

Deciding that was enough self-pity for a Saturday morning, Paolo tried again to move his head. As he shifted position he was convinced he could feel his brain sloshing in fluid. Nausea struck and he hurled himself from the bed, lurching into the bathroom. By the time he came out again, nearly twenty minutes later, he felt slightly more human and in desperate need of coffee.

While waiting for the water to boil for the cafetiere, he smiled as he recalled the antics of his team in the restaurant. Why did cop celebrations always end up featuring furry handcuffs and suggestive truncheons? But CC had been right – the team needed a reason to celebrate. Not only were they too struggling to come to terms with Dave's loss, but the lack of progress in their latest case was bringing down morale.

Two weeks of day and night surveillance had achieved precisely nothing, apart from giving Jack another reason to gripe about his part in it. The only thing the surveillance had confirmed was that the bouncer was selective in who he let in and who he kept out. Any attractive, or even passable, female went through the doors without being bothered by the muscle-bound heavy, but he was far more choosey when it came to the male of the species.

Paolo looked down at his tracksuit bottoms and scruffy tee-shirt and smiled. Even dressed in better clothes, he doubted he would make it into the club without showing his badge first.

He downed his second cup of coffee and felt better able to face the day. A shower would do him the world of good, he decided. After that, he'd head into the office. CC's words resounded in his head, telling him he shouldn't be working seven days a week, but what was the alternative? Stay home and watch *Saturday Kitchen*?

As he headed back towards the bathroom he heard the faint tones of his mobile. Cursing, he searched for it among the clothes he'd scattered across the floor last night as he'd staggered to bed in his drunken stupor. Finally, unearthing the phone from under the bed where he must have kicked it, he looked at the name displayed on the face. Could he cope with his ex-wife the way he felt right now?

He was saved from having to make that decision when the ring tone abruptly ended. Not that he had a problem with Lydia. Far from it. They'd somehow managed to forge a friendship out of what had promised to be an acrimonious divorce, but he just wasn't in the mood to chat to anyone this morning. He promised himself he'd call her back later.

Halfway to the bathroom, his landline rang. Moving back into the bedroom, he wondered if he'd ever get the shower he wanted so badly. He snatched up the receiver and sat on the bed.

'Sterling.'

'Paolo? Why aren't you answering your mobile? I've been calling you.'

Her voice hit all the wrong notes for his fragile brain and his voice came out more sharply than he intended.

'I tried, Lydia, but you rang off too quickly.'

'Okay, sorry, don't bite my head off. I only called to congratulate you on your promotion. Mind you, it would have been nice if you'd told me about it. I only found out because I got an email from Katy yesterday.'

'Lucky you,' Paolo said, deliberately ignoring Lydia's dig about not telling her he'd been promoted. 'I haven't heard from her for a couple of weeks. She okay?'

'She seems to be, but I wish she'd come home. I hate the idea of her running around Africa without us there to keep her safe.'

Paolo felt the same way, but had no intention of enlarging on the theme. Katy was doing what she needed to do and they just had to put up with it.

'Anyway, thanks for the call, but I need to get to the office. Can I catch up with you later?'

'Oh, you have to work today? I was kind of hoping we could meet for a coffee this morning.'

There was something in her voice that told him she wasn't suggesting meeting up just for a social chat.

'Have you got a problem, Lydia? Something you need my help with?'

She laughed. 'I never get anything past you. There is something, but it's not for me. One of the girls I work with thinks she's being stalked. I thought maybe you could give me some advice to pass on to her.'

'I doubt I could improve on whatever you've already told her, but yeah, we could meet in town. Where did you have in mind?'

There was silence at the other end of the phone.

'Lydia, you still there or am I talking to myself?'

She laughed. 'I'm here. I was just thinking about where we could talk without being overheard. Everywhere is crowded on a Saturday morning. What about you coming over here? I could put together some bacon and eggs if you'd like.'

Paolo's queasy stomach did a somersault at the thought of a cooked breakfast.

'Just coffee and maybe some toast will be fine. Give me time to shower and get dressed and I'll be with you as soon as I can.'

Three-quarters of an hour later Paolo, feeling better than he'd believed possible when he woke up, was ringing the doorbell at Lydia's. When she opened the door, he was reminded once again why he'd fallen in love with her all those years ago. Her smile still had the power to wrench his heart and tie his tongue in knots.

'Come in,' she said, standing back so that he could pass. 'Coffee's ready. Grab yourself a cup while I get the toast sorted. Marmalade okay? I'm out of jam. I don't keep half the supplies I used to when Katy was living here.'

He headed for the smell of freshly made nectar, poured a cup and took it over to the table. As he pulled out a chair, he studied Lydia's face. She looked more serious than he'd expected from the way she'd sounded earlier.

'Something happen since we spoke?'

The toaster pinged and Lydia turned to grab the slices as they popped up.

'Yes, Sasha just called me. How did you guess?'

'The expression on your face gave it away. I take it Sasha is the girl you're so worried about?'

She slid the toast rack towards him and put the butter and marmalade in easy reach before sitting down opposite.

'Yes, she's the one. She went out last night to meet up with some of her friends at one of the local clubs they go to a lot and said she had a feeling while she was waiting to go in that someone was staring at her. She told her friends, when she found them inside, but they wouldn't take her seriously.'

'Why not?'

17

Lydia smiled. 'They were probably halfway to getting plastered and too intent on having a good time.'

'And Sasha wasn't?'

'Wasn't what? Drunk or trying to have a good time? She's a young woman, Paolo, just wanting to enjoy life, but some creep is freaking her out.'

'Has she seen him?'

Lydia shook her head. 'No, but she is convinced someone followed her home from the bus stop. She only felt safe once she was inside the apartment lobby with the door locked.'

'Did she see the person?'

'No, but she'd heard footsteps that seemed to be keeping time with hers. They stopped when she looked back, but sped up when she ran for home. It's not the first time it's happened.'

Paolo looked up. 'Always when she's coming home from a night out?'

'No, this was the first time at night. When I tried to reassure her that it was probably nothing to worry about she said it had happened a few times during the day as well. When she went to pay her rent this month she was certain someone had followed her. Every time she looked back, there was a man with a baseball cap pulled low over his face looking into shop windows.'

'That could be a coincidence. Maybe the guy was genuinely window shopping.'

Lydia frowned. 'You really believe that?'

'It's possible, but I agree it's more probable someone is following her. Has anyone contacted her? Made threats?'

She shook her head again. 'I asked her that. The only other thing that's happened is she's had a few odd calls to her landline.'

'Odd in what way?'

'She answers the phone and it immediately goes dead. It makes her feel like someone is checking to make sure she's home.'

'The caller doesn't say anything?'

'No. Sasha answers it and the person hangs up.'

'Then I don't see how I can help, Lydia. The only advice I can give her isn't what she, or you, would want to hear.'

'What advice is that?'

'She should stop going to the places that make her feel uncomfortable.'

'Stay home and act like a nun?' Lydia said.

Paolo sighed. He'd expected that reaction. 'No, that wasn't what I meant and you know it.' He drained his cup and got up for a refill. 'What I'm saying is if she feels uneasy in the club, try going somewhere else for a while. See if she gets the same feeling of being watched in a different environment. What's the name of the place she goes to?'

'She did tell me, but I can't remember exactly. You may have noticed that I'm not at the age to go clubbing any more,' she said, grinning at him. 'Hang on, it's coming to me. It's a weird name. Doesn't sound like a club. I remember when she told me I thought it was more like somewhere plumbers would hang out.'

Paolo walked back to the table, cup in hand. 'It wasn't The Pipe by any chance?'

'Yes, that was it! How did you guess?'

'It's one of the places that comes up on the radar from time to time.'

She gave Paolo a look that he knew meant tell me more. Not a good idea.

'So what exactly do you want me to do for your young friend?'

'I want you to look into it.'

He took a sip of coffee before answering. As he put his cup down, he thought how nice it was to be sharing this moment with Lydia. Especially as he knew he was about to ruin it.

'I can't, Lydia. You haven't given me anything to go on. All I know is the girl's first name.'

'I can give you her full name,' she said.

'You didn't give me chance to finish. Even with her full name, all I've got to go on is that she feels like she's being watched, but she doesn't know who it might be, or even if she really is being followed. You're not giving me anything concrete. Has she had any weird phone calls to her mobile, or just to the landline?'

Lydia shook her head. 'She hasn't mentioned any.'

'Texts? Requests from strangers to hook up online?'

'Not as far as I know. Paolo, please, she's scared. She's a young woman living alone here. All her family are up north and she has no one to talk to other than me and I can't do anything.'

Paolo sighed. He knew when he was beaten. 'Give me her details. I'll talk to her and see if there is anything we can do.'

Lydia's face lit up. 'Thank you.'

'Just bear in mind, unless she can be more specific, there's very little action I can take. With all the cuts in our budget I can't spare the manpower to watch her 24/7 without a definite threat to her well-being.'

She got up and came round to his side of the table. Leaning forward, she kissed his cheek. Paolo felt the urge to reach out and pull her into his arms, but resisted. They'd been down that road too many times in the past and it always resulted in misery.

He looked up and smiled. 'You'd better give me Sasha's phone number and address. I'll try to get to see her over the weekend.'

She took the magnetic pad off the fridge and searched for a pen. 'I've only got her landline number, but you won't be able to call her until Monday night. She was completely freaked out; she said she was going home to her parents for the rest of the weekend and would only be back Monday evening.'

Chapter Five

Monday

Boy parked round the back of Sasha's block, so that he could see her windows, and waited for the light to come on to show she'd come home from work.

'I know you're the special one,' he whispered. He couldn't bear it if Sasha let him down, but he'd come prepared, just in case.

As he waited, he ran through the way he hoped the evening would go. She'd be a little surprised to see him. That was to be expected. But once she realised how much he loved her, how much he was prepared to sacrifice to be with her, she'd fall into his arms and be prepared to live with him and take Grammy's place at the heart of his home.

He smiled, picturing their life together. She'd have to give up work. No partner of his was going to slave outside the home and be too tired to be a proper wife. No, she'd be happy to stay in the house, making nice meals and keeping the place perfect. That's the way Grammy and Grandpa had raised him. A woman should be ready to please her man whenever he needed her.

Not that he'd had a chance to tell Sasha how he felt. Not yet. Tonight all that was going to change. Tonight they'd finally be together. He'd thought for a while that she might not be the one, but last week she'd given him the signal he'd been waiting for. He'd planned to come over on Saturday, but she hadn't answered her phone when he called. Angry bile rose in his throat. Where had she been? Why hadn't she been home when he needed her? Bitch! But he'd forgive her this time. It wasn't her fault she hadn't been trained. Boy smiled.

He'd use a different technique to Grandpa. Grammy had spent too much time in the cellar. Boy was certain he'd never need to use it. He'd teach Sasha to love him so much she'd never do anything he wouldn't like.

He reached to the passenger seat and pulled the bag over to check, once again, that he had all he needed. He unzipped it and lifted out the roses. The florist had looked at him strangely when he'd insisted she remove all the thorns, but he didn't want Sasha to hurt herself when she arranged them just like Grammy had. They looked a bit the worse for wear, but would soon freshen up when Sasha put them into a vase. He wondered what her flat looked like inside and hoped it wasn't too modern. He didn't like all that minimalist crap. Grandpa had liked dark wood and Grammy had made sure it gleamed with scented wax. He hoped Sasha would be able to keep to Grammy's high standards, but wasn't too worried if she couldn't at first. He'd seen how Grandpa had done things and vowed to treat his love differently. Punishment and praise, Grandpa always said, that's what does the trick with women, punishment and praise. Whip them hard when they get things wrong, then give them roses when they finally get it right. Well, he was never going to do that! He was only going to shower Sasha with flowers to show his love. It would be all praise and no punishment.

Sasha would get her first posy tonight. She'd earned it by giving him the signal on Friday.

He glanced over to the apartment block, but no light shone in her window. Where was she? He'd left work early just for her. His hand gripped the flower stems so tight he could feel each strand of string tying them together. Forcing himself to relax, he dropped the roses back into the bag. Shaking his head, he closed the zip, shutting them from view.

She didn't know yet she had to come straight home and not keep him waiting. That would be the first lesson he'd teach her. Some understanding of her role would be in order before he handed over the posy of roses.

Another five minutes passed and still no welcoming light showed in her window. He reached into his pocket and pulled out a bag of sweets. They had always been Grammy's favourites, but he liked them because each one carried a special message. He wondered which one he would need for tonight. When he'd first arrived, he was convinced it could only be 'She Loves Me' but now that she'd kept him waiting for so long, maybe he'd have to sort out a different love heart.

Breathe, he told himself; don't let her selfishness ruin the evening. He would soon encourage her to become a better person.

Just as he thought he would have to throw away the roses and come back the following night, the light finally came on in her flat. He reached for the pay as you go mobile he'd bought after she'd given him the signal and dialled her landline. He knew she'd been waiting for him to make contact, because her number was in the phonebook. The last one he'd thought might have been perfect had kept her number ex-directory.

'Hello.'

Sasha's voice sent his heart soaring. He could barely breathe. Concentrate! He had to concentrate.

'Hello?' she repeated. 'Who is this?'

'Miss Carmichael? This is Mark Stacey from Harlow and Griffin,' he said, putting on the poshest accent he could and reading from the business card he'd picked up in her estate agent's office. He'd been following her for days before she went into the agency and he was worried she was planning to move, so he hung around outside pretending to look at the properties on offer. He peered through the window and saw her hand over what looked like a cheque and was given a receipt. She chatted for a bit with the girl at the desk and then stood up.

As she was leaving, she called out. 'See you next month!'

She walked off and he followed; she was completely oblivious that her one true love was there to protect her from other men. She hadn't even noticed him when he'd stood close behind her at the bus stop. He remembered the floral fragrance that had invaded his senses.

Cheap whore perfume sending out an invitation to any man close enough to smell it. From now on the only fragrance he'd allow would be from the roses he gave her.

'Oh, hi. Is there a problem with my dad's cheque? There shouldn't be.' Her words brought him back to the present.

'No, nothing like that,' he said. 'We have received a call from the gas supply company. It seems there is a very slight possibility of a leak and they are sending out an engineer this evening to check all the pipes in your block.'

'Gas leak? Should I vacate the place?'

'No need for that. They say it's nothing to worry about. It's just a precaution. The engineer is on his way and should be with you shortly. I just wanted to let you know someone was coming so that you would know it was okay to let them in.'

'Are you sure it's safe for me to be here?'

He fought to keep his temper in check. 'The gas company have assured me you are in no danger. Sending an engineer out is purely a precaution.'

'Oh. Okay. Thank you for letting me know, Mr Stacey. Good-night.'

'Goodnight,' he said and ended the call.

Getting out of the car, he smiled. Their new life was about to start. He couldn't wait to take her home.

He crossed the road and walked around to the front entrance of the apartment block. Sasha was on the third floor. His heart felt like it was pounding its way into his throat. This must be what love feels like, he thought. So exciting I'm almost throwing up. He hadn't been able to get close enough to the others. That's how he'd known they weren't his true love hearts. Sasha had made it so easy for him; she had to be the one.

Pressing her number on the intercom, he waited to hear her won-derful voice.

'Hello?'

'Miss Carmichael? I'm from the gas company and need to carry out an inspection. I believe you are expecting me.'

24

'Yes,' she said. 'Come on up.'

The door clicked open and he went in, heading for the stairs. He would have to teach Sasha not to be so trusting in future. So many lessons for her to absorb, but they had the rest of their lives. He felt sad that Grammy wasn't still alive to help him teach Sasha. She'd already annoyed him by coming home late and now she'd been stupid enough to let a stranger into her home. After tonight, she'd better not invite any other men into the place. Grandpa hadn't even allowed Grammy out to visit friends and family. Boy promised himself he wouldn't keep Sasha a prisoner like that. But speaking to other men without permission was different. Sasha had a lot to learn.

Chapter Six

Paolo walked through the main office on Monday morning still thinking about the time he'd spent with Lydia over the weekend. They'd once been inseparable, but then everything fell apart. At least now they were able to be in the same room and enjoy each other's company again. They'd come a long way since the divorce.

His musings came to an abrupt halt when Jack stood up and called out.

'You're wanted upstairs, *sir*,' he said and Paolo winced at the unspoken sarcasm in the way Jack addressed him.

He forced himself not to rise to Jack's bait. 'I'll go up shortly.'

'The way the Chief sounded when I was with him, you'd be better off going straight up.'

Jack smiled and Paolo wanted to wipe the smirk from his face. Now what's he been up to?

He nodded and walked on, catching sight of CC's frown as he went past her desk. Clearly she had a gripe with Jack as well, but Paolo couldn't afford to take sides. *Who was he kidding?* He'd been taking sides against Jack from the time the man had made Dave's life a misery.

Paolo entered his office and shut the door, tempted to make a point of ignoring Jack's advice, but then he realised how childish he was being. If the Chief wanted to see him it would be for a valid reason. He chucked the newspapers he'd intended to read before starting work onto his desk and headed upstairs.

He arrived at Chief Willows, door slightly out of breath, having taken the stairs rather than the lift. After he'd settled his breathing, he tapped on the door and opened it when he heard Willows bark to come in. Shit, Paolo thought. He doesn't sound in a good mood.

'Good morning, sir,' he said, taking the seat Willows was pointing to and waiting for him to finish his call.

'Yes, Mr Mendip, we are doing all we can. Yes, I have my best officers on it. Yes, we will get to the bottom of it.' He nodded. 'I'll keep you informed of any progress. Once again, my condolences.'

He ended the call and glared at Paolo.

'I take it you know who that was?'

Paolo nodded. 'Sally Mendip's father.'

'He's not happy, Paolo, and I don't blame him. He's grieving over the loss of his daughter and expects us to find the piece of slime who gave her the drugs that killed her. I've told him my best men are on it, but are they?'

'You know we're doing our best.'

'I'm not so sure. I bumped into young Jack Cummings in the car park this morning. He tells me he's been on stake-out night after night at The Pipe and feels it's pointless. Why aren't you making better use of him, Paolo? He's a first-rate officer and deserves more from you than being sent to watch people queuing to get in a night-club. He feels he's being sidelined.'

Paolo took a deep breath before answering. He knew the Chief was partially right. Not that he'd sent Jack to The Pipe to sideline him, but if he was honest, he much preferred the office without Jack in it.

'I wasn't aware Jack felt so strongly. He's not said anything to me.'

'Well, Paolo, that's the other thing. I told Jack he has to communicate with you about this, but he didn't want to cause a fuss.'

'He hasn't made any attempt to speak to me on this subject.'

Willows shrugged. 'As I said, Paolo, he didn't want to cause a fuss. He told me how much he admires you as a commanding officer and wants to emulate your methods. He feels he could do more on the team and expressed a desire to go out with you on interviews. Perhaps you could take him along in place of DS Connors from time to time. He needs your guiding hand.'

Paolo stood up. 'Yes, sir. I'll bear that in mind. Thank you for bringing it to my attention.'

He managed to get halfway down the stairs before he let loose with a string of swear words he couldn't have used in front of Willows. Having let out some of his frustration he carried on downstairs and entered the main office to find Jack leaning against his desk as if waiting for Paolo. In fact, judging by the look of satisfaction on his face, he'd definitely been waiting to see what Paolo did.

'Jack, could you please come into my office?' Paolo said as he walked past.

He'd barely sat down before Jack bounded in after him looking for all the world like a child about to receive the Christmas present he'd always wanted.

'Sit down,' Paolo said, pointing to one of the chairs opposite him.

He waited until Jack was seated and then smiled. 'Jack, it seems I've been treating you unfairly by sending you out on nightly surveillance.'

Jack remained silent, but his smirk grew.

'So I've decided to change things about a bit. I want you to go home and get a good sleep. From tomorrow you're on daytime surveillance and will replace DC Sharp.'

Paolo tried not to be pleased at the shocked look on Jack's face, but couldn't quite achieve it.

'But . . . but . . .'

'Yes?' Paolo said. 'But?'

'You know that's not what the Chief meant when he . . .'

'When he what, Jack? Let's get one thing clear – if you have a gripe with me, be a man and deal with it. Don't go running to the Chief and expect me to fall in line with whatever it is you've got planned in that devious head of yours. You are a good copper when you want to be, but sucking up to the Chief and twisting the facts isn't the way to go if you want to be part of my team.'

Jack stood up. 'Who said I want to be part of your team? Fuck you!'

Paolo watched as Jack stormed out. *Great. Well done, Paolo*, he thought. *You really handled that like an adult. You've made him even more single-minded in his attempt to undermine your authority.*

If only Jack had been prepared to temper his ambition, he had the makings of a good cop, but it seemed to Paolo that he was determined to climb the ranks as fast as he could by whatever devious means possible. Paolo picked up the newspaper and turned it over to see the headline. *Drug Death Debacle*, the headline screamed. He was about to start reading when the phone rang.

'Hello, DCI Sterling, Hardwick here from the *Bradchester Gazette*. I wondered if you had any comment to make on today's lead story.'

'I've only seen the headline so far. Nicely alliterative.'

'Where are you in your investigation into the untimely demise of our local MP's daughter?'

'We are following a number of leads,' Paolo said.

'But you don't appear to be getting anywhere, according to our sources,' Hardwick said.

'Obviously I can't share sensitive information with you, but we are, as I've already said, following a number of leads.'

'Mr Mendip seems to feel you aren't doing enough.'

Paolo sighed. 'We are doing everything possible. I understand how Mr Mendip feels –'

'Yes, I'm sure you do,' Hardwick said, interrupting Paolo, 'having lost a daughter yourself, you must feel a strong connection with the grieving father.'

Don't rise to the bait. Don't rise to the bait. Paolo clenched his fist until he could feel his nails digging into his palms. As always, when Sarah's name came up, he saw again the car speeding towards him, Sarah at his side. He moved to push her to safety, but was a fraction of a second too late. The car mounted the pavement and swerved, missing Paolo by millimetres and hitting Sarah full on. He shuddered, remembering how the car had reversed, dragging Sarah's body into the street.

'I'm sure our readers would sympathise with you on this case, bringing back, as it must, the trauma of your own loss.'

'At this stage we don't have any comment to make. Our enquiries are ongoing. Thank you for your interest.'

Paolo ended the call before Hardwick could say anything else. The fucking weasel would use anything to get his story, but there was no way Paolo was going to let him use Sarah's death to worm his way in.

He managed to get through the day without encountering anyone else who seemed hell bent on getting under his skin and was about to leave his office when he remembered his promise to Lydia. He walked back to his desk and searched for the phone number she'd given him.

Slumping on the chair as the tone rang out without an answer, he realised how very tired he was. He'd wait half an hour or so and then try again. He ended the call, put the phone in his pocket, lay his head on the desk and fell instantly asleep.

Chapter Seven

Boy walked to the lift and sighed. He hadn't wanted their life together to start like this. She'd spoiled their first night. She would have to prove her love before he gave her the posy of roses.

As he reached her floor, he stopped and took a deep breath. This was the first time he'd approached a woman. What should he say? Sweat seeped from his pores under the gas fitter's suit. He could feel it running down his back. He couldn't go through with it. He couldn't face being rejected because then he'd have to . . . If he couldn't even put into words in his head what he'd need to do, would he be able to do it when the time came?

He heard a noise from one of the floors above. A door slammed and footsteps sounded from the stairwell. He needed to move.

Boy approached Sasha's door, put his thumb partly over the photograph and held the fake gas fitter's card so she'd be able to see it through the spyhole, and rang the bell.

When Sasha opened the door, Boy's knees almost gave way. She was so beautiful. Even lovelier face to face, up close like this.

'I've been expecting you,' she said. 'Come in.'

Every breath in his body seemed to leave him at those words. How perfect was this? She'd given him another sign.

He headed into the apartment and heard the door close behind him.

'Do I know you?' Sasha asked, following him into the kitchen.

He turned to face her. 'I don't think so.'

'You look familiar. I'm sure I've seen you before, but I can't place where.'

She suddenly looked unsure and edged out of the kitchen.

'I'll leave you to it,' she said.

He picked up a tremor in her voice, as if she was unsure. Boy didn't want to scare her. Not ever. He wanted her to love him.

He pulled the bag of love heart sweets from his pocket and offered the open bag. She shook her head.

'No, thank you. I don't eat sweets.'

'You took one saying He Loves Me.'

Why was she looking at him like that?

'I know where I've seen you before.'

She was ruining their first night together.

'Why are you pretending to be a gas fitter?'

The phone rang on the far side of the hall and she sprinted towards it, but he got there first and held down the receiver so that she couldn't lift it. Fear shone in her eyes. She was spoiling everything. But he could still fix it. He moved so that he stood between her and the front door.

'Tell me,' he said, as she stepped backwards, 'do you believe in love at first sight?'

'What do you mean? I want you to leave.'

'I love you and want to take care of you.'

Boy watched Sasha's eyes darting from side to side, as if trying to decide which way to run.

'Please,' she whispered, 'please don't hurt me.'

He put out his hand to soothe her and she smacked it aside.

'Don't touch me! Get out!'

Boy tried to control his anger, but it was hard. She wasn't doing this right at all.

'You gave me the signal. Don't pretend you didn't.'

Tears streamed down Sasha's cheeks. 'What signal? I didn't do anything. I don't understand.'

Boy stepped forward. 'Liar! You took the fucking sweet! Don't tell me you didn't know what it meant.'

'Oh my God, it was just a sweet.'

Rage flooded his mind. 'Just a sweet? Grammy's love rests in those sweets and you didn't just take one, you picked out He Loves Me. What was that if it wasn't a signal to say you wanted to be with me?'

'Please,' she whimpered. 'Just leave. I promise I'll never tell anyone you were here. I didn't mean anything when I chose that sweet. I just thought it was funny.'

'Funny?' Boy hissed, taking her throat in his hands. 'You thought it was funny to lead me on? You've got lessons to learn, starting right now.'

As he squeezed, the power flowed into Boy's hands. He tightened his grip. A spasm began in his groin and spread until his entire body trembled. His knees buckled as Sasha went limp. Stumbling to the floor, he fell on her soft body, unable to let go of the grip on her neck. The spasms grew in intensity. Building, building, building until he couldn't breathe. He sucked in air, desperate for release. His body moved backwards and forwards.

'Oh God, oh God,' he yelled, as waves of glorious heat coursed through his body.

Chapter Eight

Boy lay on the floor next to Sasha until his breathing settled and the incredible sensations disappeared completely. Dear God, he would do that every day from now on. Sasha would learn to enjoy it as much as he did. He forced himself to his feet and staggered to the kitchen sink. Grabbing handfuls of kitchen towels, he set about cleaning himself up, wondering if that was one of the routines Grammy used to share with Grandpa. He'd always known there were rituals that excluded him, but hadn't realised how special they must have been. Did Grandpa experience that sensation every time he choked Grammy? No, he couldn't have done. At least, never when Boy had been in the room.

He threw the used kitchen towels in the bin and turned back to his sleeping love. She hadn't moved since she'd collapsed, so he shook her.

'Sasha, darling, wake up.'

She should have woken by now. Grammy only ever blacked out for a minute at most when Grandpa chastised her. Why wouldn't the stupid girl move? He put his hand to her mouth, but couldn't feel any breath. Leaning forward, he rested his ear on her chest. Nothing! She couldn't be dead. He loved her too much to lose her now.

But maybe it was because she wasn't the one for him after all. She'd led him on, but then rejected him. She was nothing but a tease. A heartless, teasing bitch.

Heartless – that's how she needed to be left.

He dragged her across the floor and then picked up her lifeless body. She flopped against him, but he managed to heave her onto the kitchen table. What now? He needed a knife. A really sharp one. Opening drawer after drawer, he swore at the useless utensils she had. Finally, the last drawer he opened contained a selection of knives. He picked the sharpest-looking one and tested it against his thumb. Perfect!

Slitting open her top and slicing through her bra brought on a resurgence of the earlier sensations, but Boy forced himself to ignore them. She wasn't the one, so he mustn't give into his urges.

He gazed on her breasts and wondered where to cut. The heart was over to the left, but maybe he should just slit her up the middle. That's what he'd do. Hand trembling, he placed the point of the blade just below her breast bone and stabbed the blade in, dragging it down.

Sasha's eyes flew open and she screamed.

Without thinking, Boy stabbed, striking again and again as the blood spurted, covering his face and hands. Within seconds she lay still, eyes staring into nothing.

Chapter Nine

Tuesday morning

Paolo banged his hand on the desk. Yet another night's surveillance wasted. If he didn't get a result soon, he was pretty sure the Chief would cut off the overtime funding. But The Pipe was the place where deals were being done. His informant was definite on that and the man had never yet given him bad information.

He gazed up at the ceiling, trying to find the inspiration to come up with a compelling reason to present to the Chief why they should continue to watch a place that hadn't so far shown any signs of criminal activity.

His mobile rang and he couldn't decide whether he was glad his thoughts had been interrupted or not. Probably it was for the best, because no flashes of brilliance had come to him.

He picked up the phone and saw his ex-wife's name on the screen.

'Hi, Lydia, what's up?'

'Hi, did you manage to get hold of Sasha last night?'

'No. I rang a few times, but she didn't answer. I assumed she must have stayed longer at her parents'.'

'She said she would be in today, but she hasn't turned up and she's not answering her landline.'

'Have you got her mobile number?'

'Yes, I got it from HR, but it rings for ages and then goes to voicemail.'

'Lydia, calm down. She probably decided to stay up north a day longer and just forgot to call in to let everyone know.'

'Oh, come on, Paolo! How likely is that?'

'You'd be surprised. We've wasted many hours searching for people who either don't want to be found, or don't realise they've been reported as missing. How old is she?'

'Eighteen, but what's that got to do with anything?'

'Lydia, she's young. Young people can sometimes be thoughtless and—'

'Paolo, will you please just listen to me? She's not thoughtless. She's a sensible, down to earth girl who enjoys her job. If she wasn't coming in, she'd have called to let us know. Please, can't you do something?'

'Okay, give me her mobile number. I'll see if our tech guys can trace the location of the phone. Will that put your mind at rest?'

Lydia thanked him and rang off, but he could hear the stress in her voice. He knew she wouldn't have pushed unless she was convinced something was wrong. He picked up his phone and punched in the numbers of Sasha's mobile. It rang for several seconds, then a young girl's voice came on.

'Sorry, can't answer now. Leave me your number and I'll call you back.'

'Hello, this is Detective Chief Inspector Paolo Sterling. Some people are concerned about you. Could you please call me back so that I can reassure them of your safety?'

Paolo added his mobile and office numbers and ended the call. He'd do as promised and get the tech team on the job. They should be able to find the phone's location, but he wasn't sure how long it would take. No way would they consider it the emergency Lydia thought it was, so his request would probably be way down their priority list.

He wrote out a reminder to keep calling Sasha's mobile every hour and set it against the files next to his office phone. That way he wouldn't forget. In the meantime, he had work to do.

Two hours later, CC knocked on his door. Paolo had been so deep in form-filling the sound startled him and he jerked upright, upsetting the piles of paperwork balanced precariously on the edge of the desk.

'Damn,' he said, as the files slithered to the floor.

'Sorry, sir, didn't mean to cause chaos,' CC said, coming in to help him pick up the scattered papers. 'Is this important?' she asked, holding up the piece of paper with Sasha's number on it which had floated into the middle of the room.

'Oh my God, yes! I need to call that number right now. Take a seat. I won't be a minute.'

He tried Sasha's landline and mobile again, but with the same result.

'CC, sorry, I just need to make another call, then I'll be with you.'

Smiling an apology at CC, he tapped Lydia's speed dial number. She answered on the second ring.

'Paolo! At last! Have you found her?'

'Calm down, Lydia. We don't know yet that she's actually missing.'

He might just as well have saved his breath because Lydia wasn't listening.

'Have you tracked her mobile? Is she at home?'

'Not yet and I don't know,' he said when Lydia paused for breath. 'I've asked our tech team to track the phone, but . . .'

'Paolo, I know something's not right. Won't you go round to her flat? Please? I promise I'll never ask another favour.'

He looked at the files CC had dumped back on his desk, knew that she wouldn't have come in unless she had something important to discuss and really wanted to say no to Lydia, but he couldn't ignore the panic in her voice.

'Okay, I'll go round today. Give me her address.'

Lydia read it out to him. 'When will you go? Will you call me once you've spoken to her?'

He sighed. This was getting ridiculous. The last time he'd heard so much panic in Lydia's voice was when she'd discovered Katy's boyfriend had a brother with a criminal past. He wondered if she was transferring her maternal fears to Sasha because Katy was overseas. As soon as the thought entered his mind he realised how unfair it was. Lydia was one of the most level-headed people he knew.

'I'll go as soon as I can leave the office and I promise I'll call you. Okay?'

'Thank you!'

He ended the call and looked up to see CC's eyes on him.

'Problem?' she asked.

Explaining Lydia's concerns, he shrugged and then nodded to the paperwork on CC's lap. 'You came in to tell me something?'

She shook her head. 'More to confirm we know nothing, sir. I've been collating reports from surveillance and we have a big fat zero when it comes to valuable information.'

He looked at the scrap of paper with Sasha's address. 'Come on, CC. I need to check this young colleague of my ex-wife is alive and well. Let's do a bit of brainstorming in the car. Maybe we can come up with an avenue we haven't yet explored.'

He laughed at the look of disbelief on CC's face.

'If there's an avenue we haven't gone down,' she said, 'I'm next in line to be pope!'

Paolo picked up his car keys and almost asked CC if she wanted to drive, but couldn't get the words out. Dave had nearly always driven when they went out on a case and Paolo wasn't ready yet for anyone else to take over that position.

He pulled up outside the block of flats just as the SatNav told him he'd arrived at his destination. As much as he hated the repetitive voice, he couldn't now imagine driving without using it. It certainly cut down on the number of times he got lost.

Getting out of the car, he looked around the area. There wasn't a single-storey building to be seen. This was clearly flatland, but looked slightly more upmarket than many of the Bradchester areas where high-rise blocks dominated the skyline. He wondered if the flats were individually owned, as in most areas landlords seemed to do the minimum amount of external maintenance and this block looked very well cared for.

He pressed the intercom for Sasha's apartment, but the call went unanswered.

'I'll try another number on her floor,' he said to CC.

After three unanswered buzzes he was finally rewarded when a querulous voice piped up.

'I don't want any. Thank you.'

Before he could speak he heard the clatter of the receiver being replaced. CC laughed.

'She didn't take to you, sir.'

'You think?' he said, reaching for the buzzer again. Not taking any chances this time, he spoke as soon as he heard the click of someone answering.

'This is the police. Could you please let us in?'

The same querulous voice came back. 'How do I know that? You could be a mad axe murderer. Go away!'

'Look!' Paolo said, holding his badge up to the monitor. 'I'm Detective Inspector Paolo Sterling.'

'Chief,' CC whispered. 'Detective Chief Inspector, sir.'

Ignoring the amusement in CC's voice, Paolo tried again with the old lady on the intercom.

'We are simply here to check up on the well-being of one of the tenants on your floor, but she isn't answering her intercom.'

'Which one?'

'Miss Carmichael in number 102.'

'Hmm,' the voice said. 'Why didn't you say so sooner? I was going to report her to the tenant's association after the racket coming from her place last night. Shouting, banging, slamming doors. That boyfriend of hers was yelling. It's not what we're used to here. That's the trouble with young people. They think they're the only ones that matter. Not like my day . . .'

Paolo jumped in before she could elaborate. 'Could you please open the door for us? I'd like to ask you about what you heard last night.'

There was a moment's silence and Paolo thought the old lady had gone, but then he heard the click of the door release. He pushed it open and signalled to CC to go in.

'She didn't mention a boyfriend to Lydia?' CC asked.

40

'No, but maybe it's one from her past. She went home for the weekend. He might have come back with her.'

Or maybe, Paolo thought, Lydia was right to worry about Sasha.

They took the lift up to Sasha's floor and discovered the woman from the intercom waiting for them at her front door. Dressed in black, arms folded and hooded eyes under a heavy frown, she looked to Paolo like a vulture ready to pounce on prey. She barely waited for Paolo and CC to reach her before launching into speech.

'I must say she's been no trouble up to now, but last night was the limit. I was glad when she left, I can tell you.'

'Did you see her leave?'

'Not her, no, but I assumed she went with her boyfriend. I haven't heard a sound since I saw him go.'

The first stirrings of real unease tickled Paolo's spine. 'Do you usually hear her moving about?'

She nodded. 'Oh yes, the walls here aren't as solid as they should be. I hear her when she's in her kitchen in the mornings and in the evenings when she gets home from work. Our kitchens back on to each other.'

'You don't hear her when she's in other rooms?'

'Well, just the bathroom noises, but my mother always said ladies don't discuss those.'

Paolo smiled. 'Your mother was right, but do you think you could make an exception for me? Have you heard Miss Carmichael in the bathroom since last night?'

She shook her head. 'Not a peep since the gas fitter left.'

'Gas fitter? I thought you said it was her boyfriend.'

'I assumed it was. He'd been yelling about love.'

'So the person you saw leave was dressed in a gas fitter's uniform? Did you notice which company he was with?'

'No, but he was very messy. I had to clean up after he'd gone.'

'How do you mean?' he asked, his uneasiness increasing by the minute.

'He left mucky footprints on the tiles and in the lift. I had to come out with a bucket of soapy water and I shouldn't have to do that at my age. That's another thing I'm going to complain about to the tenant's association.'

'Do you happen to know which estate agent Miss Carmichael rents through?'

She nodded. 'Of course I do. I own most of the apartments on this floor. My late husband bought them as our retirement fund. He was very clever like that. Do you know—'

Paolo couldn't help himself; his inner voice was screaming at him to stop her from rambling. 'I'm sorry to interrupt, but it's really important that we get access to Miss Carmichael's flat. Do you have a key?'

She shook her head, clearly annoyed at not being able to finish her story. Paolo thought she looked more like a vulture than ever.

'I don't keep the keys. I employ Harlow and Griffin in the High Street. They vet the tenants and collect the rents on my behalf. However, I can tell you right now that if that boyfriend is going to be a regular visitor, Miss Carmichael's lease will not be renewed.'

She glared at Paolo and CC as if they'd been responsible for the previous night's disturbances.

'One last question and then we'll leave you in peace for now. Do you have the estate agent's phone number?'

'I've got a card somewhere. Wait here,' she said, making it quite clear they were not welcome to cross her threshold.

A couple of minutes later she returned clutching a business card. 'I want it back,' she said, looking them both up and down. Satisfied they'd got the message, she turned on her heels and went inside her apartment. The door closed with a snap and Paolo heard the sound of bolts and chains being put in place.

Giggles escaped from CC and Paolo had difficulty controlling his own urge to laugh.

'She *really* didn't take to you, sir,' CC said.

'Can't imagine why,' he said, reaching into his pocket for his phone. 'I'm such a charming fellow.' He waited while the estate agent's number rang. 'Ah, yes,' he said when a voice asked if she could help him. 'This is Detective Chief Inspector Paolo Sterling. I need someone to bring the key to 102, Carminster Mansions in Howarth Road. No, I cannot wait until this afternoon. Okay, I'll send someone round for it. No, we don't need a warrant. We have reason to believe Miss Carmichael might be in need of assistance. Thank you.'

He handed CC his car keys. 'There's only the receptionist there. Pop over and grab the keys. In the meantime I'm going to knock on some of the other doors. Maybe one of her neighbours also saw or heard something. Then,' he sighed, 'I'm going to brave our charming informant and get her to give a statement.'

CC waved the keys. 'Rather you than me, sir, but do you really think something's wrong?'

He nodded. 'Unfortunately, I do.'

Chapter Ten

Paolo waited impatiently for CC to return. He'd knocked on all the doors on the floor above and below as well as those on Sasha's level, but few of the neighbours were home. Those who were hadn't seen or heard anything out of the ordinary the previous night, although one thought he'd seen someone who might have been wearing a gas fitter's uniform leave the block. But he'd only glimpsed him from his window and wasn't able to give a description. He hadn't even been sure of the man's height, build or colouring.

Paolo heard voices coming from the stairwell and moved over to open the door. Whoever was speaking didn't sound at all pleased.

'This is most irregular. Most irregular.'

'I realise that, sir, but we are concerned about Miss Carmichael's well-being.' From the tone of CC's voice it was clear she'd said the same words several times already.

CC and a tall gangly man appeared round the bend in the stairs. Although the suit was clearly of exceptionally good quality, the wearer was one of those unfortunate individuals who looked like he'd been dressed in someone else's clothes. His face was bright red, whether from exertion or anger, Paolo wasn't sure.

'I take it you're from the estate agency,' Paolo said, moving forward and showing his warrant card. 'Thank you for coming.'

The man nodded. 'George Griffin of Harlow and Griffin. This is most irregular. I'm not at all happy about opening Miss Carmichael's apartment without her consent. Not at all happy. It's most—'

'Irregular,' Paolo cut in. 'Yes, I know, but as my colleague explained, we are concerned about Miss Carmichael's well-being. So, if you wouldn't mind, sir, perhaps you could open the door for us.'

George Griffin muttered something under his breath that sounded very much like living in a police state. Paolo saw CC move towards the man and shook his head. There was no point in making matters worse. If they opened the door and found nothing untoward Griffin was going to create merry hell.

The estate agent made a big show of finding the right key and sighing before inserting it into the lock. As the door opened, a faint smell wafted out. It was one Paolo knew all too well.

'I think it's best if you wait outside, please,' he said, putting a restraining hand on the man's arm.

George shook it off. 'Really, this is the limit. If you think—'

'What I think, *sir*, is that this might well be a crime scene. I have tried to be polite, but I am now telling you not to go inside. I'd like the keys, please,' Paolo said, holding out his hand.

The bluster seemed to leave the man at the words crime scene and he meekly handed over the key ring.

'If you could wait here in the corridor for a few minutes, Mr Griffin, we'd like to speak to you about Miss Carmichael. CC, let's go.'

Paolo slipped the key into his pocket and then pulled on some protective gloves.

The hallway had four doors leading off from it. All were closed. There were smudges in the carpet that could be blood. Paolo stepped around them and moved to the door on the left. It opened onto a bathroom. Here there were clear signs of blood, but not as if someone had bled in there. It looked more like the splashes from someone cleaning up.

'CC, go and call this in, please. We're going to need forensics.'

He closed the door and moved across to the first on the right. Opening it, he was relieved to see the room looked in perfect order. A double bed, overloaded with pale lilac scatter cushions, dominated the room. On the bedside table was a family photograph. Presumably, Sasha Carmichael and her parents.

Paolo backed out and closed the door. Moving along the hallway, he opened the door directly opposite the front door. This opened into a pretty lounge with picture windows taking up most of one wall. The view wasn't spectacular, but it gave a feeling of space and made the room seem bigger than it really was.

That left only the one room to explore. Paolo could see it was a fire door, which was standard for a kitchen. As he opened it, the faint odour which had been tickling his sense of smell suddenly became overpowering. He held his arm across his nose and looked in from the entrance.

No way could he go in there without contaminating the scene. Blood covered most of the floor and walls. In the midst of the carnage was the kitchen table. Sprawled across it lay the decomposing remains of a young woman. Bizarrely, there were flower petals, stalks and leaves scattered around the room. It looked as though someone had ripped a bouquet of flowers to pieces. Her body was partially turned away from the doorway, making it appear as if she wanted to shield herself from prying eyes. Paolo could see she was still dressed, but that didn't mean the crime wasn't sexually motivated.

He stepped back and closed the door. As he walked towards the front door he could hear CC dealing with the plaintive moaning of the estate agent. Paolo felt himself begin to shake and stopped to compose his temper before going to join them. The pillock was whinging about this taking up his valuable time when a young girl had lost her life. But going out there and shaking the idiot, although appealing, was not going to help. Paolo took a deep breath and went out.

'Is she in there? What's going on?' George Griffin demanded. 'How much longer am I expected to remain here? I have clients to see.'

'I understand that, sir,' Paolo said, 'but it appears a crime has been committed on these premises, so it would be very helpful if you could answer a few questions.'

'What crime?'

Paolo shook his head. 'I'm not at liberty to answer that at the moment. CC, take Mr Griffin back to his office. I'll wait here for SOCO.' He turned back to the estate agent. 'My detective sergeant will need to ask you and anyone who dealt with Miss Carmichael a few questions.'

'Well, I don't see how any of us can help you, but if you insist I suppose we'll have to cooperate.'

Again, there was that underlying message that Griffin felt he was living in a police state. Paolo forced himself to smile. 'Thank you. It's important that we gather as much information about Miss Carmichael as we can. Often, it is something that appears trivial and unconnected that enables us to solve crimes. Of course, if you prefer, we could insist everyone comes to the station to answer our questions. However, that would mean closing your office for a considerable period of time.'

Paolo took a small measure of satisfaction at the look of horror on the man's face as he came up with several reasons why that wouldn't be a good idea.

'Perhaps you could take the lift downstairs and wait for my colleague?'

'I don't go in elevators, thank you!' He glared at CC. 'I hope you're not going to keep me waiting too long. I am a very busy man.'

He stalked off. Paolo kept quiet until the man had left the floor before turning to CC. 'Nasty business in there. Blood everywhere. Seems like Sasha was right. Someone was after her. Did forensics say who they'd be sending out?'

CC nodded. 'Dr Royston.'

'Good. Barbara's the best there is. Sorry to land you with the charming Griffin and his associates, but you never know, they might have seen someone hanging around when Sasha went in to pay her rent.'

'That's odd, isn't it?' CC said.

'What is?'

'Going in to pay each month. I'd have thought she'd have set up a direct debit or standing order. I pay my rent online each month.'

'Good point. Find out why she didn't. Might be nothing, but worth checking.'

While he waited for Barbara Royston and her team to arrive, Paolo called Lydia. She'd asked for his help and he'd let her and Sasha down.

'Lydia, could you come to the station later today?'

Lydia's sharp intake of breath was the only indication she'd heard him. The silence raged on for what seemed like eternity and Paolo knew he'd have to break it.

'Did you hear me?'

'What? Sorry, yes. Paolo, this doesn't sound good. Have you found her? Is she . . .?'

'I can't answer any questions at this stage, but it would be very useful if you could give a statement about her fears that someone was following her? Any info you have will help.'

'Paolo, tell me!'

'Lydia, you know I can't give you any information about an active case. We need you to provide any background information you might have.'

He heard her sigh. 'I'll come in and make a statement as soon as I finish work. See you later.'

As he ended the call he heard the sounds he'd been waiting for. Barbara Royston and her team had arrived.

Chapter Eleven

Paolo took off his protective shoe covers as he left the apartment with Barbara. He'd witnessed many crime scenes, but never one as gory as this. What kind of monster were they looking for?

'Barbara, please tell me that poor girl died from the first stab wound.'

'Sorry, Paolo, judging by the blood splatter she was alive for at least two of the blows.'

Paolo shook his head. 'Why so much blood? It's everywhere in that room!'

Barbara nodded. 'Yes, I know. That's because the perpetrator hit her jugular with one of the blows.'

'And that's the cause of death?'

'Looks like she was strangled as well, but—'

'I know,' he interrupted, 'you need to carry out the autopsy to be certain. Look, I know he stabbed her to death, but why strangle her and then put her up on the kitchen table to do it?'

She stared at him for a moment before answering. 'I can't even begin to guess.'

Paolo shuddered. How angry did someone have to be to do something like that? He shook off the thought and asked the question that Lydia hadn't been able to put into words.

'Was she sexually assaulted?'

Barbara shook her head. 'It doesn't appear so. She was still fully dressed and there were no signs her underwear had been tampered with, but again, I can only say for sure after the autopsy. It looks as though he cut open her clothes to get at her chest, but whether or not that was sexual, your guess is as good as mine. Who knows, he might get off on that and not need penetration.'

'What do you make of the flowers?' Paolo asked. 'Think this was a romance gone wrong?'

Before she could answer, one of the SOCO team, still covered from head to toe in his protective clothing, came to join them.

'Excuse me for intruding. We've found a load of kitchen towels in the bin. Looks like they've been used to clean up semen.'

Paolo glanced over at Barbara. 'Well, that answers the sex question. At least we have something to test for DNA.'

Barbara grimaced. 'Assuming it's the perpetrator's and not a boyfriend's, but we should be able to determine how long the semen has been there.'

'There's also this, sir,' the officer said. 'We found it on the floor under the table.'

Paolo put his hand out and the man gave him a small evidence bag. It held a round disk-shaped sweet.

The sweet was pale pink with words picked out in red. Paolo could just about make out the message through the blood stains. It read *She Loves Me Not*.

Chapter Twelve

Boy kicked a kitchen chair so hard it flew across the room. One of the wooden legs snapped as it hit the opposite wall. How could he have been so stupid? Just because she'd taken a sweet didn't mean she was the one. He'd thought that was the signal, but he'd been wrong. So how was he supposed to know when he found the right one?

He needed a double signal; that was clear. The next one had to take a sweet and do something else to let him know she wanted to be with him – but what? A smile wasn't enough. Lots of girls smiled at him. He had that kind of face. Grammy always said he had a face to love, so it must be true.

'You're as handsome as your father,' she used to say when Grandpa wasn't around.

His stomach heaved as he remembered the anger that had consumed him the night before. When Sasha turned him down, he'd known then he didn't want her, but hadn't expected the sense of outrage he'd felt at her rejection. His hands had closed round her throat of their own accord and he'd lifted her off the floor and slammed her against the wall – just like Grandpa had done to him so many times. At the time, it had felt good to have that power, but he didn't want to be like Grandpa. He wanted someone to love him, not be frightened all the time. But then again, Grammy had loved Grandpa, even though she was so scared of him she never went against his word. Although, thinking about it, she must have done so sometimes, because he remembered her coming to visit before his parents had died.

His head dropped as he remembered Sasha's limp body. He'd never meant to kill her, just show her the way things were meant to be, that was all.

Tears coursed down his cheeks as he recalled his feelings of remorse when he'd looked down on her bloodied corpse. He shouldn't have done that, but he was glad he'd destroyed the roses. She didn't deserve his love.

Wimp! You're a wimp, Boy. You couldn't even get her heart.

'I tried!'

Tried! You are such a weakling. I'd have opened up her chest and ripped it out with my bare hands.

Boy knew he had to block out Grandpa's voice or he'd never break free of him. What went wrong with Sasha? If he could concentrate on that, maybe he could stop the old bastard from getting inside his head.

Would Sasha have come to love him if they'd had more time together? Perhaps he'd taken her too much by surprise. He needed to get to know the next one properly before they got married. He'd make sure she was the right one for him. But how could he do that unless they were already living together?

He'd have to keep her in the punishment room until he was sure she loved him enough to take Grammy's place in the house. That's if Grandpa had left him the house. Who knew what the old bastard might have done. But that was tomorrow's problem. He'd find out when the will was read.

He walked down the stairs and unlocked the cellar door. He'd spent many hours in here when Grandpa wanted him out of the way, but he hadn't minded because he always thought of it as Grammy's room. He went inside and looked around. Everything was covered in dust. It was years since he'd been in here, so he'd need to get the place cleaned up, but he could make it perfect once again. The bed needed new linen and he'd get pretty towels to hang outside the shower cubicle. His new love would be comfortable while she was getting to know him better.

He stood in the middle of the room and closed his eyes, praying as he'd never prayed before. In answer, Grammy's voice came through to him.

You're a good boy. You deserve to be happy.

'Please God, let me keep the house,' he whispered.

He'd need to smarten it up, but if the house was his, he knew he could make it perfect.

Chapter Thirteen

Paolo put the last of the crime scene pictures on the board and then turned to his team. Almost involuntarily his eyes moved to where Dave should be sitting and he had to stop himself from yelling at DC Drake to move and find somewhere else to sit. He forced himself to focus on CC instead.

'The victim worked with my ex-wife who will be in shortly to give us whatever assistance she can. In the meantime, we know she felt she was being stalked, but had no evidence to support that.'

'There's plenty of evidence now,' Jack Cummings muttered.

Paolo swallowed the angry words he wanted to hurl at Jack. 'Possibly, but we don't yet know for certain the person who killed her is the same one who was shadowing her, do we?'

'What's the chances of there being two weirdos out there after the same bird?'

'*Woman*,' Paolo said, glaring at Jack. 'She wasn't a bird, she was a young woman.'

Jack waved his fingers in a gesture Paolo felt could be taken several ways. He decided to look on it as a gesture of apology, even though it probably wasn't any such thing.

'Dr Royston will be carrying out the autopsy on Friday, but has given an approximate time of death for us to work with. She was killed between six and nine on Monday evening.'

He looked around the room. Apart from Jack, he had a good team, but they were already stretched to the limit. It was going to be tough to cover Sasha's murder and The Pipe surveillance.

'Our ongoing drug case has to run side by side with this one. We don't have the resources to devote an entire team to each case, but I'd like the officers who have been running surveillance at The Pipe to continue.'

Jack had been leaning back so that his chair was balanced on two legs, but at Paolo's words he dropped forward.

'What? No, we should run shifts on the surveillance. I don't want to be hanging around that place knowing nothing's going to happen when there's a juicy murder to work on.'

Juicy murder? What kind of police officer looked on the killing of an innocent young woman as a juicy murder? Paolo resisted the urge to take Jack by the scruff of his neck and shake some sense into him.

'When this briefing is over, I'd like to see you in my office, Jack. Understand?'

Jack's head barely moved, but it was enough to signal he'd heard.

'One thing we do know about Sasha is that she was a frequent visitor to The Pipe, so we will have to visit the club, but in such a way that it doesn't compromise our surveillance. CC, you and I will go out there after Lydia has been in and I have a clearer idea of which days she went and who she might have gone with. There might be a connection there between her stalker and/or her killer, if they are not one and the same,' he said with a glance in Jack's direction.

'Okay, CC, the floor's yours. What did you find out at the estate agents?'

'They knew her quite well because she went in each month to pay her rent by cheque.'

'That's unusual in this day and age,' Paolo said. 'As you said, it would be more normal to pay via bank transfer.'

CC nodded. 'I expect she would have done so, but the cheques were not from her account. It appears her father was paying the rent. Sasha told one of the staff that he'd given her a batch of post-dated cheques made out to the estate agency when she moved down here. All she had to do was bring in the correct one each time.'

'That explains how she could afford to stay in such an upmarket development on an office worker's salary,' Paolo said. 'Anything else?'

CC nodded. 'Yes, but it's ironic. Sasha told the agency staff her father insisted on paying the rent so that she would be safe and not have to live in a dangerous area. Apparently, he was very old school about banking. Sasha told the estate agent her dad wouldn't have anything to do with online banking and didn't trust direct debits. Hence the post-dated cheques. Do her parents know yet, sir?'

'I haven't spoken to them yet as I wanted to wait until they heard the news in person. I've arranged for a family liaison officer to go out from their local station. As soon as I hear back from them, I'll call the house to see if Sasha told them anything that might help us track down her killer.'

'Any news back from tech on her phone, sir?'

'Nothing yet. She had it password protected, so it might be a while before they can get into it. Right, as there is nothing else at the moment, Jack, I'd like you to come with me.'

Paolo headed for his office without bothering to look in Jack's direction. He already knew the man would take his time getting to his feet and couldn't bear to see the look of long-suffering Jack was able to bring to his miserable face. The sooner he could get rid of him the better.

He'd just settled himself at his desk when Jack sauntered in.

'Close the door,' Paolo said, noting the look of contempt on Jack's face as he turned back to obey.

Jack moved forward and sat down, looking at Paolo with just a hint of a smile on his face. How had Jack managed to convince the Chief that he'd been Dave's best friend when he'd been the one to goad Dave so mercilessly? That was something Paolo would never understand. The Chief seemed to feel Paolo didn't care that Dave had died, but what he didn't understand was that Paolo couldn't put into words how he felt about losing his partner – and closest friend. He still felt physically sick about it.

'I get the impression you're not happy here,' Paolo said, 'so I'm putting you in for a transfer to another unit. I think you'll do better under someone else's command.'

'I don't think I want to go anywhere, sir,' he said, with that inflexion on the sir that made Paolo's blood boil. 'I want to stay right here. The Chief seems to have taken a shine to me, so why would I move away?'

'Cards on the table?' Paolo said leaning forward to emphasise his words. 'I don't want you here. You drove Dave into reckless behaviour by your constant harping on his relationship to the Chief. Every day you hounded him and now you have the gall to use his uncle as a shield. You could be a good copper, but you're lazy and lack discipline. If you choose to stay here, you do things my way.'

Jack stood up, still with a smile lurking. 'Paolo, you can do what the fuck you want but I am not leaving. Transfer me? You can try, but you won't succeed. I intend to make sure the old man upstairs thinks the sun shines out of my arse. I've told him how close me and his precious nephew were. He laps up my stories about the good times Dave and I had together.'

Paolo stood up to face Jack across the desk. 'One word from me about the way you really treated Dave and he'd soon see through you.'

Jack laughed. 'Go for it! I'd love to be a fly on the wall when you do that. As far as the Chief is concerned I was Dave's best friend. I even told the Chief that Dave had confided to me how much he felt intimidated by you. Said that was why Dave went off on his own and got himself killed. Put the blame right at your door. Willows didn't believe it at first, but after a few subtle hints, he began to see you were the reason Dave ended up buried by that nutter. He isn't at all happy about it.'

Paolo felt the pulse in his temple throbbing. He wanted nothing more than to reach out and drag Jack across the desk and beat the crap out of him. Gripping the edge of his desk, he managed to control his anger.

'Get out of my sight!'

Jack sauntered over to the door, then turned and looked Paolo in the eye.

'One day I'll be standing right where you are now. You'll have been demoted by then and will be under my command, providing you still have a job, that is. I'm slowly but surely getting in with the Chief and pushing you out. It's as simple as that. See ya.'

Chapter Fourteen

Damn the man to hell, Paolo thought, banging his fist on the desk. *How dare he use Dave's memory to advance his career!* Not only that, but he'd also clearly been undermining Paolo's standing with the Chief. So many things now made sense. Paolo had been surprised the Chief hadn't said much beyond a curt well done when the news of Paolo's promotion had come through. He hadn't really thought about it before, but now Paolo realised the distance between himself and the Chief had been growing since Dave's funeral seven months earlier.

That was when Jack had made his first move by telling Willows he wanted to be taken under Paolo's wing when he'd wanted no such thing. It had all been a ruse to get closer to the Chief while he was vulnerable.

He shook his head. There was no point in worrying about any of that. Dave was dead. Jack would do whatever he'd set out to do and achieve it or not. Paolo had to concentrate on things that really mattered, like finding the bastard who'd taken that young woman's life.

He looked at his watch, wondering when Lydia would come in. Almost as if thinking about her made her appear out of thin air, there was a gentle tap on the door and it opened.

'They told me downstairs to come up,' Lydia said, coming into the office and closing the door behind her.

'Thanks for coming, Lydia. Take a seat.'

'Paolo, she's dead, isn't she?'

There was no point in him trying to deny it, but he couldn't confirm anything before Sasha's parents had been informed.

'I'm sorry, Lydia. You know I can't comment at this stage.'

'You don't need to. I can see it on your face. I can't believe this. She was so young. The same age as Katy. Only a few years older than Sarah when she died.'

Paolo felt his heart contract as it always did at the mention of his eldest daughter's name. It was a pain that never went away. He managed to force a smile.

'She was right, though, wasn't she?' Lydia said. 'There was a stalker.'

Paolo pulled a pad towards him and picked up his pen. 'We still don't know that for certain, but it seems likely.'

'How can I help?' Lydia asked. 'She was such a sweet girl. Always laughing and joking with everyone.'

'Did she have any special friends at work?'

Lydia shook her head. 'Not really. She was so much younger than the rest of us. She was friendly with all the staff, but not friends with anyone as such.'

'What do you know about her social life? Did she mention anyone's name? Boyfriend? Girlfriends she went out with?'

'I know she went to the gym a couple of times a week because she used to say I should go with her. Apparently it's a good place to meet men.'

Paolo was surprised at the rush of jealousy that swept through him . . . He shook off that thought. Now wasn't the time to worry about her love life. He looked up to see Lydia frowning.

'Where did you go just now?' she asked.

'How do you mean?'

She shrugged. 'I know you well enough, Paolo. Whatever you were thinking had nothing to do with Sasha.'

He smiled. 'You're right. Sorry. Let's get back on track. Which gym did she use?'

'I'm not sure. There's one not far from our offices, but I don't think she went there. I've a feeling she used one closer to where she lived. I believe there was a man there she fancied, but I don't know how far that went.'

Paolo scribbled that down. 'Names of girlfriends?'

Lydia fished in her bag for a tissue and wiped her eyes. 'Sorry, I need a moment. She was such a lovely girl.'

'Take your time,' Paolo said.

Paolo watched as Lydia battled with her emotions, wishing he could simply take her in his arms, but that closeness was long gone from their relationship.

Lydia gave a final sniff, stood up and walked over to drop the sopping tissue into the wastepaper bin. As she sat down again, a tremulous smile rewarded Paolo's patience.

'She used to get calls from time to time, but not very often and I can't remember any names. You know what it's like now, Paolo. Hardly anyone calls on the landline. We all have mobile phones. Can't you get the names and numbers from Sasha's? I'm sure that would tell you far more than I could.'

Paolo sighed. 'I know, but while I'm waiting for the tech guys to unlock her phone, I was hoping you could give me something to follow up on. What's the set up where you work? Do you each have your own work station? Is there somewhere Sasha might have left personal stuff?'

Lydia nodded. 'We use whichever computer is available, so don't tend to personalise any particular space, but we each have a small locker. There might be something in Sasha's to help you.'

'Will you be going straight back to the office when you leave here?'

Lydia shrugged. 'I wasn't going to, but I can.'

'It would be helpful. I'll get CC to follow you in her car. She can have a look through Sasha's locker and bring back anything useful. If you think of anything while you're with CC, let her know and we'll follow up on it.'

Lydia smiled and Paolo was struck as always by memories of their shared past. She'd been his first love and he knew he'd never really stopped loving her – not even during the bad times.

'Paolo!'

He jumped. 'Sorry, I was thinking about something else.'

'Clearly,' she said. 'I asked you three times if you'd heard from Katy and you just looked straight through me.'

'Last time I heard from her was a few weeks back. Why? Are you concerned about anything?'

'Not really,' she said, 'but this business with Sasha makes me wish Katy would come home and settle down. I hate not knowing where she is or what trouble she might be in.'

Paolo stood up and walked around to Lydia's side of the desk, holding out a hand to help Lydia get up.

'She's a big girl now, Lydia,' he said. 'We have to let her do her own thing until she's ready to come back to us.'

As she moved closer to him, Paolo caught a hint of her perfume. He recognised it as one she'd used when they'd been together. What a waste they'd made of a perfect love affair. He shook his head. Why was he thinking so much about what should have been?

'Jesus, Paolo, what is wrong with you today? That's the third time you've drifted off on me.'

'Sorry, Lydia, what did I miss this time?'

'Just me saying goodbye. Nothing important.' She shrugged. 'This isn't like you, Paolo. Are you okay?'

He was about to give a standard 'I'm fine' answer when there was a knock on the door. Less than a second later it opened and CC came in.

'Hi, Lydia, how are you?' she said before turning to Paolo. 'Good news, sir. The tech guys have managed to get into Sasha's phone.'

Paolo smiled. 'At last! Anything useful on it?'

'Mike is bringing the info up for you, but he said there are a couple of messages that might help, plus a contact list that should keep us busy for a while. It seems she was a popular girl.'

'I'm not surprised,' Lydia said. 'As I've just been telling Paolo, everyone at work liked her. She had a way of making you feel she was giving you her complete attention. You know you can talk to some people and you're sure they are thinking of other things at the same time? Sasha never did that.'

Paolo wondered if that was a dig at him, but decided not to rise to the bait.

'CC, would you please follow Lydia back to her office? She'll show you Sasha's locker. There might be something in there we can tie in with her phone records. Lydia, thanks so much for coming in.'

'I just wish there'd been more I could tell you,' she said, reaching out to touch his arm. 'I know you'll get this creep, Paolo.'

She looked as if she wanted to say something more, but remained silent. Paolo had the impression whatever it was had little to do with Sasha. Maybe she too was thinking about what they'd thrown away.

As he closed the door behind CC and Lydia, for the first time since Sarah had died, Paolo realised he was allowing his personal life to intrude on the job. Losing his eldest daughter was a different matter, though. It had been understandable that he'd fallen apart back then, but not now. *For fuck's sake*, he thought, *pull yourself together*.

While waiting for Mike to arrive, he tried to concentrate on the ongoing, but sadly stalled, drug-running investigation. For once his mind refused to cooperate. He found himself looking back over the last few years and wondering what the future held. For some reason this depressed him, so he was relieved to hear a knock on his office door.

'Come in.'

The door opened and Mike shuffled in. Paolo forced his face to remain passive, but he could feel a grin trying to force its way to the surface. Mike was wearing his usual mix of corduroy trousers, long-sleeved shirt and tie, and a cardigan Paolo's grandfather would have thought too old-fashioned to wear. On the twenty-five-year-old technical whizz kid the outfit made him look as if he'd raided an OAP's wardrobe.

Mike pushed his unruly hair out of his eyes with the back of the hand holding Sasha's phone in a plastic bag and held out a sheaf of papers with the other.

'Lots to go through here, Paolo. Not sure how much will help but hope some does.'

'Take a seat, Mike. Tell me what you've uncovered.'

'She had all her social accounts linked to her phone and it seemed that was the way she kept in touch with most people. Actual phone activity is minimal. A few outgoing calls and some messages, but mainly she seems to have used WhatsApp and a few other messaging apps. You might find this voicemail useful though.'

He took the phone out of its protective plastic bag and fiddled with the settings. Paolo wished he could be as competent on his own phone, never mind being able to work around all the different smartphones out there. For Paolo, what his phone could do outside of making and receiving calls was still a mystery.

Mike put Sasha's phone on the desk and touched the screen. A young woman's voice, slurred but shouting, could just about be heard over heavy background music.

'Hey, Sash, where the hell are you? I've been in The Pipe for fucking hours waiting for you. You said you'd come tonight. Bitch, I bet you're out with that fucker from the gym. Spud was looking for you. Call me!'

'There's another one,' Mike said. 'Same person, but much drunker.'

He touched the screen again.

'Sash, wha' you? I'm fuckin' pissed . . . an' you . . . not here. Thought . . . you were . . . friend. Goin' holi . . . day . . . Can . . . Can . . . fuck it. Can . . . a . . . da morrow. You sposed to dri' me to air . . . airpaw. Caw me.'

'This is the last one.' Mike pressed the phone again and the same voice could be heard, sounding more sober, but very fragile.

'Sash, it's me. God, my head feels shit. Why do I drink like that? I needed you to stop me. Where are you? Look, when you get this don't feel bad. Spud is coming over to take me to the airport. But you'd better be there to pick me up when I get back or it's the end of our friendship. Just kidding. See you then!'

The room seemed really quiet when the message ended.

'When were the messages sent?' Paolo asked.

Mike looked at the sheet of paper on top of the pile. 'I knew you'd want to know that. Monday evening. The first one came in just before ten and the second one just after midnight. The last one was timed just after six in the morning.'

Paolo sighed. 'Sasha was already dead before the first message came in. What's the caller's name?'

Mike glanced down again. 'Muff. Although that's probably Sasha's nickname for her. I doubt her parents christened her Muff.'

'Whatever her real name, at least I can call her.'

Mike shook his head. 'Already tested the number and got a recorded message to say her phone is out of the network range. She might have decided not to run up roaming charges, or could even be using a local sim while she's away.'

'Damn. I'll just have to keep trying. Is there any way of finding out her real name?'

'I can get in touch with her service provider, but they won't give out the information easily. Data protection and all that.'

Paolo sighed. 'What about the person Muff mentioned? Spud? Is he in Sasha's contact list?'

Again Mike shook his head. 'Nope. That was the first thing I checked. Loads of names beginning with S, but no Spud in there. Taking all her accounts together with her phone contacts, you're looking at hundreds of names to go through. On Twitter alone she has nearly a thousand followers. Several hundred friends on various social media sites. There's some overlap, but from what I can see, you've got a mountain of information to sort through.'

Paolo looked down at the papers littering his desk. 'How can she have so many friends? She hasn't even been living here that long.'

Mike smiled. 'I take it you don't use social media? The friends aren't necessarily people she's met, or even people she knows. They're just people she would've connected with in some way online. I'll have some of my people trawling through her accounts to see if anything jumps out as threatening or creepy, but you know what it's like, most of these sites are reluctant to allow us access.'

Paolo wondered if everyone other than him knew about social media. An ache filled his heart. Katy would have known how to explain it to him so that he understood the lure, but she was halfway across the world.

Paolo shook off the poor me feeling and smiled at Mike. 'You've done a great job. Keep me in the loop with anything new.'

Mike stood up. 'Will do, but it's possible her killer only knew her in the real world and there might be nothing to find.'

As the door closed behind Mike, Paolo vowed, no matter how tough it was, he would track down the person who'd taken that young life as if it had had no value.

Chapter Fifteen

Boy left the solicitor's office and managed to hold his temper in check until he reached the car park. 'Fuck that bastard,' he hissed as he clicked the remote to release the central locking. He climbed into the car and tried to relax. He knew he couldn't turn up at work in this state, but he was so angry he could barely breathe.

How could Grandpa have done that to him? For years he'd believed he was completely beholden to Grandpa for everything – food, clothes, the roof over his head. As that last thought came into his head he hammered on the steering wheel until a knock on the car window made him look up to see a traffic warden peering in at him and gesticulating to open the window.

He pressed the switch and the glass slid down.

'Are you okay, sir?'

The warden leaned forward. Boy wondered if he was trying to smell for alcohol.

'I'm fine,' he said. 'I've just had some news that shook me up a bit that's all.'

The warden looked unconvinced. 'As long as you're sure, sir. I see from your ticket that your time is almost up here. You do know that you cannot pay for more time for another two hours, don't you?'

Boy forced a smile. 'I'm leaving. Thank you for your concern.'

He started the engine and managed to pull away without jamming the gears, or doing anything else stupid. That was him, stupid Boy. Grandpa was right. He was stupid. Stupid enough to be fooled into thinking he was a charity case.

He'd gone into the solicitor's office not knowing what to expect from the will, but sure Grandpa would have left him something. As it turned out, Grandpa had left everything he owned to the local cats' home.

Remembering the solicitor's words made his blood boil again. It was no good, he couldn't drive like this. He'd end up hitting something or someone. As he turned the corner into Camberwell Street he saw a car pulling out of a parking bay. He drove up and parked in the space, going through many more manoeuvres than he should have, but his mind was on fire.

'I leave my full estate to the Bradchester Charity for Unwanted Cats,' the solicitor had said. 'To my grandson, I leave nothing as he meant nothing to me.'

Mr Clerkenwell's hands shook as he read the words and Boy almost felt sorry for him, but when the words penetrated he jumped up, reaching forward to try to snatch the will.

The solicitor pulled it into his chest.

'He can't do that, can he?' Boy begged. He'd be homeless and penniless, apart from the money he'd found in the old man's bedroom and that wouldn't go far.

'I'm afraid he can,' Mr Clerkenwell said. 'Of course, you can contest the will on the grounds of mental instability or a number of other issues, but it would be costly to do so, although you would not have to worry about that, being as financially sound as you are. However, there is no guarantee you could get the clause overturned.'

Boy slumped back into the chair. What on earth did the old fool mean about being financially sound? He earned a good salary, but was far from well off. He couldn't afford to contest the will.

'How long have I got?' he asked.

'I'm sorry, I don't quite understand.'

Boy wanted to shake the antiquated old fart. 'To stay in the house. How long before I have to leave?'

If anything, Mr Clerkenwell looked even more confused. 'Why would you need to leave the house?'

'Well, I can't stay there if it belongs to the cats' home, can I!'

'I'm sorry, I don't quite follow you. The house is yours. It has been for a number of years. Since your grandmother died, in fact. Didn't you know?'

Boy shook his head.

'Ah,' said Mr Clerkenwell, 'now I see where the misunderstanding has come in. Really, your grandfather should have told you, but I understand the two of you were somewhat estranged.' He gave a thin smile. 'Your grandmother inherited the house on the death of the last member of her family – her father. I believe your great-grandparents were not enamoured of your grandfather and had a clause in their wills whereby your grandfather was excluded from any inheritance.'

'So how come no one told me I owned the house? I had no idea.'

Mr Clerkenwell gave another smile. He looked so smug Boy wanted to throw something at him.

'Your grandmother left everything in trust for you. Until you reach the age of thirty, which I believe is next month; your grandfather and I were made trustees of your inheritance. Your grandfather has drawn down a monthly amount since your grandmother died to cover your living expenses and also the costs of running the house – maintenance and such like.'

Boy thought back to all the times Grandpa had called him a parasite. The bastard had been collecting money for him every month and kept quiet about it.

'So the house becomes mine next month?'

'The house has been yours since your grandmother died, as has the money she inherited from her parents. It has all been held in trust for you and will be passed over to your control when you attain the age of thirty. I do apologise, I assumed your grandfather would have told you all this. Without consulting the documents, I am unable to give you exact figures, but you will be receiving something in the region of four hundred thousand pounds.'

Boy came back to the present. Four hundred thousand! He could afford to do whatever was needed to make the cellar even more

68

comfortable. His true love had already shown she wanted him by taking the special sweet. It was tempting to call in and quit his job, but he knew he would never do that. A man needed to work. Grandpa always said that and, although he hated agreeing with anything the old bastard said, Boy knew he'd been right on that one.

Feeling calmer now, he started the engine and pulled out into the slow-moving traffic. The cats' home could have Grandpa's estate. Grammy had shown once again how much she'd loved him.

When Marissa came back from her work trip it would be time for her to take Grammy's place and stay home. He couldn't wait to pick her up at the train station. She must want to be with him, or why would she have told her friend what train she was getting while he was listening? He wouldn't allow her to work once he had her in his care.

69

Chapter Sixteen

When Paolo's phone rang he jumped. He must have drifted off again. What the hell was wrong with him? He fumbled the swipe a couple of times, but finally managed to answer the call.

'Is that DCI Sterling?'

'Yes, who is speaking?'

'Sorry, sir, I should have identified myself immediately. I'm PC Collins, the family liaison officer dealing with the Carmichaels. I have explained the situation to them and both parents want to help in any way they can. Would you be okay with me putting you on speaker phone, sir?'

'Yes, of course. Please do.'

Paolo waited. Of all the tasks the police had to carry out, dealing with the bereaved ranked as one of the hardest. He knew how it felt to lose a daughter, but couldn't allow his own emotions to get in the way. It wasn't fair to the Carmichaels.

'We are ready for you now, sir.'

Paolo cleared his throat. 'Thank you. Firstly, I would like to offer my sincere condolences on your loss.'

Over the sound of Mr Carmichael's thanks, Paolo heard the soft weeping of Sasha's mother.

'I know how distressing this must be for you, so I will keep my questions to the minimum. I understand Sasha came home last weekend. Did she mention anyone to you who might have caused her some anxiety?'

'Not to me, but she and Shirley are . . . were . . . very close. Tell the officer what Sasha told you, sweetheart.'

'She . . . she . . . I'm sorry . . .'

Paolo heard Mr Carmichael soothing his wife and urging her to go on.

'She said she . . . she said she thought the bus driver was a creep.'

'Bus driver?' Paolo asked, scribbling on his pad. 'She took the bus to work?'

'She did,' said Mr Carmichael, 'but that's not the driver she meant. She told my wife the driver of the night bus that she and her friends travelled on to go home after visiting some dance place used inappropriate language. She said he gave her the creeps.'

'A pervert! She said he was a pervert!' Mrs Carmichael said. 'I told her to report him, but she didn't want to get him in trouble and now he's killed my baby girl.'

The only sound coming through for a minute after that was Mrs Carmichael's sobbing. Then the speaker phone was switched off and Mr Carmichael came on the phone.

'I think it's best if I answer your questions. If I don't know I can ask Shirley, but she's not doing very well at the moment. What else do you need to know?'

'Do either of you know the real name or address of Sasha's friend? The one she called Muff?'

'I'm afraid not. She never mentioned anyone of that name to us.'

'Is there anything else you can think of that might help us find out who attacked your daughter?'

A massive sigh drifted down the line. 'No. You have no idea how much I wish I'd never agreed to pay her rent, or had tried harder to stop her from leaving home. You said earlier you know how distressing it must be for us. Unless you've lost a child, you have no idea what it's like.'

Paolo wanted to scream that he knew exactly what it felt like, but now wasn't the time to say so. It would be an intrusion on Mr Carmichael's grief.

'You're right. I'm sorry, I shouldn't have said that. Please, if you think of anything, no matter how insignificant it seems, please call me.'

He gave his mobile and office numbers and ended the call. Getting up from his desk, he moved over to the door and opened it. He looked around the main office for CC, then remembered she'd gone to Sasha's place of work. Andrea was working through Sasha's social media contacts. The only person apparently with time on his hands was Jack. Paolo walked over to him.

'Can you find out which bus company runs the night service that picks up patrons from The Pipe?'

Jack grinned. 'Oh, so now I'm on this case, am I?'

Paolo couldn't be bothered to fight. 'Yes, so find out and bring me the details.'

He returned to his office and tried to work on the reports littering his desk. A few minutes later, Jack sauntered in and dropped a piece of paper on Paolo's desk, then turned and left without uttering a word.

'Arsehole,' Paolo muttered as the door closed behind Jack.

He dialled the number on the piece of paper. Paolo was told his call was important to the company and would be answered as soon as an operator was available, but was given no indication of when that might be. After what seemed like a lifetime, a mechanical voice told him his call was about to be connected.

'Bradchester Sprints. Thank you for calling. How may we help you today?'

Paolo gave his name and rank. 'Could you please give me details on the regular driver for the night service which runs past The Pipe nightclub?'

'I'm afraid I can't do that. You need to come in and talk to our HR executive.'

'Could you put me through to her, please?'

'Him. He's a him, but he won't tell you nothing over the phone.'

'Regardless, I'd like to speak to him, please.'

'As you like,' she said. 'Hang on a jiffy and I'll put you through.'

But a fruitless five minutes later Paolo ended the call. He'd have to call in at the bus company's offices if he wanted to find out anything at all about any member of staff. He had no choice; with CC away, he'd have to take Jack.

He'd got as far as his door, when he heard CC's voice in the outer office. Relieved at being able to avoid Jack's company, Paolo opened the door.

'CC, you're back just in time. Come with me.'

'Don't you want to know what I've found out, sir?'

'You can tell me in the car on the way to the bus company.'

'I do the dog work but the new favourite gets to go out!' Jack hissed under his breath, but loud enough for Paolo to hear.

Judging by the look on CC's face she'd heard it too. Paolo stepped in before CC could react. In any scrap he'd put his money on CC, but had no intention of allowing an argument in the first place.

'Come on,' he said, heading to the door and not bothering to look to see if she was following him. He knew she was too professional to let Jack get under her skin.

'Do you want to drive?' he asked once they were outside the building and heading towards his car.

'I don't mind, sir. You usually don't trust me with your keys,' she said, but the grin on her face took any sting out of the words.

'Dave always drove. That's the only reason I've not wanted you or anyone else behind the wheel.'

'And now?'

Paolo shrugged. 'I guess we all need to move on.' He handed her the keys. 'Just don't drive my car the way you drive your own. I've seen you when you leave here. Bat out of hell doesn't even come close.'

She laughed. 'I'll go slow. Promise. But where are we going? Which bus company?'

He gave her the address and she entered it in the SatNav. Once they were on the way, Paolo pulled out his notebook.

'I spoke to Sasha's parents. I didn't get much from them, apart from the fact that she found a bus driver creepy. What did you discover in the locker?'

73

'I found some info on her gym. Lydia was right, Sasha didn't go to the one near where she worked. She went to one close to her flat. I've got the details.'

Paolo nodded. 'Great. We'll go there after we've finished at the bus company. Anything else?'

'Yes, I found details for her friend's trip to Canada. Clearly she was supposed to take her to the airport and then pick her up on the return flight.'

'Okay, that's great. We can have someone meet the friend on her return. I don't suppose the girl's name was shown anywhere?'

CC shook her head. 'No, it says "Muff's holiday" at the top of the paper.'

Paolo sighed. 'If we don't find out her real name before she gets back, Jack can stand in the arrivals hall holding up a sign saying he's there to meet Muff!'

CC's laughter was overlaid by the voice of the SatNav telling them they had reached their destination. She manoeuvred the car into a vacant parking slot clearly marked Chairman. Paolo grinned. He would have done the same.

The building did nothing for Paolo. It was one of the newer constructions, all glass and steel. Not at all what one would expect for a bus company. Once inside, he realised Bradchester Sprints was just one of several companies housed in the building. Under a massive sign showing the name of the holding company, All Global Logistics, a list ranging from coach travel to ferry services covered most of one wall.

The receptionist looked up and held up a hand in the universal gesture meaning stop. She finished her call and then smiled.

'Good afternoon. How may I help you?'

Paolo showed his identification. 'I'm Detective Chief Inspector Paolo Sterling. This is Detective Sergeant Cathy Connors. We need to speak to someone in the HR department for Bradchester Sprints. I called earlier.'

She nodded, as if she had been expecting them. 'Please take a seat and I will call in a moment to see if he is available.'

'We'll stand, thank you. Perhaps you could call whoever it is immediately.'

Her eyes flew open at Paolo's tone and she nodded.

'Yes, of course.'

Paolo and CC stepped away from the desk and waited. Within a few seconds, the receptionist called out.

'If you would like to take the lift up to the fifth floor, Mr Goodstone will see you.'

They thanked her and headed to the elevators. When the doors opened on the fifth floor they were greeted by someone Paolo mentally tagged as a corporate climber. He was immaculately dressed in a suit that was so understated it screamed class. No way was this man languishing in HR.

The man held out a hand. 'Good afternoon, my name is Goodstone. I'm part of the legal department. Come through to my office and tell me how I can help you.'

Paolo gave himself a pat on the back. He'd known the man had to be someone important just by the way he was dressed. The question was, why was the legal department involved?

Chapter Seventeen

Paolo looked around at the plush furnishings, black leather couches, sleek desk, oriental rugs and a standard lamp that probably cost more than a month of Paolo's salary. This wasn't just someone from the legal department. This was the top bod. Paolo's bullshit antenna quivered. They were about to be told a pack of lies.

'Please sit down. Would you like refreshments of some kind? My secretary can organise drinks,' Goodstone said, holding a finger above a button on the phone on his desk.

'Nothing for me, thank you,' Paolo said, looking over at CC.

'Nor me,' she added.

Goodstone took his hand away from the phone and smiled. 'How can I help you?'

Paolo sat on the smaller of the three sofas. CC elected to remain standing, notebook at the ready. Paolo smiled. She could intimidate even the most hardened criminals simply by looking them up and down. He wondered what technique she'd use on Goodstone.

'Well, you can start by telling me what your driver has done in the past.'

'I'm sorry? I don't quite follow you.'

'One,' CC said.

Goodstone looked in her direction and raised an eyebrow.

'Excuse me?' he said.

CC raised her own eyebrows as a return gesture, but didn't explain.

'You are clearly a person of importance in this organisation. You

76

would not have been called in to deal with us if there wasn't some sort of previous wrongdoing to cover up.'

'This is preposterous! I can assure you there is no question of covering up any wrongdoing by any of our employees.'

'Two,' CC said.

Paolo grinned as Goodstone's head spun to face CC and he glared at her.

'What are you doing?' he demanded.

She shrugged. 'Just counting out loud.'

'Would you be so good as to tell me why?'

'I will shortly, but let's press on. I can see DCI Sterling has more questions for you.'

The man looked as if he wanted to order CC out of the room, but he managed to plaster on another smile. 'Of course,' he said, turning back to Paolo, 'but do tell me, what is it you wish to know?'

'We are investigating the murder of a young woman who regularly used your night bus service when she left The Pipe nightclub. She told her parents that the driver had made inappropriate comments which left her feeling vulnerable. We would like to interview the driver and would appreciate his contact details.'

'I'm not sure which driver that would be. I believe the routes were reassigned a little while ago.'

'Three,' CC said, nodding to Paolo.

Goodstone didn't bother to hide his annoyance this time. 'I am not answering any more questions until you explain to me exactly what you are counting.'

'Lies,' Paolo said. 'Every time you tell a lie, even a slight twisting of the truth, Detective Sergeant Connor picks it up.'

'I can assure you I haven't told any lies,' he spluttered.

'Four,' CC said. 'That was another lie.'

Paolo leaned forward. 'You know exactly which driver we mean. It's my belief you have had complaints from the public about him and so have moved him from that particular route. Why not cut the crap and give us his details so that we can either arrest him or eliminate him from our enquiries.'

'We could insist on a court order,' Goodstone said.

'You could,' Paolo said, 'but then the press might find out that you refused to cooperate with a murder enquiry in order to protect one of your employees. It's amazing how reporters love to protect their sources, but at the same time will rip companies to shreds if they try to hide the names of people the press consider the public has a right to know.'

'That's blackmail.'

'What is?' Paolo said. 'I didn't say I would let out information and I'm quite sure DS Connors is absolutely trustworthy, but these things happen.'

Goodstone sat quietly for a few seconds, then pulled open the top drawer of his desk and removed a personnel file.

'This is confidential information and I really don't want it to go further than this room, but we are being sued by a passenger. She claims the driver exposed himself to her while driving.'

'How could he do that?' Paolo asked. 'I'd have thought he would need both hands to drive the bus. Did he stand up when the bus was stationary?'

Goodstone shook his head. 'Look, we only have her word against his, but she claimed he'd rigged up some sort of mirror system that was focused on his genital area and his penis was exposed between one stop and the next. Naturally, we investigated, but couldn't find any sign of such a system on the bus. However, he has been suspended until this is resolved.'

'And was this the first time a complaint had been lodged against him?'

'Yes, of course,' Goodstone said.

'Five,' said CC.

He glared at her.

'How many complaints?' Paolo asked.

Goodstone hesitated, then looked over at CC, as if weighing his answer.

'I am afraid I cannot answer that,' he said, 'as it could prejudice our legal position.'

Paolo stood up. 'From what you've *not* said it is clear you employed a sexual predator to drive young women home late at night. If you received earlier complaints and didn't act on them you will have more to worry about than a single lawsuit. Are you going to make me come back with a court order, or are you going to furnish me with the man's name and address?'

'I think we'll leave the gym until after we've spoken to the driver, Tom Sidcup,' Paolo said as he reached over to fix his seatbelt. 'By the way, how did you know when Goodstone was lying?'

CC grinned. 'His lips were moving.' She reached towards the SatNav. 'What's the address, sir?'

Paolo looked down at the sheet of paper Goodstone had grudgingly handed over. 'West Castle Street, number 43. Seems a bit odd,' he said.

'What is?'

Paolo shrugged. 'It's an affluent part of town. Why would someone who can afford to live there drive a night bus?'

CC reversed the car out of the parking spot. 'It provides good opportunities to eye up young and probably drunk young women?' she suggested.

He sighed. 'You may be right, but let's give him the benefit of the doubt for now. What other reason could there be?'

CC didn't answer, but Paolo hadn't really expected one.

As the car pulled up into West Castle Street he asked himself the question once again. Why would someone who belonged here want to drive a night bus? It was an area of detached houses, each one architecturally different from its neighbour. Although many were protected by high hedges, wrought-iron gates allowed Paolo glimpses of the properties as CC drove slowly along the road searching for number 43. The houses were not massive, but still bigger than the average three-bed semi in better-off parts of Bradchester.

As the SatNav told them they'd arrived at their destination, Paolo looked through the gates of number 43. A short drive led from the street to the front door of a mock-Tudor property. Paolo had never understood why anyone would want to live in a pretend period house, particularly as most of them were completely modern on the inside.

CC switched off the engine and moved to get out of the car.

'Hold on a minute, CC. I think it would be best if you conducted this interview. Let's see how he deals with a woman questioning him.'

'Right you are, sir,' she said, grinning at him. 'How do you want me to be? Sweet and innocent, or dark and disturbing?'

Paolo laughed. 'Neither! Just be yourself. I want to see how he reacts to you.'

As they got out of the car Paolo wondered again about the man's choice of occupation. 'This is solicitor and banking territory,' he said. 'Nice safe place to live and raise children.'

'I don't suppose they get many opportunistic crimes around here,' CC said as she clicked the button to activate the central locking. 'But I don't want to be responsible for your car getting pinched.'

Paolo walked over to the gate and pressed the bell next to the intercom. After a few moments a voice demanded to know what they wanted. Paolo nodded to CC and she stepped forward.

'I'm Detective Sergeant Cathy Connors. I'm here with my colleague to ask about someone who has travelled on your route several times recently.'

'That woman who says I exposed myself? She's lying! I didn't do it!'

'That's why we need to come in, Mr Sidcup. We can clear up any misunderstandings,' CC said.

'My solicitor says I don't have to talk to you.'

'No, of course you don't, but we might be able to help you if you tell us your side of things.'

There was a long silence. Paolo was about to step forward and take over when the gates opened. They walked up to the house past well-kept flower beds. Either Sidcup was a keen gardener, or he employed someone to do it for him. The place reeked of middle-class money. This wasn't an area for the super-rich, but neither was it bus-driver territory.

A man stood on the doorstep. He was about six feet and looked in need of a good meal. His clothes hung loosely on a gangly frame.

Paolo put his age at about thirty. His hairline was just starting to recede, but he still had a good head of dark brown hair.

'I suppose you'd better come in. I don't know why the company feels the need to bring the police in. My solicitor said it was only going to be a civil case.'

They moved into a spacious hallway.

'In there,' he said, pointing towards an open door. 'Do you want anything to drink? Tea? Coffee? Water?'

Paolo walked into the room, but looked back to answer Tom. 'Nothing for me, thank you. We won't keep you long.'

As he'd expected, the interior of the house bore no relation to the exterior. There wasn't an exposed beam or Tudor feature in sight. In fact, Paolo thought, if he had to describe the room the word he'd have to use would be bland. Magnolia walls, biscuit-coloured lounge suite, brown curtains and rugs, and not a spark of colour anywhere. It was the most depressing room he'd been in for some time. What made it worse was the fact that the furnishings were clearly good quality.

Tom stood just inside the doorway, almost as if he didn't belong in the room. Paolo sat in one of the two armchairs and CC took the other.

'Please come in and sit down,' she said, almost as if she were the hostess and Tom the visitor.

He shuffled into the room and sat on the edge of the three-seater couch. Paolo was interested to see he'd positioned himself as far from CC as possible.

'I didn't do it, you know,' he said, looking at Paolo. 'That woman said I exposed myself, but I was driving the bus. How could I do that if I was driving the bus?'

'Don't worry,' CC said, 'we haven't come to ask you questions about that.'

Tom's head shot round. 'Then why are you here? You said it was about that.' He turned back to Paolo. 'She said it was about that. Why did she say it if it wasn't true?'

Paolo didn't answer. Clearly CC was having an effect on Tom, so he'd leave her to it.

She stood up and walked over to Tom. 'Do you remember this young woman?' she asked, showing him a picture of Sasha.

Tom shrank back. 'Please don't get so close. I don't like people in my personal space.'

CC put the photo on the coffee table directly in front of him and then moved back to sit down again.

'I'm sorry,' she said. 'I didn't mean to intrude. Could you tell me if you know this young woman?'

'I don't know her,' he said, 'but she's been on my bus a few times. She comes on with two friends. Well, sometimes it's two friends and sometimes only one. I pick them up outside that club.'

'When did you last see her?' CC asked.

'I don't know. Maybe a couple of weeks ago. I've been suspended since that woman told her pack of lies.'

'How have you been spending your time since then? Don't you get bored rattling around in this place alone?'

His head snapped up and Paolo thought he looked almost haunted.

'I like being on my own. It's peaceful,' he said.

'No Mrs Sidcup?' CC asked.

'Not yet,' Tom said, 'maybe one day.'

'What do you do in the evenings?'

Paolo studied Tom's face as he considered CC's question. A number of emotions seemed to flicker before he answered.

'I watch TV and play video games.'

'Every night?' CC asked.

'Yes, why shouldn't I?'

CC smiled. 'No reason. So you were watching TV last night?'

He nodded. 'I told you. That's what I do.'

'What about Monday night? Were you home then?'

He nodded, but Paolo thought he looked uneasy. Maybe it was time to step in.

'Could anyone confirm that?' he asked.

At the sound of Paolo's voice, Tom stood up. 'Why are you harassing me? I want you to leave now. Go on, get out. I don't have to talk to you.'

Paolo signalled to CC to get up. 'Thank you for your time, Mr Sidcup. Is it okay if we come back again if we have any other questions?'

'Yes, no, I don't know. I'll ask my solicitor. She said I didn't have to talk to anyone.'

'Your solicitor is quite right, Mr Sidcup,' Paolo said. 'You don't have to talk to us, but I hope you will.'

As they moved towards the door CC stopped to pick up the photo of Sasha.

'What happened to her?' Tom asked.

CC lifted the photograph. 'Why do you ask? We never said anything had happened to her.'

Tom shrugged. 'People think I'm slow, but I'm not stupid. You wouldn't be asking questions and showing that photo unless something had happened to her. Is she dead?'

CC nodded. 'Is there something you want to tell us?'

He shrugged again. 'She was kind. Her two friends could be bitches, laughing at people and being mean, but she never was.'

Tom walked with them to the front door and pressed a button to open the gates. Paolo didn't look back, but he could feel the man's gaze on him until they were back in the car.

'What do you think, sir?' CC asked, turning the key to start the car. 'Is he our man?'

'I don't know yet,' Paolo answered, 'but he was clearly up to something on Monday night.'

Chapter Eighteen

'Fit to Go Gym in March Street next, sir?'

'Where do they come up with these names? What's wrong with calling it March Street Gym? Oh God, I'm sounding more like my dad every day. Someone shoot me.'

CC laughed and manoeuvred the car away from the kerb. 'I promise to do you that favour just as soon as I'm issued with a fire-arm, sir.'

'Just make sure you do,' Paolo said. 'Now, what do we know about this gym, if anything?'

'Only what I found in Sasha's locker, which was her membership card and a few flyers for special events. She'd written on one of them with a yes and four exclamation marks, so must have been keen to go to that one.'

'What was it promoting?'

'One-to-one sessions with a fitness trainer. First session free. Pre-sumably to encourage members to pay for a course afterwards.'

Paolo thought of his own diminishing fitness level and tried not to feel old. 'Let's hope they kept records of who each member was paired with. I like Tom Sidcup as a suspect, but there could be others we need to look into.'

Twenty minutes later CC pulled into the Fit to Go car park.

'Plenty of spaces, CC. Maybe the gym isn't doing so well.'

'It's mid-afternoon, sir. Probably the quietest time for a gym. They get early-morning users, lunchtime fitness fanatics, and those who come after work. I would imagine this time of the day the gym is probably greyed out.'

Paolo climbed out and peered at CC over the top of the car. 'Greyed out?'

She laughed. 'You'll see, sir, once we get inside.'

The gym was bigger inside than Paolo had expected from the façade. The entrance was quite small and dominated by a fancy spiral staircase next to a long unmanned desk. Behind the desk on the wall were posters promising everything from boundless health and energy to eternal life. The reception area opened into a massive room holding what looked like torture instruments to Paolo. Things to pull on, straps to strain against, rowing machines without the water, treadmills and other pieces of machinery whose use he didn't even want to guess at.

Then he realised what most of the people trying to kill themselves had in common and laughed.

'I get it now, CC. This is the retirement brigade trying to hold back time.'

'You've got it in one, sir. Most gyms offer special discounts for older members at certain hours of the day.'

'I'm almost scared to ask, CC, but how do you know so much about the way these places operate? I thought martial arts was your thing?'

She nodded. 'It is, sir, but I also run in the mornings and go to my local gym whenever the job allows. You should try it.'

Paolo sucked in his stomach. 'I think I'll give it a miss.' He looked around again. 'You'd think there'd be someone here to make sure only members use the equipment.'

As he said the words, a man came down the spiral staircase. He was dressed in a suit, so probably not one of the fitness trainers, Paolo decided.

'Can I help you? I'm the manager, Callum Jennens,' he said.

Paolo held out his identification. 'Detective Chief Inspector Paolo Sterling. This is my colleague, Detective Sergeant Cathy Connors. We understand Sasha Carmichael was a member here.'

The manager shrugged. 'Possibly. Without checking our system

I couldn't say offhand. We have hundreds of members, but very few come on a regular basis, so not all names ring bells. May I ask why you need to know?'

'I'd rather not say at this stage. We believe Sasha came along for your free event to try the one-to-one training. I'm sure you would have kept a record of that day, if only to follow up on promotions.'

Callum smiled and moved towards the desk and positioned himself behind a computer monitor. 'One moment and I'll check for you. What did you say her surname was again?'

'Carmichael,' Paolo said and spelled it out for him.

'Carmichael, Carmichael, yes! Here she is. She had a half hour session with Brad Cooper and then booked a five-week course with him. She was supposed to be here yesterday, but I can see from our records that she didn't turn up. I hope nothing's happened to her?'

Paolo heard the question in Callum's voice, but didn't answer it. He glanced into the main room where puffing and panting OAPs were straining their pacemakers. A few of them had young and fit men and women murmuring words of encouragement as they lifted and stretched.

'We would like to speak to Mr Cooper. Could you call him over, please?'

The manager shook his head. 'I'm afraid not. He only works three evenings a week. He'll be here tonight. Perhaps you could come back later?'

Paolo nodded. 'Do your members have to log in? Is there any way of knowing how often Sasha came to work out?'

Callum smiled. 'They have to swipe their membership card to gain access to any machine. They are all non-operational unless activated by a current membership card. Just a moment and I'll be able to tell you what you want to know.'

He checked the computer again. 'She was a regular user. From what I can see she came in at least three times a week.'

Paolo frowned. 'Just now you said you'd know the names of regular users.'

Callum looked taken aback. 'No, I didn't say that. What I said is that not all names ring bells. There was no reason for me to be aware of her. It's the troublemakers, the ones who want more for their money than a standard membership entitles them to that I take notice of. Believe me, some of these senior members seem to think their age should give them all the privileges of elite membership while only paying for the basics and all at a reduced pensioner's fee. I could give you the names of most of *them*,' he said, raising his eyes skywards. 'I'm rarely down here so don't get to meet many members, but I do recognise the names of those who complain a lot.'

'Who is usually at the desk?'

'My assistant manager. While I prefer to stay upstairs in the office, he likes being down here. He is very hands on.'

Callum stood at the desk, the polite smile on his face clearly indicating he wasn't going anywhere until Paolo and CC left. Paolo thanked him and promised to return that evening when Brad would be on duty.

Back in the car, Paolo sighed. He'd been looking forward to a night in for a change. Maybe watch some unrealistic cop show on TV, order in a pizza, and just veg out. Oh well, that would have to wait for another night.

'Station, sir?' CC asked.

He nodded. 'I don't feel we've achieved very much, but maybe Mike and his IT bods will have something else for us to go on.'

As they walked into the main office, Paolo caught sight of Jack's face. The smirk was enough to know the man had been up to something. Ignore him, Paolo ordered himself, but knew he wouldn't be able to. Jack had the ability to get under his skin. He walked over to the white board.

'Listen up, everyone. I want to bring you up to date on what we know so far.'

'You're wanted upstairs, sir,' Jack called out with that irritating inflexion on the sir that made Paolo want to lash out.

'Thank you, Jack. I'll go up as soon as I've filled you all in.'

'As you wish, *sir*, but the Chief did say you should go up the

87

second you get in. He asked me to pass on the message, so I'm just carrying out his instructions.'

Paolo counted to ten silently. He couldn't trust himself to speak until he'd calmed down. Feeling CC's eyes on him, he looked over at her. She was gently shaking her head from side to side. Paolo breathed out. She was right. He needed to keep his temper in check.

'Thank you again, Jack. I'll go up now. CC, would you please come up and share what we've learned this afternoon? Please also arrange surveillance on Tom Sidcup. We need to keep a close watch on him.' He looked up and smiled. 'I'll leave you in CC's capable hands.'

He left the room with as much dignity as he could muster, but still felt like a naughty schoolboy who'd been reprimanded in front of the class and sent to the head to complete the humiliation.

Chapter Nineteen

Paolo took the stairs up to Chief Constable Willows' office. The smirk on Jack's face told him whatever the Chief had to say, Paolo wouldn't like hearing it.

He reached the top floor slightly out of breath. He was even less fit than he'd thought he was. Maybe he should join a gym? Get down there with the silver-haired brigade and do some weights. He smiled as he realised the OAPs he'd seen could probably outdo him on every fitness level.

The door to Willows' office was half open. Through the gap Paolo could see the Chief gesticulating while talking on the phone. The man did not look happy. Standing just outside the door, Paolo could hear the Chief didn't sound at all thrilled with whatever he was hearing. *Great, just what I need,* Paolo thought, *a dressing down from Willows when he's in this sort of mood.*

Willows looked up and waved Paolo in, pointing to a chair on the other side of his desk. Paolo felt even more like a naughty schoolkid facing the head.

'No, I bloody don't,' Willows barked into the phone. 'Any more cuts to our budget and we might just as well put an ad in the paper telling the criminals to do what the fuck they want because we won't be doing a thing to stop them!'

Paolo winced. He could count on the fingers of one hand the number of times he'd heard Willows swear.

'Fine! Noted! Just don't be surprised if the crime rate in Bradchester goes up.'

He ended the call and threw the phone down onto his desk, looking across at Paolo as if he blamed him for whatever he'd just been told. In fact, he looked as if he blamed Paolo for all the ills of the world.

'Sir,' Paolo said. 'You wanted to see me?'

'Yes, I want to know what the bloody hell you're up to, Paolo! I bumped into young Jack Cummings again on my way in this morning. Why aren't you using him on the murder?'

So that was how Jack was inching his way in, Paolo thought. He's been hanging around in the mornings in order to bump into the Chief. Paolo forced himself to hold back the words racing round his head.

'He is actively involved on the surveillance operation at The Pipe.'

Willows shook his head. 'Not any more he isn't. As of this moment that line of investigation is closed.'

Paolo sat forward. 'Why? We need to find out who is moving the drugs around and we know it's someone at that club.'

'We don't have the money to continue a surveillance operation that isn't bringing in results. We've already wasted valuable resources on it that could have been better employed elsewhere. And that brings me to the reason I wanted to talk to you.' He sighed. 'You've always done well with the youngsters, Paolo, but you're not doing right by Jack Cummings. If you remember, I asked you at Dave's funeral to take Cummings under your wing. I can see a bright future for him.'

Paolo thought for a moment and then decided to tell Willows the real reason he couldn't get on with Jack.

'Look, sir, I have kept this to myself because I didn't want to cause you more distress than you'd already suffered when we lost Dave, but Jack was partly responsible for –'

'Don't you dare continue, Paolo. Jack has told me how the two men were well on the way to becoming firm friends but it was your interference that caused a rift between them.' He held up his hand as Paolo tried to speak. 'I have no intention of going into that. I am sure it was no more than a misunderstanding. What I will say is that I have always admired the way you have been able to engender respect and loyalty from your team. I'd like to think you don't make exceptions.'

Paolo swallowed his anger. What was the point in trying to explain when the Chief had been brainwashed?

Willows nodded. 'I want you to nurture Cummings, Paolo. He has the makings of an outstanding officer, but he needs your guidance. I can't think of anyone better than you to mould him and smooth off his rough edges.'

Paolo inclined his head slightly. If Willows wanted to take that as a nod it was up to him.

'Now what's the latest on the murder of that young woman?'

'There is very little to report, sir. Barbara Royston is doing the autopsy on Friday, so we might have something to go on after that. CC is arranging someone to watch the only suspect we have so far, but other than that, we have nothing. This evening I'm going back to the gym Sasha used to interview her personal trainer.'

'Take Jack with you.'

'I had intended to take CC,' Paolo said.

Willows' bushy eyebrows disappeared into his hairline. 'Did I just waste my breath? Take Cummings with you. He needs to see first-hand how you work. He really is keen to learn from you.'

Paolo stood up. 'Yes, sir. I'll do that.'

He managed to get out of the office and down one flight of stairs before the anger he felt flowed out.

'Fuck, fuck, fuck, fuck, fuck! Sorry, that wasn't aimed at you,' he said to a young woman running up the stairs towards his position on the landing.

She grinned and waved a hand as she passed, showing she hadn't taken it personally. Oh, well, time to do as he was told. He just hoped Jack would be able to keep the smirk off his face when he realised he'd won this time.

Paolo swung the car into the gym's parking area. Jack had offered to drive, but there was no way Paolo would ever let him take Dave's place behind the wheel. It was bad enough he'd had to put up with the bastard's gloating smile when he'd been told he would be coming with Paolo to interview Brad Cooper.

In contrast to the abundance of spaces earlier that day, Paolo had to hunt to find an empty bay. He switched off the engine and turned to Jack.

'I'll lead the interview. I want you taking notes. If there is anything you think I should have asked, but didn't, feel free to jump in, but don't talk over me. Wait for the right time. Got that?'

Jack grinned and nodded. 'Anything you say, *sir*.'

Paolo forced himself yet again not to rise to Jack's deliberate provocation. If the Chief could only see and hear his golden boy in action, he'd soon change his mind. They walked from the car to the gym in silence and Paolo again had to bite his tongue when Jack waved him in through the door first as if conferring a favour.

As they entered the gym, Callum Jennens walked towards them.

'Hello again. I saw you in the car park on our CCTV,' he said. 'I take it you've come to talk to Brad? He's over by the rowing machines. Would you mind if I asked him to talk to you in my office, rather than on the floor? I don't want the members upset and thinking there is anything suspect going on here.'

Paolo shrugged. 'That's fine.'

Callum pointed to the spiral staircase. 'If you go up to the top you'll see two doors. One is a private changing room for our trainers and staff. The other is my office. I'll send Brad up.'

Paolo murmured his thanks and headed for the stairs with Jack close behind. As promised, at the top were two doors side by side. Paolo opened the one marked office and entered a room with a picture window taking up most of the wall overlooking the gym. On the left wall were three monitors. One showed the reception area. Callum was still there, this time chatting to a man. The second monitor was trained on the car park and the third showed what looked like a utility area. It was a walled-off section with rubbish bins, a clothes-airing rack, and various cardboard boxes stacked haphazardly next to a door, which probably led out to the street behind the gym. Clearly the manager was expected to keep an eye on what was happening in and around the building.

In front of the wall to the right was Callum's desk. Opposite the desk were two low-slung armchairs, the kind Paolo knew he'd have difficulty getting out of once he'd sunk into it. He decided to pull out the office chair to the side of the desk and sit on that. Jack and, presumably, Brad were young enough to manage the low armchairs without going into contortions.

After a couple of minutes Paolo heard footsteps ascending. The door he'd left ajar opened fully and a tall, athletic man came in. He was dressed in running shorts and a vest that barely covered his muscular torso.

He held out his hand to Paolo. 'Hi, I'm Brad. The manager said you wanted to see me?'

Paolo shook his hand and nodded. 'Yes, thanks for coming up. Please take a seat.'

'Will this take long? I'm supposed to be working with a client and she gets sniffy if I don't give her my full attention. I take it this is about the petty thefts from the lockers? I'm surprised you lot are taking it so seriously.'

'Petty thefts?' Paolo asked.

'Some idiot stole some clothes and other stuff from one of our members. The member was right miffed about it – went off like a nutter. Callum said he was going to report it to the police, but I didn't think they'd send CID round.'

Paolo shook his head. 'We're not here about that.'

'Okay,' Brad said. 'What's it about then? My client won't like it if I don't get back down there pronto.'

'This shouldn't take more than a few minutes,' Paolo said. 'It is in connection with one of your other clients. I believe you worked with Sasha Carmichael?'

Brad smiled. 'Yes, that's right. She's only recently started her programme, but didn't turn up this week. I'm afraid that happens a lot. People come along all enthusiastic, saying they want to change their lives. You know, give up smoking, eat right, stop taking whatever dope or booze they've been using to destroy their bodies, but it turns out to be more like hard work than they'd expected. Then we never see them again.' He shrugged. 'I didn't think Sasha fell into that category, but you can never tell. I don't really know her that well, but I'm happy to answer any questions.'

Paolo's internal antenna quivered. Brad had given far more information than was necessary to answer a simple question.

'How long did you work with Sasha?'

Brad's forehead creased into a frown. 'Let me think. She came along for three out of a twelve-session programme. This week would have been her fourth visit. Is she in some sort of trouble?'

Paolo ignored the question. 'Did you know her outside of here?'

Brad shook his head. As he did so Paolo noticed Jack sit up straighter, almost as if he wanted to contest Brad's answer. Paolo looked over and waited to see if Jack had a question to ask, but when nothing was forthcoming he turned back to Brad.

'Did she associate with anyone in particular?'

Brad laughed. 'A friend came in with her from time to time. I don't know her name, but if you give me a card and she comes in again I can ask her to call you.'

'No one else? No one you saw her talking to on a regular basis?'

Brad shook his head. 'Not as far as I saw, but then I wasn't watching her unless we were on a one-to-one session.'

Paolo thought that was probably a lie, but let it pass. 'Did you notice anyone you thought she might be trying to avoid?'

'I wouldn't call it avoid as such. She was a good-looking girl and one of our regulars had the hots for her.'

'I'd like his name, please.'

Brad smiled. 'No problem, but would you mind if I called the manager up? I don't want to get into trouble for giving out information without his knowledge.'

'No need to call him up,' Paolo said, glancing at the screen opposite. 'It looks like he is heading our way.'

A few seconds later Callum appeared at the door. 'Everything okay?'

Brad stood up. 'The police wanted to know if there was anyone who showed an interest in Sasha Carmichael.'

Callum looked over at Paolo. 'Before I answer that, I think it's time I knew why you are so interested in her.'

Paolo tried to keep both men in his sight as he answered. 'I'm afraid Miss Carmichael was murdered. We are trying to trace her friends and, if she had any, her enemies. Any assistance you can give us would be appreciated.'

Neither man looked particularly shocked, Paolo thought, although both made all the right noises. He turned to the manager.

'You almost seem to have been expecting that announcement,' Paolo said.

Callum nodded. 'It wasn't hard to work out. The news of a young woman's death in suspicious circumstances has been on the local news and in the papers. You come in asking questions about a young woman. Two and two really did make four in this case.' He moved behind his desk and tapped on the computer keyboard. 'What was the name you wanted to give the police, Brad?'

'Darius Nelson used to tease her. I got the feeling she didn't like the attention from him but was too polite to tell him where to get off.'

'Yes, I'm afraid Darius likes to hit on all the pretty girls. I haven't had any complaints, but it wouldn't surprise me if some of our female members found his attentions annoying.' He looked over at Brad and raised his eyebrows. 'You didn't think to mention Greg Mallory? He's another one who spends more time chatting than working out when there is a young woman around.'

Callum typed some more and then looked up. 'I'm afraid I can't give you their details, you know, data protection and all that, but Darius is a Friday night regular, as is Greg. If you come back this time on Friday you would be able to speak to both of them.'

'We'll do that. Thank you.'

Paolo pulled out his cards and handed one to Brad. 'If Sasha's friend comes in, please ask her to contact me.'

Brad promised he would. 'Look, I'm sorry, I've got to get back downstairs before my client goes apeshit.'

'Tell her she can have an additional hour with you to make up for it,' Callum said. 'The gym will cover the cost.'

95

'Before you go,' Paolo said, 'where were you on Monday evening?'

'Where I always am on Monday nights. Right here,' Brad said. 'I hope you're not accusing me of killing her?'

Paolo shook his head. 'It's standard police procedure. We have to establish the whereabouts of everyone she might have come into contact with.' He turned to Callum. 'I take it you can confirm Brad was here.'

Callum checked the computer. 'Yes, he had clients from six right through to ten.'

Paolo turned back to Brad. 'Please don't take it personally. I don't have you down as a suspect.'

Brad shrugged. 'Anything I can do to help,' he said and left.

Paolo nodded to Callum. 'And you, sir. Where were you on Monday evening?'

'I was also here. Mondays are often quieter nights than most, so it's when I catch up with the previous week's paperwork.'

Paolo felt a moment's envy, imagining a time quiet enough to get through the mound of files on his desk. He forced a smile.

'Thank you for your assistance.'

'Not at all. We'll do anything we can to help you find her killer, but I really don't think you'll find the answer here. Everyone seems so normal.'

Paolo looked out through the picture window at the sweating bodies straining and contorting themselves in agony and decided Callum's idea of normal was a world away from his.

'Who looks after the place when you're not here? I take it you don't work from early morning until last thing at night?'

'No, I have an assistant manager, John Soames. We split the shifts between us.'

'When would be the best time for me to talk to him?'

Callum frowned. 'Why would you need to see him?'

'Just routine,' Paolo answered. 'We need to chat to anyone who might have known Sasha.'

'If you come back this time tomorrow John will be here. It's my evening off.'

Paolo waited until they were in the car and then turned to face Jack. 'Did you want to jump in with a question up there?'

'No,' Jack said. 'When?'

'When I asked Brad if he knew Sasha outside of the gym. You sat forward as if you had something to say.'

Jack shook his head. 'Nope. Can't even remember the moment.'

Paolo looked at the smile playing around Jack's lips. He had no idea what was going through the man's head, but one thing he knew for sure was that Jack was lying.

Chapter Twenty

Friday

Boy stood in the middle of the lounge and looked around, satisfied that even Grammy couldn't have cleaned the furniture better. He ran his fingers along the mahogany sideboard. It had been in Grammy's family for ever. She'd told him once her parents had passed it on to her when she'd married Grandpa, so she'd treasured it.

The satin-covered sofas and armchairs were in their proper positions, just as Grammy would have wanted. The scent of freshly cut roses perfumed the air. Boy was ready to bring Marissa home and was finding it harder than he'd imagined waiting for the days to pass until she came back from her trip.

He wandered out into the hall where the lemon scent of furniture polish still lingered. Walking along the hallway, he wondered how long it would take before he would be able to allow Marissa to take over these jobs. He planned to keep her in the training room for as short a time as possible.

Opening the door to the stairway leading down to the cellar, he smiled at the thought of the day she would be queen of his home and heart. Grammy had adored Grandpa and would do anything for him. That's what he expected from Marissa once she was with him. Absolute obedience and a willingness to kiss his feet if that's what he wanted, but would she love him enough for that?

Of course she will love you that much.

Grammy's voice soothed away his fears.

He reached the bottom of the stairs and stretched his hand up for the key hanging next to the door frame. Opening the door, he peered in and smiled.

The bed was covered in pretty linen, the shower was sparkling clean and the pink towels looked fluffy and welcoming.

Marissa was going to be very comfortable.

Paolo stood flanked by CC and Jack as Barbara Royston concluded the autopsy. As she moved away from the table, stripping off her gloves and throwing them into the bin marked for incineration, Paolo studied her face. Usually he could pick up clues from her expression, but she seemed almost preoccupied. As if the dead girl was of secondary importance, which was completely out of character.

'Cause of death was the stab wound to her heart,' she said, 'but the marks and trauma to the neck show she had been violently strangled prior to death. I believe the fingerprints at the crime scene have been processed and match those lifted from her body. What do you make of it, Paolo?'

'I wish I knew. The flowers and the sweet suggest a prearranged date, but from what I've heard from Lydia and Sasha's parents, she wasn't dating anyone and was highly unlikely to let a stranger into her home. We've contacted all the gas companies in the area, but none of them had any record of a gas fitter being called out to the premises. There was a number on Sasha's landline from a pay-as-you-go phone. That got our hopes up for a while.'

'And then? No good?'

Paolo shook his head. 'We managed to trace it to a bin in the next street. He must have chucked it when he left. It had smudged fingerprints on it, but none we could use. We checked out the shop where it was purchased, but they don't keep proper records and have no idea who bought it, or even when!'

Barbara moved over to the sink and turned on the tap. 'So, where do you go from here?' she asked, looking over her shoulder as she washed her hands.

'We might learn a bit more tonight,' Paolo said. 'Jack and I are going to interview a couple of gym members who were apparently keener on Sasha than she was on either of them.'

Paolo was aware of CC stiffening next to him. Damn Willows. He'd far rather have CC on the interviews than Jack any day. She had a way of picking up nuances most people would prefer to keep hidden. Well, why not? There was nothing to say he couldn't take both with him.

'And CC, of course, I expect you to come with us.'

'Yes, sir,' she said.

Paolo heard a muttered exclamation coming from his other side, but ignored it. If Jack didn't like CC coming along he could stay behind.

'Nothing else you can tell us, Barbara?'

She shook her head. 'Only that the knife wounds look as if they were delivered either in a great rage or total panic. It's hard to tell, but whichever it was, the perpetrator had lost control when he stabbed her.'

'Thanks, Barbara,' Paolo said. 'Even though everything I know goes against it being the case, I still hope this was a romance gone wrong. If it wasn't, who knows if or when the bastard will strike again?'

He turned to go, but Barbara called him back. 'Have you got a moment, Paolo?'

'Of course.' Signalling to the other two to go on without him, he followed Barbara to her office.

'Coffee?' she asked, one hand on the snazzy coffee machine Paolo coveted every time he saw it.

He smiled. 'Need you ask?' Settling down onto one of the armchairs, he wondered what it was that was troubling Barbara. They'd gone from almost lovers to friends over the years, but now rarely saw each other outside of work hours. His fear was that the cancer she'd beaten so triumphantly had returned.

'Everything okay?' he asked.

She turned from pouring the coffee into cups and smiled. 'Everything's fine. I have a favour to ask you and it's a biggie.'

Paolo released the breath he hadn't even realised he'd been holding.

'Anything. You name it.'

She laughed as she brought the two cups across and put them on the low table in front of Paolo's armchair. She sat opposite, suddenly looking so serious again that Paolo's heart quailed.

'Come on, Barbara, spit it out. You're worrying me.'

'I've kept it quiet, but I've been seeing someone for over a year.'

Paolo smiled. He knew how protective of her private life Barbara was, but there had to be more to it than a revelation of an ongoing love affair.

'And?' he prompted.

'I don't know if I've ever told you, but my parents are both dead. They were in an accident in Durban. An overloaded taxi pushed their car off the road.'

'I'm sorry,' Paolo said. He would have continued but Barbara shook her head.

'It was a long time ago. I miss them every day, but that's not why I mentioned it. Gareth has asked me to marry him and I've accepted.'

'Congratulations,' he said, pleased to find there was no hint of the jealousy that had hit him last time Barbara had been involved with someone. 'When's the big day?'

'That's just it,' she said. 'We don't want a big day. Gareth has been married before and already had an over the top wedding. I don't have any real family to invite and just want a quiet event with close friends and Gareth's family. The thing is, Paolo . . .' She stopped and looked embarrassed.

Was Barbara going to tell him he wouldn't be receiving an invitation? He tried not to feel hurt, but the feeling of complete rejection hit him so hard he could barely breathe. Their short affair was long in the past, but he'd always thought their friendship would last for ever. He was aware of Barbara speaking, but was concentrating so hard on not letting his emotions show that he missed whatever she'd said.

He looked up and smiled, hoping she wouldn't realise how much he was hurting.

'Well?' she said.

'Well what?' he asked.

'Will you do it?'

'Do what?'

'Paolo, I don't believe you. You didn't listen to a word I said.'

'I'm sorry,' he said. 'I'm listening now. What is it you want me to do?'

'Will you give me away?'

Chapter Twenty-one

Paolo arrived back at the office still in a daze. He wasn't sure if it was the fact that Barbara was getting married, or that he'd agreed to walk her down the aisle, affecting him the most. One thing was certain, her future husband was one lucky man.

As he walked through the main office he glanced over at the murder board. That young woman would never get the chance to find love. He made a silent promise to her smiling picture that he would find her killer and make sure he paid for taking away her future.

'She was a stunner, wasn't she, sir?'

Paolo turned to find Jack standing just behind him. For once he hadn't put the sarcastic emphasis on sir. Paolo wondered if he would ever be able to forgive him for the way he'd goaded Dave. Inwardly he sighed, knowing it would be up to him to make the first move if they were ever going to forge some sort of professional working partnership.

'She was,' he agreed. 'I was just thinking how sad it was that she wouldn't get the chance to fulfil any of her dreams. Let's hope we find out something useful at the gym this evening.'

Jack nodded. 'Well, I'm sure super CC will help, *sir*.'

And there it was again. That bloody annoying way he had of niggling Paolo just when he'd been on the verge of offering an olive branch.

'Do you have a problem with CC going with us?'

'Me, *sir*, oh no, *sir*.'

Paolo stared at Jack until the smirk left his face. 'Don't you think it's time you grew up, Jack?'

He didn't wait for an answer, just headed towards his own office. As he reached the door his mobile rang. Fishing it out of his pocket with one hand, he pushed his door closed with the other.

'Hi, Lydia, I don't have any news yet.'

'I didn't expect you to, Paolo. I'm not calling about Sasha. It's Katy.'

He walked over to his desk and leaned against the edge. 'What about her? Is she okay?'

'Well, you've just answered my question. Clearly you haven't heard from her either.'

He tried to think back to the last email he'd had from her. Was it a week, or longer? It suddenly hit him that it must be three weeks or more.

'Paolo, are you still there?'

'Yes, of course I am. Why are you worried? Has something happened?'

Paolo heard a long drawn-out sigh. 'Not as far as I know,' she said. 'It's this business with Sasha. It's made me realise all over again how vulnerable young women are and our Katy is out in Africa somewhere. We don't even know exactly where she is. I haven't had a call or email for nearly a month and I'm worried about her. Her phone goes straight to voicemail and she's either not getting my texts or she's ignoring them.'

'Calm down, Lydia. I'm sure Katy is just fine. She's done this before, remember? Last time we got stressed because we hadn't heard from her for a few days she went ballistic because we tracked her down in some remote village where she was helping in the bush hospital. We've got to give her space.'

'I know that, Paolo. It's just . . . what if something happened to her? She's all we have left. Please, won't you find out? Make sure she's okay?'

'I'll see what I can do,' he promised, ending the call.

Sighing, he turned and put the phone on his desk next to a pile of reports while he rummaged through the loose papers until he found the page he needed. He'd give the volunteer service Katy was with a call. They'd know for sure if there was anything to worry about.

Picking up his phone, he wondered why Lydia hadn't called the service herself. It wasn't as if they would tell him more than they would have told her. Shrugging, he decided if he lived to be a hundred he would never understand the workings of his ex-wife's mind.

The woman on the phone promised to check into Katy's well-being.

'But you do realise, Mr Sterling, that our volunteers go into remote regions where there is often no phone coverage and certainly no internet service. It isn't unusual for them to be out of contact for several weeks at a time.'

'Yes, I am aware of that,' Paolo said, 'but Katy's mother is concerned, so any information you can give would be appreciated.'

'I will do my best, but I doubt I will be able to tell you anything before Monday at the earliest.'

Paolo thanked her and ended the call. He looked at his watch as he moved around the desk. There was still an hour before leaving for the gym. Maybe, if he didn't get any other interruptions, he could get through some of the paperwork he hated so much.

Paolo drove into the gym parking area and slowed the car down to a crawl looking for somewhere to park. Just as he was about to give up and double park, a car reversed out, leaving a gap right next to the front doors.

He edged into the space, turned off the engine and climbed out, silently thanking the universe for small mercies. The atmosphere inside the vehicle couldn't have been colder if his car had been used as a refrigerated storage unit. CC had tried to talk to Jack, but he'd replied in monosyllables, making it quite clear he resented her presence. CC had spent the rest of the journey in a silence so loud it had almost been deafening.

As the other two emerged from the car, Paolo called them over.

'Do you think we could leave the kindergarten behind? You're both experienced police officers, not children. Act like it!'

He didn't wait to see what effect his words had, but strode towards the gym entrance.

John Soames was waiting for them. 'Good evening, Inspector. Callum told me to expect you. Both of the men you want to interview are here. Callum said to use the office again. We would far rather you did that, if you don't mind.'

'Yes, of course,' Paolo said. 'That makes sense. We need to have a word with you in private. Can you come up now?'

'It's tricky for me to leave the floor at the moment. As you can see, we're packed. Callum did tell me about your visit so I've had a chance to think about things. I barely interacted with Sasha Carmichael, so I'm not sure I can tell you anything you don't already know.'

'Fair enough. One thing, though, can you tell me where you were on Monday evening?'

John looked relieved and Paolo wondered why. 'Monday? Yes, no problem. I was here.'

'All evening?'

'Yes. I didn't leave until almost midnight.'

'And the manager? Was he here?'

John nodded. 'Monday is when he catches up on his paperwork while I look after things down in the gym and reception.'

Paolo nodded. 'Thank you. We'll go on up now. Would you please bring the two men up one at a time? Don't say what it is in connection with. It's better if that comes from us. Is Brad here?'

John shook his head. 'No, he works somewhere else Friday and Saturday.'

'Another gym?' Paolo asked.

'No, I don't think so. I'm not sure where he is over the weekend, to be quite honest,' John said. 'It's not really any of my business.'

Paolo was about to head towards the stairs when he caught sight of Jack's face. He looked like the proverbial cat with the cream. Making a mental note to ask him about it, Paolo sighed. Teachers dealing with delinquent children probably had it easier than him.

As before, Paolo pulled out the manager's office chair to sit on. He glanced up at the screens on the wall opposite the desk. The views were from slightly different angles than the day before. There must be more than one camera in each location, he thought.

Within minutes, footsteps sounded on the stairs and the door was pushed fully open. John came in with a man dressed in deep purple lycra running shorts and a white tee-shirt. He could have been a poster boy for the keep fit brigade, Paolo thought. Dark hair flopping over one eye and a handsome face in the mould of a very young Hugh Grant. He had an air of self-satisfied charm and Paolo could imagine him expecting every woman to fall at his feet in adoration.

'Inspector, this is Darius Nelson. Is it okay if I leave you to it? There are people below who want to sign up for some of our exercise special events.'

He left without waiting for an answer, but that was fine because Paolo would have asked him to leave anyway.

'Please take a seat, Mr Nelson. I'm Detective Chief Inspector Paolo Sterling and these are my colleagues, Detective Sergeant Connors and Detective Constable Cummings.'

Darius raised an eyebrow. 'Sounds serious and mysterious,' he said, smiling at CC as he passed her on his way to sit down. 'What do you want to talk to me about?'

'We're following up on the movements of Sasha Carmichael and will be speaking to everyone who knew her.'

'Who's she?' Darius said.

'She worked out here. I believe you showed an interest in her.'

Darius laughed. 'I show an interest in all the fit ones, but I don't remember anyone of that name. What's she look like?'

Paolo glanced over at CC and she pulled out the photograph they had enlarged from Sasha's phone. She passed it to Darius.

'Oh, her!' he said. 'Stuck-up cow thought she was too good for me. I tried chatting to her, but she brushed me off.' He winked at CC. 'Plenty more fish in the sea, hey, babe?'

'Detective Sergeant Connors to you, *babe*,' CC said.

The ice in her voice could have frozen a lava flow, Paolo thought. It seemed to have the same effect on Darius because he looked back at Paolo as if seeking protection.

'Look, I didn't know her and didn't really want to know her. I offered to buy her a drink once and she turned me down.'

'Do you come to the gym every evening?' Paolo asked.

Darius nodded. 'As often as I can. Sometimes I finish work late if there's a longer than usual operation, so I don't always feel like it.'

'What do you do?'

'I'm a theatre nurse at Bradchester General.'

'Did you come here on Monday evening?'

Darius looked at the ceiling as if the answer he needed was written there. 'Monday? No, my car broke down on Monday. By the time I got it sorted I didn't feel like doing anything apart from vegging out in front of the box.'

'Can anyone confirm that?' Paolo asked.

'What? That my car broke down? Yeah, the AA came out to fix it.'

'At what time?'

'I don't know. Half five maybe six. Look, I've answered your questions. What the fuck is this about?'

Paolo smiled. 'Just one more question and then I'll answer yours. Were you alone watching TV or did you have someone with you?'

'I was on my own. Why? Is that a crime now? I want to know why I'm being asked all these questions.'

'We're investigating Sasha Carmichael's murder, so the more information you can give us about your movements on Monday evening, the quicker we can clear you of any involvement.'

Paolo watched the blood leave Darius's face.

'I . . . I've got the AA report at home. It . . . er . . . it will have the time on it. Fuck! I didn't know her. Honestly, all I did was try to buy her a drink. That's it.'

'Perhaps you could bring in the AA report to the station? I'm sure we'll soon be able to take your name off the list. Could you give Detective Sergeant Connors your address and phone number? Just in case we need to ask you one or two more questions.'

Darius gave CC his details and left, looking a hell of a lot less sure of himself than when he'd come in.

The next man to arrive couldn't have provided a greater contrast to Darius. His gym gear had seen better days and his light brown hair, far from flopping stylishly over one eye, was cut close to his head.

'I'm Greg Mallory. The assistant manager sent me up,' he said. 'He seemed to think you wanted to see me, but I can't think why. I've done nothing.'

'Please take a seat, Mr Mallory,' Paolo said. 'We need to ask you a couple of questions about a fellow gym member.'

As Greg moved to sit down Paolo glanced across at Jack, who so far had contributed nothing to the process. He hadn't even bothered to take notes, so it was just as well CC had been keeping up.

The look on Jack's face seemed completely at odds with where they were and what was going on. Jack looked as if he had a winning lottery ticket. He must have become aware of Paolo's eyes on him because he suddenly wiped the look of glee from his face. What the hell was he up to now?

'Jack, perhaps you'd like to lead the questioning,' Paolo said.

'No, I would rather observe, sir,' he said.

'Mr Mallory, do you know another gym member by the name of Sasha Carmichael?'

'Call me Greg,' he said. 'Yeah, I know Sasha.'

'Okay, Greg,' Paolo said with a smile. 'Were you friends? Did you see each other outside of the gym?'

Greg shook his head. 'Nah, not really. I delivered pizza to her place once, but she didn't even recognise me.'

'Is that your job?' Paolo asked.

Greg nodded. 'It is at the moment, yeah. I do motorbike deliveries for that pizza place in the High Street. It's just temporary though. I'm saving for better things.'

Paolo smiled. 'Such as?'

'Doing a year abroad somewhere. Don't know where yet, but that's the aim.'

'I hope you do it,' Paolo said. 'Were you working on Monday evening?'

Greg nodded. 'Yeah, I do deliveries Monday, Tuesday and

Wednesday evenings. I work daytime hours Thursday and Friday. Why do you want to know? What's my job got to do with Sasha?'

'Would your employer be able to confirm your working hours?'

'Oh, Jesus, please don't go causing trouble for me at work. The bastard who runs the place is itching to get rid of me, but the owner is a mate of my dad, so he can't.'

Paolo smiled again. 'Don't worry; we'll make it quite clear you are not in any trouble. I'm sorry to tell you that Sasha was murdered and we need to establish where people were at the time of her death.'

'When?' Greg asked. 'When did it happen?'

'I'd rather not say at the moment,' Paolo said. 'Would you please give your contact details to Detective Sergeant Connors just in case we need to get in touch with you later?'

Paolo stood up and held out his hand to Greg. 'You have been most helpful. Thank you.'

Once again, the expression on Jack's face made Paolo wonder what was going on in the man's head. He was staring at Greg as if he wanted to commit his face to memory.

They followed Greg down the stairs. John Soames was standing next to the reception desk, speaking on the phone. He mimed a question to Paolo, his gestures clearly asking if Paolo needed to speak to him. Paolo shook his head and mouthed his thanks.

As soon as they were outside, he grabbed Jack's arm and swung him round to face him.

'What was going on up there?'

Jack shrugged his arm free. 'I don't know what you mean.'

'You were staring at Greg Mallory as if you knew something about him. Whatever it is, I want to know. I'm not having my officers keeping information back when it could impact on the investigation. If you want to be part of my team, you need to share.'

'I've told you already, *sir*, I have no idea what you're on about.'

As Jack strode towards the car, Paolo looked over at CC. She nodded.

'I saw it too,' she said, keeping her voice low. 'He either knows something about Mallory, or he picked up on something we missed.'

Chapter Twenty-two

Paolo waited until everyone in the room had stopped shuffling papers, checking their phones, and scribbling notes. He needed their full attention.

'Right, listen up. We're getting nowhere on the few suspects we had in the frame. It's been a week since we interviewed Darius Nelson and Greg Mallory and we're still no further forward.'

CC tapped her pen on the desk. 'But either one could still be our man, sir.'

Paolo nodded. 'Unfortunately that's true as neither of them have a watertight alibi. Although the AA part has been verified, Darius says he was at home on his own for the rest of the night, but really could have been anywhere.'

He turned to the board and pointed to the next name on the list.

'The pizza delivery guy, Greg Mallory, was out making deliveries as he claimed, but according to his boss he took far more time than was necessary. Now that could be as Mallory said, his boss has it in for him and wants to fire him but can't. On the other hand it means he had spare time he couldn't account for.'

Jack leaned forward. 'Didn't he say the delivery bike gave him trouble?'

Paolo nodded. 'He did, but the boss said he's always making that excuse. It seems Greg Mallory is the slowest pizza delivery man in Bradchester. The manager is forever getting complaints about pizzas arriving long after they should. He'd fire Mallory in a shot if he could, but the owner won't hear of it because of his friendship with Mallory's father.'

'What about the bus driver, Tom Sidcup?' CC asked. 'Any news from surveillance?'

Paolo sighed. 'Tom Sidcup appears to be leading a blameless life. He hasn't taken a step outside his home without someone watching his every move. The man doesn't see anyone and doesn't even pass the time of day with his neighbours. I'm keeping surveillance on him for a few more days, but unless we can come up with a good reason the Chief is not going to allow the cost to continue for much longer.

'We might be in a better position after talking to Angelica Macduff. Mike from tech was able to establish she is the female we only knew as Muff who left the various messages on Sasha's phone the night she was killed. CC and I will be going out to the airport to meet her flight on Sunday.'

Paolo expected a negative reaction from Jack at being excluded from the airport trip, but he seemed to accept the situation. Once again Paolo wondered what was going on. Ever since the interviews at the gym Jack had been even more secretive than usual about his movements. He looked pretty pleased with himself as well. Paolo knew he was up to something, but decided life was too short to try to fathom the workings of Jack's mind.

'Did Mike have anything else for us from Sasha's phone?' CC asked Andrea.

She shook her head. 'His guys are still cross-checking her social media accounts, but haven't yet found anything even remotely suspicious. He's sent up this list of names and numbers,' Andrea said, handing over a sheaf of papers to Paolo to distribute.

'Please work out between you who will be calling which contact,' Paolo said. 'We don't want one person receiving ten calls while the killer's phone never rings.'

He felt his phone vibrate in his pocket. Nodding to the team, he retrieved the phone and saw Lydia's name on the screen. Sighing, he answered it as he walked towards his office.

'Have you heard anything?' she asked.

Paolo went in and closed the door with his foot.

'Nothing at all, Lydia. I told you I'd call you as soon as I heard anything. The woman at the volunteer centre said she's been in contact with the people Katy is with and they have no reason to think anything is wrong.'

'You're right. I know I'm just being stupid,' she said, but Paolo could hear the tremor in her voice.

'Are you okay, Lydia?'

A sob answered him.

'Lydia, come on. I'm sure Katy is fine. She's gone AWOL like this before, you know that.'

The only reply was that of Lydia softly weeping and it broke his heart.

'Are you at home or at work?'

'Home,' she whispered.

Paolo looked at his watch. It was almost lunchtime. Maybe he could take her out for a bite to eat.

'Lydia, listen up. I'm coming over. Okay?'

'Yes,' she said and ended the call, but not before a shuddering sob broke from her.

Lydia must have been watching out for his car because the front door opened as he pulled in to park. As he walked into the house and closed the door Lydia fell into his arms.

'I know I'm being an idiot, but Sasha's murder has me thinking all sorts of horrible things. I can't bear not knowing where Katy is or what she's doing. I keep imagining her lying dead somewhere and we won't even know about it,' she said.

Paolo tightened his arms around her in an attempt to calm her. Lydia's body was shaking with emotion.

'Don't do that to yourself, Lydia,' he said. 'Katy is in good hands with that group. If anything had happened to her we would have been told.'

As he spoke he pulled her in closer and stroked her back. The tears stopped, but the trembling continued. Making soothing noises, Paolo edged Lydia into the kitchen.

'Let me make you some coffee,' he said.

She clung tighter. 'No, don't let me go, Paolo. I feel safe like this.'

Paolo felt every fibre in his body respond when she rested her head against his chest and sighed. This wasn't what he'd intended to happen, but it felt so good to have her in his arms again. He kissed the top of her head.

'Don't worry. I'm here for you.'

She lifted her face to his and it seemed the most natural thing in the world to kiss away her tears. His lips barely touched her eyelids and then their mouths met. After a kiss that seemed to last for ever his brain screamed a question at him: *what on earth were they doing?*

He pulled away, but Lydia's hand came up behind his head and drew him close again.

'Kiss me again,' she whispered. 'God, Paolo, I've missed you.'

Paolo knew there was nothing he wanted more than to continue the embrace, but his head wouldn't let him. They'd been down this road too many times before. Gently guiding her to one of the breakfast bar stools, he shook his head.

'I'm sorry, Lydia. I shouldn't have done that.'

She smiled up at him. 'Why not? It's what we do in between the times when we can't stand the sight of each other.'

He shook his head. 'I've never felt I couldn't stand the sight of you. I just sometimes needed to escape from the firing line.'

She held out a hand. 'There's no firing line at the moment. Why did you stop?'

He took her hand in his. 'You know why.'

Lydia gave a watery laugh. 'No, I don't. I need you, Paolo. Let's go upstairs.'

He let go of her hand and turned away to put the kettle on. 'You're upset about Katy and not thinking straight. Going to bed with me is the last thing you need.'

She laughed. 'There was a time when you would have carried me up the stairs after an invitation like that.'

He looked back. 'You're so right, but I've never taken advantage of a damsel in distress and I'm not going to start now. I'll make a pot of coffee and we'll sit and drink it like two civilised divorced people worried about our daughter. Then I'm going back to the office to work on Sasha's murder case. Okay?'

'Okay.' She nodded.

Paolo could see the invitation lingering in her eyes and cursed silently at his own stupidity.

Chapter Twenty-three

Boy took one final look around the cellar. It was perfect. It wasn't how he'd wanted his life with Marissa to start out, but he had to give her time to get used to being with him.

Fixed into the wall between the bed and the shower he'd attached a solid iron ring with a long chain running from it. Boy hated the idea of tethering his love like this, but she'd soon come to love him and then he could set her free. He picked up the end of the chain and felt the inside of the restraint she'd be wearing on her ankle. Smiling, he thought how much she would appreciate the care he'd taken to line it with felt so that it wouldn't chafe her delicate skin. Boy double-checked she would be able to reach the shower area. Grammy always kept herself immaculate for Grandpa. He walked around the cellar and smiled; she'd be able to get to each corner. He didn't want her to feel trapped down here.

It had taken longer than he'd anticipated to get the place ready, but for Marissa he had to do whatever it took to make her love him.

Looking at his watch, he realised it was time to set out for the station. Her train was due in twenty-five minutes and he needed to be there when she saw her tyres had been slashed. He was going to be her knight in shining armour.

Boy parked two streets away from the station. He positioned himself just outside the entrance to the car park and waited for Marissa to arrive. If he hadn't heard her talking to her friend, he wouldn't have been able to plan it as well as this. As Grammy would have said, it was meant to be.

He wasn't sure what her job entailed, but she'd said she'd be away for two weeks staying in various hotels around the country. That would have to stop once she became his. Grandpa never let Grammy go anywhere without him and look how much Grammy adored him for it. Even though Boy had no intention of ever being like Grandpa, sometimes it was necessary to do stuff that felt wrong because the end result was worth the pain of getting there. That's the way it would be with him and Marissa.

He heard the train pull in and doors slamming. It suddenly hit him that someone from the train might come to the car park with Marissa and offer to help. A cold rage filled his body. She wasn't even his yet and already she was probably making eyes at some bastard on the train. If she came through with a man he'd never forgive her.

Footsteps sounded. He peered through the bush and saw Marissa pulling a case behind her. She was alone. But that didn't mean she hadn't been with someone while she was away. He'd question her about that later. She strode towards her car and stopped dead.

'Oh, fuck! No!'

That was his cue. He walked around the perimeter fence and entered the car park.

'Hi, I was going past and heard you. Do you need help?'

Her head whipped round, fear on her face until she recognised him.

'Oh, hello. Unless you happen to have some tyres hidden away, no, I don't think you can. Some idiot has slashed my rear two.'

Boy looked at the car and gave what he hoped was a sign of surprise.

'Who the hell would do something like that?' he said. 'No, sorry, no tyres, but I can call for a tow truck for you.'

Marissa shook her head. 'Thanks, but there's no need. My insurance company will send someone out.'

Boy struggled to keep his emotions under control. Why was she being so difficult?

'Listen, my friend has a garage and tow truck. He'll give you a great deal on the tyres and probably pick up the car free of charge if I ask him. What's the excess on your policy? I bet he could do the

117

job for you under the excess amount and you won't lose your no claims bonus.'

Marissa smiled. 'That would be great. Do you think he'll be able to come over tonight? It's really late.'

Boy nodded. 'I'm sure he will. Let me call him.'

He made a pretence of looking up a number and then turned his back on her.

'Hey, Gary, how you doing? Great, thanks. Listen, I've got a problem. Any chance you could come out tonight to pick up a car from the station? Some bastard has slashed a couple of tyres on a friend's car.'

He turned back and smiled at Marissa. 'Tomorrow bright and early? No problem. I'll get her to meet you here with the keys. Thanks. Chat later, yeah?'

Putting the phone back in his pocket, he took a step towards Marissa.

'Gary will be here tomorrow at eight. Can you get here with the keys for then?'

She nodded. 'I'll get a taxi home. Thanks so much for organising the recovery truck.'

Boy shrugged. 'No problem at all. Glad I happened to be passing. Listen, I'm on my way home from visiting friends. My car is only a couple of streets away. Why don't I give you a lift?'

'I couldn't possibly put you to so much trouble. I've got a minicab number on my phone.'

Boy picked up her suitcase. 'I insist. What's your address?'

He turned towards the exit, leaving her no choice but to follow. Smiling, he thought Grammy would approve. He was taking action!

'Look, really, I can call for a car.'

Boy quickened his pace slightly. 'It's no bother at all. I'll have you home in no time.'

He could hear her uneven steps as she struggled with her high heels in her hurry to catch up with him, but he made no attempt to slow down. He had to get her case in the boot of his car before she could stop him. Once it was safely locked away she was more likely to give in and climb in the car.

'Wait,' she called.

He stopped next to his car and looked back. She wasn't as far behind as he'd hoped. Pressing the release on his key fob, he unlocked the car, lifted the boot and only just managed to place her case inside before she reached him.

Slightly breathless, she smiled, but it looked more of an effort than it had earlier.

'Honestly,' she said, 'I can . . .'

While she paused for breath, Boy opened the passenger car door. 'Jump in.'

Marissa hesitated and then seemed to resign herself. 'Thank you,' she said and climbed in.

Boy shut the door and raced around to the driver's side. It was essential he got in before she realised the handle had been removed from the passenger door. As he slammed his door shut and put the key in the ignition he breathed a sigh of relief. At last he had his love all to himself.

'I live over in Bradchester East,' she said. 'I'm sure it's miles out of your way.'

Boy shook his head. 'Nothing is too much trouble for you, my love.'

'Sorry? What did you say?'

'I said nothing is too much trouble for you, my love. I covered over the CCTV camera, you know. I did that before I slashed your tyres.'

'What? Are you some kind of nut?'

'No, although I am crazy about you. We are going to be so happy together. I know you love me.'

'I don't even know you apart from to say hello to.'

'Then you shouldn't have taken the love heart, should you?'

'What?'

'I think you heard me. Grammy always said people should listen properly but they never do. I hope you are a quick learner. I want you to be just like her, Marissa.'

'What the fuck are you on about?' she said.

He saw her hand searching the door panel, and laughed.

'It's gone,' he said. 'I took the handles off your side of the car.'

'This isn't funny. Stop the car and let me out. I'll call a cab,' she said as she pulled her phone out of her handbag.

Boy reached out and snatched it from her hand. 'I'll look after that for you,' he said, slipping it into his pocket.

'Are you mad? Let me go!'

Marissa lunged across him, hand reaching for his pocket. Boy almost lost control of the car. He pulled over to the side of the road and slapped her face.

'You will do as I tell you!' he screamed.

'Fuck you! Let me out!'

Her fingers became claws as they reached towards his face. Boy put his hands around her throat and squeezed. The drumming in his head grew louder and louder as he pressed his thumbs and fingers into her flesh. Suddenly she went limp and he let her go.

He fought to get his breathing back under control. He couldn't have killed her. Not his Marissa. Feeling her pulse, he shuddered with relief. She was alive. He had to get her home as quickly as he could.

Boy started the car again and pulled out. Fortunately, there was no other traffic on the road. If it had been earlier there probably would have been witnesses. Fucking bitch had ruined their first night together.

Chapter Twenty-four

Saturday morning

Paolo woke to the unwelcome sound of his mobile phone vibrating across his bedside table not quite in time with the ringtone. As he fumbled for the light switch with one hand, he stopped the racket his phone was making with the other.

'Sterling,' he mumbled, voice not yet up to speed.

'Sorry, sir, CC here. I'm afraid I've got some news you're really not going to like.'

Paolo sat up and shook his head to clear it. 'What is it?'

'I've just heard back from the surveillance on Tom Sidcup. It seems the officer on watch fell asleep in his car last night. He claims it was just for a couple of minutes but it was obviously long enough for Sidcup to leave because the officer woke up just in time to see Sidcup's car go up the drive and the automatic door on Sidcup's garage opening and closing.'

'Damn it! What time was this?'

'Close on eleven last night, sir. The problem is we don't know how long Sidcup was out or where he went. He could have nipped to the nearest all-night supermarket for some booze and snacks, or he could have been gone for hours.'

'Are you at the station?'

'I am, sir. I came in early to type up a couple of reports and saw the surveillance log, so thought I'd better let you know.'

'Thanks, CC. I'll be there in under an hour.'

★

Paolo pulled up outside the station just as Jack was getting out of his car. Although not pleased to see him, Paolo knew he had to give the man credit for putting in the hours. If nothing else, he often worked over the weekend when most took every opportunity to have a few hours away from the job.

Paolo laughed quietly. Right, when was the last time *he'd* taken a few hours off? Better not to think along those lines. He climbed out and shut the car door with more force than he needed. It made a satisfying clunk. Great, now he was taking out his mood on inanimate objects. He'd be talking to the walls next!

By the time he reached the main office Jack was already at his desk, seemingly focused on his laptop screen. Paolo gave a general good morning to the room at large and then nodded to CC.

'Listen up, everyone. CC has some crap news to share.'

Loud groans filled the air as CC explained the surveillance lapse.

Jack looked up from his laptop. 'We don't know he's our guy though, do we?'

Paolo shook his head. 'No, but we still need to know where he goes and what he gets up to if only to rule him out.'

Jack looked as if he had more to say, but to Paolo's relief his phone rang.

'Sterling.'

His relief soon vanished when he heard George Mendip's voice. He'd want an update on his daughter's death and Paolo had nothing to give him. They were no further forward on finding who had supplied the drugs to Sally.

'Do you have any news for me? Anything at all?'

Paolo heard the heartbreak in Mendip's voice and hated having to deliver the bad news that the case had been put on ice until further notice.

'I'm afraid not, Mr Mendip. I wish there was something I could –'

'That's why I'm calling. I think I might have something for you. I've been going through Sally's things and found a diary I didn't know she kept. There's not much in it, but she wrote about some boy, man, whatever, she met at the gym. His name's Greg. I can't be sure of the last name. Looks like it might be Melluny, or something like that. Sally never was the neatest writer.'

'Greg?' Paolo said. 'Greg Mallory?'

'Yes, it could be. Do you know him?'

'What does she say about him in the diary?' Paolo said, avoiding answering Mendip's question.

'That's the point,' Mendip said. 'It's a series of dates and times where she met him at The Pipe. The place where she was given the bad drugs. I've checked against a calendar and every meeting took place on a Saturday night. Tell me, Sterling, can you act on it?'

Paolo, aware of the Chief's words on the subject, knew he couldn't do anything officially, but that didn't mean he couldn't do a bit of checking up in his spare time.

'Give me the dates and times, Mr Mendip. I'll do my best to look into it for you.'

Paolo scribbled down the information and ended the call.

'I thought that investigation had been dropped,' Jack said.

'It has, but we've been given a new lead. One which crosses our murder investigation, so maybe we can look at both at the same time.'

'So what's the connection?' Jack asked.

'Greg Mallory, the pizza delivery guy. Sally Mendip kept a record of all the Saturday nights she met up with him at the club. I think I might take a wander out there tonight and see if I can spot anything going on.'

Jack stood so quickly, his chair spun away from him.

'I'll do it.'

Paolo saw the flush of excitement on Jack's face and wondered what was going on in his head.

'Why? Why now when you couldn't wait to get away from surveillance there not that long ago.'

Jack shrugged. 'I know the place well enough. I'm more likely to pick up something untoward than you or anyone else. Unless you have something more pressing for me to do, *sir*?'

And there it was, Paolo thought. That slight stress on the word that turned it into an insult.

'Maybe I should come out with you,' Paolo said, trying not to enjoy the look of horror on Jack's face.

'I think it would be better if I went alone,' Jack said. 'I know all the hiding places around the club and none of them are big enough for two.'

'If you're happy to take a drive out there, fine,' Paolo said. 'But don't get involved in anything other than observation. For all we know Sally Mendip was in a relationship with Greg Mallory.'

'Yeah, right,' Jack said. 'She was a stunner from the right side of town. He's a loser from the wrong side. Can't see them coming together in some great romance.'

Paolo shrugged. 'Stranger things have happened. But if Mallory *is* dealing, it would be good to know. Although, even if he is, I doubt he's the boss of the operation. So, take notes, Jack, but don't spook him. We need to know who's supplying him.'

Saturday evening

Paolo flicked between channels. Dancing or singing. Those were the choices for a Saturday night's viewing. Neither appealed. His mind kept going back to Jack's enthusiasm to spend the night watching a place he swore he'd never go near ever again. He was up to something. The more Paolo thought about it, the more he was convinced Jack knew more than he was letting on. At the gym he'd acted weird during the Mallory interview, even though he'd denied it later.

Pressing the off button on the remote, Paolo stood up. No way could he concentrate on the crap on television. He'd go out and keep Jack company, whether he wanted him there or not. Maybe Willows was right and he should give Jack more credit.

Paolo laughed. He must be getting soft in the head if he thought Jack was out for anything other than his own advancement. Still, it wouldn't do any harm to have two watching the club.

He picked up his phone and called Jack's mobile.

'Yes?' Jack whispered. 'I can't speak up in case someone hears me.'

'Listen, Jack, I'm coming over to do a spot of surveillance with you.'

'Why?'

'What do you mean, why? Because I think the two of us are less likely to miss something than one alone.'

After a brief silence when Paolo thought Jack might have ended the call, his voice came through again.

'Are you saying you don't think I can manage this alone?' he hissed.

Paolo sighed. 'No, that's not what I said, but if you want to take it that way be my guest. I'm coming over regardless of what you might think. Where are you? I don't want to trip over you when I get there.'

There was another silence.

'Jack, stop pissing about and tell me where to find you.'

'I'm in the car park opposite the club, but don't park there. I've left my car a few blocks over.'

'Fine,' Paolo said. 'I'll be with you in about twenty minutes.'

'Great! I can hardly wait.'

The sarcasm dripping from Jack's words was unmistakeable, but Paolo decided to let it go. What was the point in antagonising the idiot still further?

Paolo pulled into a space four streets away from the club and made his way on foot. As he walked, he thought about the connection to Sally Mendip's death and Sasha Carmichael's murder. The gym and the club were frequented by someone they both knew, but did that mean there was more than a coincidental connection? Probably not. Both women lived in the same part of town and were similar ages, so it would have been more surprising if they didn't have at least one person or place in common.

On the other hand, he had to bear in mind that Greg Mallory's name had cropped up in both investigations. If nothing else, it was worth keeping tabs on Mallory's movements.

Paolo was so deep in thought he arrived at the street before the club almost without realising how much ground he'd covered. He slowed his pace and looked around. Jack should be in the car park somewhere, but Paolo didn't want to go over to look.

He stopped on the corner opposite the club's car park next to a kebab restaurant. Pretending to look at the menu lit up in the window, he used the reflection to scan the area on the other side of the street. No sign of Jack, but the usual queue of people lined the pavement waiting to get into the club.

He recognised the bouncer controlling the crowd, although Brad Cooper looked very different in his street clothes to the way he'd appeared at the gym. No wonder Jack had looked like the cat that got the cream when they'd interviewed Brad. He'd known all along there was a connection with this place. Paolo watched Brad for a few moments as he singled out the good-looking girls and allowed them in ahead of the young men in the queue. It didn't look as if anyone was complaining and Brad was totally in control of the situation. Maybe that was the way it always worked here.

So, where was Jack hiding? Paolo knew he couldn't stand looking at the menu for much longer without drawing attention to himself. Just as he was about to move away, a pizza delivery bike screeched to a halt outside the club. Greg Mallory jumped off and sauntered over to Brad. They shook hands and Greg must have said something because Brad smiled and nodded.

Did something pass between them during the handshake? Paolo couldn't be sure, but his gut told him it had. If Jack was here somewhere he could continue to watch the club on his own, which is what he'd wanted all along. Paolo needed to get back to his car in time to follow Greg. If he was delivering, he must be getting his supply from somewhere and maybe Paolo could follow him to the source if he was quick enough.

He walked away from the kebab restaurant and waited until he was out of sight of the club before breaking into a run. As he passed an alleyway he heard someone groaning in agony. Determined not to be side-tracked, he continued for a few paces, but then his conscience kicked in. He could get one of his team to track Greg's movements. Whoever was in that alley had sounded pretty desperate.

Paolo turned and ran back to where he'd heard the noise. The alley was completely dark – the street light didn't penetrate and there didn't appear to be any windows in the walls on either side. If there were, there was no light coming from them.

Paolo tapped the torch app on his phone and edged his way forward. The groaning had stopped, which probably wasn't a good sign. Sweeping his phone from side to side he searched for the person in distress. It wasn't until the beam reached the dead end at the back of the alley that he saw a bundle of clothes. It took a few moments before he realised it was a man. His limbs were bent into shapes no human was designed to achieve.

Rushing forward, Paolo felt for a pulse. It was barely there. He hit speed dial and waited for the emergency services to answer. The man's face was bloodied and bruised, but still recognisable. It was no wonder he hadn't been able to spot Jack in the car park. He'd been beaten almost to a pulp in this alley and left for dead.

Paolo had never been so relieved to hear the sound of a siren and rushed out of the alley to flag down the ambulance.

'Police officer at the back of the alley,' he said to the first medic on the scene. 'He's in a bad way.'

'And you are?' a voice asked behind Paolo as another medic ran past him.

He turned to see who'd spoken and found himself under the scrutiny of a young woman who looked barely older than Katy.

'Detective Chief Inspector Paolo Sterling,' he said, showing his identification.

'Can you tell us anything that might help our assessment of your colleague?'

Paolo shook his head. 'I was going past and heard him groaning. As soon as I saw the state he was in I called for help.'

'You weren't together?' she asked, looking down at Paolo's clothes.

Wondering why, he glanced down himself and saw he had bloodstains on his jacket from where he'd leant over Jack trying to find a pulse.

'No, we arrived separately. I'd been looking for Jack, DC Cummings, and was about to return to my car when I heard him.'

She nodded, but couldn't have looked more suspicious if she'd been a police officer. Paolo smiled to himself. That must be the way he appeared to others.

There was a shout from within the alley and moments later the two men came out carrying Jack on a stretcher.

'How is he?' Paolo asked as they rushed past.

'Too soon to tell,' the leading medic answered.

'Not looking good,' the other said.

Paolo nodded to the young woman and sprinted for his car. Even as he worried about Jack's chances, he wondered what he'd found out that had put his life in danger. Someone had been prepared to commit murder to stop him from passing on whatever he'd learned.

Chapter Twenty-five

Paolo paced up and down the hospital corridor, his emotions alternating between anger and frustration. As he turned back towards the lift for the fiftieth time, the doors opened and Chief Inspector Willows stepped out.

Paolo covered the short distance between them, but before he could speak Willows let fly.

'What the hell happened last night, Paolo?'

Paolo looked at Willows and wished he had an answer for him. What had happened to Jack? Until he recovered, *if* he recovered, they were unlikely to find out. Jack was still in surgery and would be there for a few more hours yet. It seemed it wasn't just his limbs that took a beating. Most of his internal organs had suffered as well.

'Well?'

'I just don't know, sir,' Paolo said.

Willows glared at him. 'I told you to drop this case and concentrate on the murder inquiry.'

'I know you did, sir, and I followed your orders, but –'

'Are you telling me Jack went rogue and set up surveillance without your knowledge?'

A porter pushed an empty trolley bed through the gap between them, saving Paolo from having to answer immediately.

'No, sir, I'm not saying that,' he said, as soon as the obstacle cleared their space. He moved away from the wall and faced Willows. 'We received a lead on the Mendip case that appeared to overlap with our murder investigation. It seemed to me to be worth pursuing. Jack chose to go out on his own.'

Willows' eyebrows almost disappeared into his hairline. 'And yet you were there?'

Paolo shrugged. 'I arrived later. I thought Jack might need help.'

'Clearly he did!' Willows said. 'I hold you entirely responsible for his condition, Paolo. Whatever happens, whether he pulls through or not, you can consider your recent promotion short-lived. In my opinion, you have forfeited any right to it.'

Paolo watched as Willows stormed towards the lift. In truth, he couldn't give a crap about being a DCI, but he cared deeply about his team – even idiots like Jack. No one deserved to be in the state Jack had been in when Paolo found him.

He looked at his watch. Two-thirty in the morning and he had to pick CC up at six to head down to Heathrow. They needed to make sure they arrived well before Angelica Macduff's flight came in. The last thing he could afford was for the flight to land early and they missed her.

He headed towards the ward duty station and waited for the nurse to finish reassuring someone on the phone that their relative was going to be just fine. As soon as she ended the call Paolo moved forward.

'Hi, I spoke to you earlier when my colleague was brought in. I just wanted to make sure you had my number if . . . if there was anything to report.'

She nodded, sympathy showing in the way she looked at him. Clearly, she wasn't expecting to be passing on good news.

'I have your mobile, home and office numbers. Someone will call you if his situation changes post-surgery.'

'Thank you.'

Paolo pressed the button for the lift and wished he could give in to the rage that was almost consuming him. He wanted to kick the lift doors, punch the walls, swear at anyone who glanced in his direction, but he couldn't do any of those things. All he could do was swallow his anger and get on with the job.

★

Paolo pulled up outside CC's apartment and climbed out of the car. As he walked round to the passenger side, she appeared in the block entranceway.

'You want me to drive, sir?' she asked as she approached the car. 'You look like crap if you don't mind my saying so. Actually, you look like crap whether you mind me saying it or not. No sleep? What's happened? Looks like something big.'

Paolo nodded and slid into the passenger seat. He waited until she was settled behind the wheel before answering her question.

'Jack's in hospital.'

'What? Is he sick?'

Paolo shook his head. 'Someone tried to beat him to death not far from The Pipe. He's in a critical condition in ICU.'

'Any idea who or why?'

'Not yet, but I will. He's far from my favourite person, but he's part of my team.'

He waited for CC to say something, but she shrugged and stayed quiet for a few minutes. When she finally spoke it was clear she wasn't going to comment on Jack's situation.

'What time is Angelica Macduff's flight due in?'

Paolo pulled out the printout Mike from IT had given him. 'Five to ten, but we should get there well before then.'

'Sir, why don't you put the seat back and have an hour's doze? You'll be in no fit state to talk to anyone if you don't rest up a bit.'

Paolo was about to decline when he suffered a yawning fit that would have given the lie to any claim of not being tired. He reached down, pulled the lever and gave in to sleep as soon as the seat reclined.

He woke an hour and a half later to find CC shaking his shoulder. His head felt like it had been drenched in treacle and his back was on fire from being twisted while he slept. Shaking his head, he pulled the lever to raise the seat back up to its normal position. By the time CC had parked Paolo was almost able to convince himself he was fully awake.

They headed into terminal five and made for the board to see if the flight was due to land on time.

'There it is, sir,' CC said. 'BA098 from Toronto due at 9:55 a.m. but delayed by twenty minutes.' She looked at her watch. 'We've got time to sort out some coffee.'

Paolo had no intention of arguing with that idea and followed CC towards the massive Starbuck's sign hanging a few hundred yards away.

As they queued Paolo looked at his notes. 'Let's hope Angelica can help. The way things stand, we have no idea who Sasha might have thought was following her. Maybe she confided in Angelica.'

CC ordered their coffee before turning to Paolo. 'She would have told someone for sure. Women share their fears more than men.'

The barista handed over two cardboard cups. Paolo picked up both and walked to the nearest free table. As he downed the coffee, life finally returned to his brain.

'Have you got the copy of Angelica's photo?' he asked.

CC nodded. 'Let's hope she hasn't changed her hairstyle and colour while she's been away.'

'I thought of that,' Paolo said and reached into his inside jacket pocket. He pulled out a folded piece of paper. 'I printed this off before leaving home,' he said, unfolding it to show CC Angelica's name emblazoned across it. He checked his watch. 'Come on, let's take this over to the gate and grab a good position.'

Nearly an hour passed before the passengers began to trickle through from the Toronto flight. Paolo spotted Angelica almost immediately and waved his printed banner in her direction. She looked surprised, but pulled her suitcase towards them.

As she neared, Paolo held up his identity card.

'What is it?' she asked. 'Please don't tell me something has happened to my mum and dad!'

Paolo shook his head. 'Nothing like that. We'd like to have a chat with you about one of your friends, if that's okay.'

Angelica shook her head. 'Right now? I was expecting someone to be here to meet me,' she said, looking around, 'but it looks like she's let me down. Sorry, I need to go and see if I can get a place on the shuttle.'

'We're from Bradchester,' CC said. 'We can give you a lift all the way home and chat in the car on the way. How does that sound?'

She smiled. 'Sounds like a deal,' she said. 'I'll get back much faster with you. The shuttle stops at so many places en route, it sometimes feels like I'll never get home. I'm already battling with the time zone change as it is.'

As they walked towards the car park Angelica seemed to catch up with Paolo's earlier words.

'You said something about one of my friends. Which one? What's happened? Not Sasha? Is that why she isn't here?'

Paolo shook his head. 'Let's wait until we're in the car.' He pointed to the press of bodies moving in all directions. 'It's impossible to talk while we're battling against all these people.'

As CC manoeuvred the car through the airport traffic Paolo explained to Angelica why they had come to meet her off the plane.

'So have you any idea who Sasha believed was stalking her?'

'She told me she thought someone was watching her, but when I asked who she said she didn't know. I can't believe she's dead. God, I wish I'd asked more questions, but to be honest I thought she was being a drama queen.' She opened her handbag and began rummaging. 'Where have I put my bloody tissues?' she said, tears streaming down her face.

Paolo leaned forward and opened the glove compartment. He pulled out a nearly full box of tissues and passed it back to Angelica.

He waited until she'd regained control of her emotions before moving on with his questions.

'On your messages to Sasha you mentioned Spud. How did she get on with him?'

Angelica gave a watery sniff. 'I don't understand. Who do you mean?'

'What was the relationship between Spud and Sasha?'

'Friends,' Angelica murmured through a fresh bout of tears. 'I introduced them and they became almost inseparable.'

'What's his real name?' Paolo asked, pencil poised over his notebook.

'Who?' Angelica asked.

Paolo wondered if she was suffering from shellshock over the news of her friend's murder.

'Spud,' he said. 'What's his real name?'

'Spud isn't a man,' Angelica said. 'She's one of my oldest friends. Her name's Marissa. Marissa Piper. We gave her the name Spud at school. It seemed funny back then. That's the same time I became Muff to my friends. We all had dumb nicknames, but only Spud's and mine stuck.' She must have seen the confusion on Paolo's face. 'My surname's Macduff, so it got shortened to Muff. Marissa's name was close to the potato, you know, Maris Piper, so she became Spud.'

'Right, I see,' said Paolo. 'You say Sasha and Marissa were close?'

Angelica nodded. 'Very close. I was meeting Sasha at The Pipe one night. Spud had never been, so she came along to see what it was like. She and Sasha hit it off straight away and met up quite often for lunch and shopping and stuff. They even joined the gym together.' She tried to smile, but it was a woeful effort. 'They tried to get me to go more often than I did, but I have to be in the mood to work out and most nights I'm too tired.'

Paolo asked for Marissa's address and contact numbers.

'What more can you tell me about Marissa? It helps if we know as much as possible before we interview someone.'

Angelica leaned forward. 'Spud can be a bit prickly. She grew up in care and doesn't have a high opinion of authority, so might be a bit stroppy with you at first, but she'll want to help you find out who did that to Sasha.'

Paolo nodded. He'd met many adults who had a low opinion of authority because of the life they'd experienced in the system. It was hardly surprising considering how badly so many were treated by those who were supposed to care for them.

'We'll drop you off at your home and then call round to see if Marissa has any idea who might have been stalking Sasha.'

Angelica sagged back against the seat. 'I hope she does.'

Paolo dialled the mobile number Angelica had given him for

Marissa, but it went straight to voicemail. He left his name and number, but said he'd call back.

Angelica looked surprised there was no answer.

'Spud's been away on a business trip, but she should be back by now. Weird that she hasn't answered. She's not like me. I didn't bother switching on my phone while I was away, but Spud is glued to hers.'

An hour later CC pulled up outside the apartment block where Angelica lived. Paolo got out and opened the car door while CC went to the boot to retrieve the suitcase.

As she got out of the car, Angelica's tears were still flowing.

'Please get whoever hurt Sasha,' she begged.

Paolo nodded. 'I intend to,' he said. 'Let's hope Marissa can give us a hand to find him.'

As CC pulled away from the curb, Paolo tried Marissa's mobile number again, but it clicked over immediately to voicemail.

Back at the station Paolo repeatedly dialled Marissa's number, always getting the same result. He tried to concentrate on working through reports, but couldn't shake off the thought that something bad had happened to Marissa.

There was a light tap on his door. When he looked up CC was standing in the doorway.

'Why don't you head home? You look shattered and it's been a long day.'

Paolo shook his head. 'I can't leave just yet,' he said, pointing to the files on his desk. 'I've got these to finish off. Then I'm going to call in at the hospital to see if there's any improvement in Jack's condition.'

She shrugged. 'Up to you, of course, sir, but you won't be helping anyone if you collapse from exhaustion. When was the last time you took a few hours off?'

Paolo forced up a smile. 'You know the answer to that one. Probably the same day you did!'

CC smiled. 'Sad pair, aren't we? God, I remember the days when

I had a social life. I need to get one back again before I forget how to have fun – and so do you! I'm off home. See you tomorrow.'

As the door closed behind her, his phone rang. *Oh bloody hell, now what?* He saw Lydia's name on the display and was tempted to ignore the call, but couldn't bring himself to do so.

'Hi, Lydia, what's up?'

'Nothing. I'm making paella and wondered if you fancied sharing it with me?'

Paolo's stomach took that moment to rumble and remind him he hadn't eaten much that day. The thought of going home and making something for himself, or stopping off for a takeaway couldn't compete with Lydia's cooking.

'Don't worry,' she said. 'It was just an idea. I'm going to freeze most of it anyway.'

Realising he'd taken too long to answer, he rushed into speech.

'No, don't do that. I'd love to come over. I've got some work to finish up here and then need to call in at the hospital. Okay if I get to you in a couple of hours?'

'Sure, but let me know if you're going to be any later, or if you can't make it.'

'I'll be there. Looking forward to it.'

As he ended the call Paolo realised he'd spoken the absolute truth. It wasn't just the food; he was looking forward to spending time with someone who knew him better than anyone else. His ex-wife was probably the one person with whom he could just be himself – a man trying to do his best and all too frequently failing.

Paolo approached Jack's room wishing he could turn the clock back and outright forbid him from going to The Pipe that night. Although, as he opened the door, he acknowledged that nothing he could have said or done would have made any difference once Jack had made up his mind.

He was about to go in when he realised there was an older woman sitting next to Jack's bed. The family resemblance was so strong, she could only be his mother.

'I'm sorry,' Paolo said softly, as she looked up. 'I didn't realise there was anyone in here.'

She stood up, put her finger to her lips and gestured towards Paolo, making it clear she wanted him to go outside. He took a step back and waited for her in the corridor. A few seconds later, the door opened again and she came out.

'I know who you are,' she hissed.

Taken aback by the venom, Paolo couldn't immediately find his voice.

'You're the one who wants my boy to fail. He's told me all about you.'

'I'm sorry, Mrs Cummings, but—'

'So you should be. He's always looked up to you. He told me all about how hard he tries to please you, but you're so high and mighty you've no time for him. Well, right now, I've no time for you. I don't want you near my son.'

Paolo watched helplessly as tears streamed down her face.

'Go on, go away and don't come back.'

She turned her back and re-entered Jack's room. Paolo stood and watched as the door closed with the softest of clicks. It felt like thunder to Paolo's ears. How could he have caused so much hatred in Jack that he was prepared to lie to his own mother?

Paolo turned and headed for the nurses' station. He'd get an update on Jack's condition and then head over to Lydia's. There was no point in staying.

Paolo put his knife and fork together and smiled.

'That was delicious,' he said. 'Shall I make us some coffee?'

Lydia shook her head. 'Let's have another glass of wine.'

'Right now there's nothing I'd like more, but I've already had enough to put me right on the limit, Lydia.'

'You could stay over. Katy's bed is made up.'

Paolo was suddenly too tired to move. Driving home felt like running a marathon, too much effort for too little reward. Why not sleep here tonight and go home early tomorrow to shower and get ready for work?

He lifted up the wine bottle and refilled their glasses.

Lydia smiled. 'Let's go through to the lounge and have this. The dishes can wait.'

Paolo wanted more than anything to spend the night, but what was in his mind was not necessarily in Lydia's. He wondered if he would ever stop wanting her, ever stop loving her.

He stood up and reached for his glass. Lydia did the same thing and he found himself just inches away from her. She looked up, a smile trembling on her lips. He put down his wine glass, took hers and placed it next to his on the table.

As he turned back to her, she melted into his arms and nothing had ever felt so right.

Chapter Twenty-six

Boy put the tray on the floor and unlocked the door into the cellar, then picked up the tray again and smiled. He'd made a special effort with Marissa's first meal in her new home. He'd even put a small bowl of love heart sweets, all with positive messages, next to the single red rose he'd picked before coming down.

As he opened the door it flew back towards him, tipping the tray from his hands. Orange juice dripped from his face and scrambled eggs covered his shoes.

He shoved hard and heard a grunt as Marissa fell backwards. Boy stepped into the room as she was picking herself up off the floor. Before he could move, she charged at him, fingers like talons reaching for his face.

'You fucking bastard. Let me out of here,' she screamed.

He managed to catch both wrists and wrestled her to the ground. How dare she attack him when all he'd done was love her? As her naked body squirmed under him he felt the heat grow in his groin. He wanted that marvellous feeling he'd had with Sasha. Why was Marissa being so stupid?

He raised himself up and punched her face.

'You took the sweet,' he yelled. 'You took the love heart.'

With each word he smacked her again and again until she lay still. Panting, he got to his feet, then reached down to lift her into his arms and carried her over to the bed.

'I'm so sorry. I never meant to hurt you. Why did you make me do that?'

He settled her on the mattress and then leaned down to touch the red welts on her face. He'd never hit her like that ever again. That wasn't who he was.

'Why did you attack me?' he whispered. 'I made a special meal for you and you ruined it.'

He sighed. He had to be patient, give her time to get used to being his. But then he heard Grandpa's voice.

You can't give her time, Boy. You have to start training her right now. Take what's yours. She belongs to you.

Boy ignored the voice. He would do what was right. Marissa was the one. He was sure of that. As he looked down at her beautiful body the urge grew again in his groin, but he didn't want to take her while she was unconscious. He shortened the chain so that she would not be able to leave the bed until he was sure she had learned her lesson, then went to the tap and poured a bowl of cold water. He walked back to the bed and dribbled some on Marissa's face.

'What the fuck?' she yelled, trying to sit up. 'What have you done to me now, you fucking monster?'

'You have a dirty mouth,' Boy said. 'Grammy never swore. She was a lady.'

Marissa kicked against the chain and Boy was glad he'd put padding on the cuff. He didn't want her delicate skin bruised.

'Marissa, if you promise to be good, I'll remove the chain. Not now, because you're a bit upset—'

'I'm not a bit upset. Fuck you, I'm raging. When I get free—'

Boy lunged forward and put his hands round her throat.

'You said you love me and now you're spoiling it!'

As he squeezed, his erection grew. He let go with one hand and found the zip on his flies. It was time for her to prove she loved him.

Marissa bucked and shoved against him. His head shot back suddenly. The bitch was pulling his hair. He put his hand back round her throat and squeezed as hard as he could. Her hand fell away from his head. He felt the heat rising, just like before. She would love him, she would! He felt Grandpa watching. Fucking bitch was making him

140

look stupid. He tried to get inside her, but it was too late. Wave after wave of orgasm wracked his body.

Boy staggered off the bed and fell to the floor.

You wimp, Boy. You can't even fuck a woman.

Boy shuffled onto his knees. Had he killed her? He crawled up to the bed and peered at Marissa's chest. Was it moving? He couldn't be sure. As he stood up, her eyes flew open.

'When I get free I'm going to kill you,' Marissa croaked. 'You are dead meat, you fucking pervert.'

Boy staggered back. 'You'll learn to love me, Marissa. You'll be like Grammy was to Grandpa. You'll see.'

'Love you? Never! You want to fuck me? You'll have to kill me first, you perverted piece of shit.'

Boy couldn't bear to listen to any more filth coming from Marissa's mouth. As he fled, all he could hear was Grandpa laughing at him.

Chapter Twenty-seven

Paolo opened his eyes and smiled. Lydia's hair was spread out on the pillow next to his and she was snuffling gently in her sleep. If he was still dreaming, he didn't want to wake up. As good as he felt, he needed coffee and was pretty sure Lydia would feel the same way. He moved to get out of bed and she turned towards him.

Her eyes opened.

'Good morning, ex-husband.'

'Good morning, ex-wife,' Paolo said. 'Coffee?'

She nodded, so Paolo went downstairs into the kitchen and put the kettle on. As the water boiled he thought back over the events of last night.

He spooned coffee into the cafetière and topped it up with boiling water, all the time wondering how he and Lydia had once again reached this point. What kind of man was he to take advantage of his ex-wife? Placing mugs, cafetière, milk and sugar on a tray, he headed back upstairs. He owed Lydia an apology.

She was sitting up in bed. Her hair was a mess and she had last night's make-up smudges under her eyes. Paolo thought she'd never looked lovelier. He put the tray on the bedside table and poured her coffee. He passed it to her with a rueful smile.

'Lydia, I'm sorry –'

She put up a hand to stop him. 'Don't apologise, Paolo. We both wanted what happened.' She grinned. 'It's about the only part of our marriage that never fell apart. Last night was great. It's always great, but let's leave it at that, shall we?'

Paolo took her hand. 'You know I never stopped loving you, don't you?'

She nodded. 'I feel the same about you, but we can't live together. It just doesn't work any more.' She squeezed his hand and laughed. 'We could be friends with benefits.'

Paolo grinned. 'I like that idea!'

Paolo stood under the shower and felt like singing for the first time in many months. On the drive home he'd thought about what Lydia had said. Friends with benefits. He could definitely live with that. As he turned the water off, he heard his phone. Damn! Water dripping, he rushed back into his bedroom and answered it.

'Sir, sorry to disturb you, but I've been waiting down here for twenty minutes.'

'Damn, sorry, CC. I lost track of time. I'll get dressed double quick and come down.'

Where the hell had the time gone? It only felt like five minutes ago that he'd woken up in Lydia's bed. Flinging on the first clothes he could find, Paolo thought it was just as well he wasn't entering a fashion parade. He grabbed his phone and wallet and rushed down to join CC. She was standing next to his car with a rueful look on her face. It was parked in so closely by other cars it looked like it had been slid in sideways.

'Getting this out is going to be tricky,' she said.

'Where are you parked?'

'In the next street.'

'Okay. Let's go in yours,' he said. 'It will be quicker than trying to get mine out. Whoever blocked me in should have left a can opener.'

Twenty minutes later they were pulling up outside Verity Venues.

'I've heard of this group,' CC said as she got out of the car. 'They set up special events all over the country. You know the type of thing, sir, country house murder mystery weeks, or haunted house weekends. Companies are big on these things now. They use them for corporate bonding.'

143

Paolo's feelings must have shown on his face because CC grinned.

'Not your cup of tea, sir?'

'No, CC, you know very well it isn't,' he said, grinning back at her and barely suppressing a shudder.

They went into the building and were greeted by a vibrant redhead yelling into her phone while holding up a hand to show she couldn't talk to them immediately. Paolo looked at the wall behind her which was covered in group photos, presumably of events they'd organised.

When she eventually ended her call, the redhead smiled up at them.

'How can Verity Venues help you today?'

Paolo held up his badge. 'I'm DCI Paolo Sterling and this is Detective Sergeant Connors. We'd like a word with Marissa Piper, please.'

The redhead rolled her eyes. 'Wouldn't we all! If you find her, tell her she'd better get her arse in here pretty bloody pronto or she'll be out of a job. She gets to go away for a few weeks staying in gorgeous hotels up and down the country and does she come back to report on her findings? Does she hell!'

'Have you spoken to her at all since she's been back?' Paolo asked.

'Not a bloody word. I've even been round to her place, but it's shut up tight. If she thinks we're going to pay over the top on hotel bills she's got another think coming!'

'How do you mean?' Paolo asked.

The redhead shrugged. 'I assume she's shacked up with someone in one of the hotels we sent her to check out.'

'Could you please give me a list of those hotels?'

'Why?'

Paolo smiled. 'She might be sick and unable to call you. We'll contact all of them to find out for you.'

The redhead didn't look convinced, but handed over a sheet of paper. 'The hotel names are in the order she would have used to visit them.'

'Thank you,' Paolo said. 'If we find her, we'll let you know.' He handed over one of his cards. 'In the meantime, if she comes in, please ask her to call me. It's important.'

'Sure thing. Will do,' she promised.

'I don't like the feel of this,' Paolo said as they reached the car.

CC shook her head. 'It seems a bit off, doesn't it?'

'Let's head back to the station and make sure she's not lying sick in one of these hotels,' Paolo said.

'You don't believe that, do you, sir?'

Paolo shook his head. 'No, not at all. I have a real bad feeling in my gut.'

Paolo ended the call on the last hotel on his list and glanced over at CC and Andrea on the other side of his desk. So far none of them had had any luck locating Marissa.

'She left five days ago? Thank you for your cooperation,' Andrea said. She put her phone on the desk and sighed. 'She certainly hasn't stayed on at any of the hotels unless she's booked in under a different name, or maybe a boyfriend's.'

'Not likely though,' Paolo said. 'I'm going to put out a missing person's report on her. I really don't like this. I'll also put out an alert for her car.'

Chapter Twenty-eight

Paolo glared at the piles of paperwork littering his desk. How come everyone else seemed to be able to stay on top of it? Chief Willows was one of those *a tidy desk is a tidy mind* people. Maybe so. That might explain why Paolo couldn't keep his thoughts in order at the moment. The drug-dealing ring at The Pipe was no closer to being shut down than it had been this time last month, which meant he still had no answers for George Mendip about who was responsible for Sally's overdose. Marissa Piper, the only person who Sasha might have confided in, had disappeared off the face of the earth. Jack was in a coma. He still hadn't heard from Katy. And he'd slept with Lydia!

Incredibly, while thinking about how amazing last night had been, his phone began to vibrate, showing Lydia's name on the screen.

He picked it up, feeling like a teenager who had to talk to a girl the morning after their first kiss. What to say? How to react?

'Paolo, I've got news about Katy.'

'Good news?'

'No, more like bad news. That boyfriend of hers is back in Bradchester. The one I never wanted her to go out with but you talked me round, if you remember.'

Paolo smiled. This was more like it. He felt far more comfortable with this version of Lydia.

'I remember.'

'I saw him this morning in the newsagent's on my way to work. I asked why he wasn't still in Africa with Katy and he said they'd broken up.'

'Did he say when Katy is coming home?' Paolo asked.

'He doesn't know! He doesn't even know where she is! It took me ages to get the truth out of that wretched young man, but he finally told me they'd had a big fight. He'd had enough of Africa and wanted to come back. Katy refused, so he left her there! Fine way for him to behave considering it was his not so brilliant idea to go out there as volunteers in the first place!'

Paolo looked up at a tap on his door. CC was standing just inside the doorway, looking serious. The fact that she didn't go away while he was clearly on a personal call told him all he needed to know.

'Lydia, I have to go. I'll call you back later. Okay?'

'It will have to be, but we need to talk about what we do next.'

'About what?' Paolo asked.

'Katy, of course. What else?'

CC held up the paper she carried and pointed to it. This was serious.

'Okay, sorry, Lydia, I really must go.'

He ended the call and gestured for CC to come in and sit down. 'What is it?'

'Marissa's car has been located, sir. It was towed from the station car park. Two of the tyres had been slashed.'

Paolo felt sick. 'No news of her?' CC shook her head. 'What about the CCTV?'

'It was covered with a black cloth. There are some images showing a man walking towards the camera, but with the cloth held in front of his face, so no way of identifying him.'

'Nothing in the street?' Paolo asked.

'There is some footage of a car slowing down, but it's too grainy to make out the number plate. I've asked Mike in IT to see if they can enhance the images. He says they should be able to tell us the make and model, even if they can't get a clear image of the number plate.'

Paolo nodded. 'At least that's something, but where the hell is Marissa Piper? I just hope to God it's not the same maniac who murdered Sasha Carmichael, but I have a horrible feeling it might be. Set up the CCTV viewing. Maybe one of us can spot something that might help.'

CC stood up. 'I'll do that right now, sir.'

Paolo followed her out of his office and into the main room. He waited until CC nodded and then sat on the edge of a desk facing the screen.

'Listen up, everyone. CC is going to put on the relevant images from the station car park the night Marissa Piper's tyres were slashed. The timing of this is important. It happened in the evening at 9:55, which is twenty minutes before the Leeds train comes in. As we now know, that was Marissa's last stopover. I want you all to concentrate on the man holding up the black cloth. I know you can't see his face, but there might be something we can fix on to help us later. Hands, shoes, trousers, anything you can see clearly, write it down. Who knows, we could get lucky. Andrea, I want you to organise a door-to-door on the properties around the station. Someone might have seen the man walking towards the camera.'

With the relevant images on a loop, Paolo was pleased to see his team making notes. 'Right, CC, put up the car images. Mike in IT is working to enhance these shots to try to get the number plate a bit clearer, but in the meantime we can see the car's shape and size. It might be nothing to do with the investigation, but we still need to check it out.'

'Looks like a Ford Fiesta to me, sir,' Andrea called out. 'My mum has one.'

'Could be a Skoda Fabia,' DC Colin Merton said. 'My girlfriend drives one and that's very similar in shape.'

Paolo nodded at Andrea and then looked over at Jack's temporary replacement. 'Both are good calls, well done, you two. Okay, pity the film is in black and white, but I think we can safely assume a dark colour. If Mike gets even a partial number, we'll have enough to do a search.'

He stood up from his position on the edge of the desk.

'Colin, I'd like you to set up a team to conduct enquiries on the houses around The Pipe. One of the neighbours might have seen something the night Jack was attacked. I'm going to the hospital now to check on his condition. Any news, anything at all, whether it's to do with our murder investigation, Marissa Piper's whereabouts, or the drug situation at The Pipe club, I want to hear about it immediately.'

Chapter Twenty-nine

Boy put the finishing touches to Marissa's tray. He'd taken such care cooking the stuffed heart, she was sure to enjoy it. She hadn't eaten for over a day, so must be really hungry by now. He felt bad that he'd had to punish her, but if she was going to behave badly, then he had no choice.

He could feel Grandpa's unwelcome presence.

You're such a wimp, Boy. You've had to attach three extra chains just so you can get close to your whore.

'Shut up,' Boy whispered, but he knew Grandpa was right. He'd fixed more chains in place so that Marissa was now held down by four of them. It was her own fault. He'd wanted to give her freedom to move around, but she'd ruined things for both of them. She had to learn. He knew she loved him, so why was she making him act like Grandpa?

You'll never be a man. You'll never amount to anything. Women need a real man, not you, Boy. Your fancy piece would soon follow my rules.

'You're dead,' he yelled. 'Grammy, where are you? I need you.'

He could hear her voice, soothing him, making everything all right again.

I'm here. Don't worry. She's just a bit scared, that's all. She'll soon learn her place.

Gradually, the sense of Grandpa sneering at him began to fade. He put a small posy of roses next to the dish of love heart sweets. Marissa would soon get used to his rules. She had been punished by being kept without food. Now he was going to show her how much he loved her with gentle words of praise.

He carried the tray down the stairs and placed it on the floor outside the cellar. He wasn't going to take any risks she might break another piece of Grammy's best china. Opening the door, he stepped cautiously inside.

Wimp! Scared of a woman. What's wrong with you? Show her you're a man.

Grandpa's voice came out of nowhere. Boy shivered. Grandpa was going to ruin everything. He peered round the door. Marissa was on the bed, still chained to the four corners. She opened her eyes and smiled at him.

'Hello,' she whispered. 'I'm so pleased you're back. I've missed you.'

This was more like it! See, Grandpa, he thought, my way works.

'Are you hungry?' he asked.

Marissa nodded. 'Very hungry. Have you brought me some food?'

'Are you ready to be good?'

She nodded again. 'I'll do whatever you want.'

Boy stepped back into the corridor. With shaking hands, he picked up the tray, ready to experience at last the love Grandpa had shared with Grammy. He carried the tray into the room and placed it on the table near the bed.

'I'm going to lengthen the chains on your wrists so that you can sit up.'

'Thank you,' she whispered.

She gave him such a look of love he felt his heart might explode. He reached over and adjusted the length of chain on the wrist attached to the far side of the bed. Then he loosened the other wrist.

'Can you sit up?'

Boy watched as she tried to get into a sitting position, but saw she needed help. He put his arm under her shoulders to raise her. The next thing he knew was a searing pain as her fingers raked down his cheek. He tried to pull away, but she'd somehow wrapped part of the chain around his neck.

His hands managed to find her throat and he squeezed.

'Fucking bitch. I've been good to you,' he yelled, increasing the pressure until she stopped struggling.

When she was finally still he listened to her heart. She was still alive. Good, now he'd take what she'd denied him. He stood up and unzipped his fly. This time he'd show her what love was all about.

He climbed on the bed and forced her legs apart. It would've been better if she was awake, but . . .

Can't fuck her unless she's out cold? What's wrong with you, Boy?

He could feel his erection failing. He wouldn't listen to Grandpa. He was dead and gone. Boy reached out and caressed Marissa's breast with his left hand, his right hand moving to bring his erection back. This was better; he'd be able to do it now.

Trembling, he was ready to enter her when he realised a noise he'd been blocking out was persisting. Someone was ringing his doorbell. He tried to ignore it, but whoever it was wouldn't stop pressing the buzzer. There was no way he could perform now.

He climbed off Marissa. There was always tomorrow and all the tomorrows for the rest of their lives. Zipping up his flies, he left the room, carefully locking the door behind him, and went to find out who the hell had ruined his moment of bliss.

Paolo stood at the end of Jack's bed and wondered what he'd seen or done for someone to beat him so severely and leave him in this state. Jack was lying completely still, no sign of life at all apart from the rise and fall of his chest and even that was assisted by the mass of equipment surrounding the bed.

As he turned to leave, a doctor he hadn't seen on previous visits, attended by two nurses, entered the room. Paolo waited outside and stopped the doctor when he came out.

'I'm DCI Paolo Sterling,' he said, showing his warrant card. 'Can you tell me how my officer is doing?'

The doctor shook his head. 'There has been no change, I'm afraid.'

'And the prognosis?' Paolo asked.

'Too soon to say. He could be in a coma for years, or come out of it tomorrow. He might never come round. I'm sorry, I can't give you anything positive. Each patient reacts differently.'

Paolo forced himself to ask the question he least wanted to hear answered.

'He took quite a beating to his head. If . . . when he comes round, will there be any damage?'

'To his brain? Impossible to say at this stage. It's certainly likely, but we have seen other cases where there has been considerable trauma and yet the patient recovers completely. I'm sorry, you must excuse me; I have to complete my rounds.'

The doctor nodded to the nurses and they huddled for a whispered conference before going into the next room. Paolo sighed. He now had to update Chief Willows on Jack's condition. Not a meeting he was looking forward to.

'Well, what's the latest?' Willows said, glaring at Paolo.

'What do you want first, sir? Where we are with the murder investigation or –'

'You know damn well what I want. How is Jack?'

'No change at all. I spoke to the doctor and he was unable to give me any kind of prognosis.'

Willows slammed his hand on the desk. 'As I told you before, Paolo, I hold you entirely responsible for the fact that one of our officers is in this state. When he first mentioned to me the feeling of being sidelined, I made it clear I didn't listen to niggles about senior officers. I told him in no uncertain terms to take it up with you.'

Paolo took a deep breath. No good would come from losing his temper.

'Leaving his feelings to one side, Jack withheld information from me and the rest of the team. I don't know if that's relevant to what happened, but there were facts he should have shared with us.'

'Like what?' Willows demanded.

'Like the fact that Jack knew both Brad Cooper and Greg Mallory from his surveillance of The Pipe, but he didn't pass that on.'

'Is that all?'

'All?' Paolo said. 'We know The Pipe is being used to supply the drugs that killed Sally Mendip and will at the very least ruin more lives, but Jack was running his own private investigation instead of working as part of a team.'

'So you say, Paolo, but it's beginning to look as if you pushed him too far out of the loop. Perhaps he felt he needed to find something solid for you to take him seriously. You know, I didn't believe him in the beginning, but now . . .'

'That is both untrue and unjust and you know it!'

'Do I? I always believed you were a good person, Paolo, but from what I've heard lately you might not have been as fair to Dave as I'd thought.'

'What? Are you mad? Dave was my right hand and a bloody good friend.'

Willows thinned his lips and shook his head.

'I want to know who attacked Jack, but apart from that leave The Pipe investigation alone. Concentrate on Sasha Carmichael's murder.'

Paolo forced himself to calm down and took a couple of deep breaths.

'On that subject, sir, we have an unpleasant development.'

He outlined what they knew so far about Marissa. As he spoke, Willows' face changed from one of irritation to outright anger.

'It seems to me, Paolo, you are dropping the ball on too many cases. I suggest you get back downstairs and get your act together.'

Paolo didn't trust himself to speak, so simply nodded and headed for the door.

'I think your recent promotion might have gone to your head. I expected better from you.'

Paolo opened the door and didn't even bother looking back. He could do without breathing in toxic air. He headed back down the stairs, trying and failing to control his anger. He hadn't wanted the promotion in the first place. In fact, he'd done all he could to persuade Willows not to put him forward for it. And now to be accused of letting it go to his head! Jack had done a better job of turning Willows against him than Paolo could ever have believed possible. He knew Jack had been dripping poison into the Chief's ear, but how the hell had it come to this? What had Jack said or implied that had somehow undone years of good feeling between Paolo and Willows?

154

He reached the main office and looked over to where CC was talking to Andrea. Thank God he had those two on his team.

'CC,' he called. 'Get your stuff; we're going to pay a visit to The Pipe.'

Whatever happened to Jack had something to do with that bloody club. It was time to dig a bit and find out what.

He was still fuming when CC pulled up outside the club. It looked pretty deserted, but Paolo knew from past surveillance the manager would be there at this time of day. It was nearly five and he'd be making sure the place was ready for when they opened in a few hours.

He climbed out of the car feeling incredibly weary. Shaking his head, he forced his mind to concentrate. As CC came over to join him, flicking the switch on the central locking without looking back, Paolo couldn't help but think of Dave's pantomime with car keys. It didn't matter that he used to put them in the same pocket every time, when it came time to find them he'd still search every other pocket first. Paolo knew he'd never stop missing his friend and colleague's company.

How dare Willows imply he hadn't treated Dave well? In reality, he knew the truth was that Jack had planted the idea and then nurtured it. Damn the man. If he came out of the coma and was able to return to work at some point in the future, Paolo would make sure he wasn't allowed to rejoin his team.

'Are we going in, sir? Or will we continue to stand outside getting wet for fun?'

Paolo came back to earth at CC's words and grinned.

'Scared of a bit of rain, CC? That's not like you.'

Before she could answer, the door to the club opened and Brad Cooper peered out.

'Are you looking for me?' he asked.

Paolo walked towards him. 'I wasn't,' he said. 'Should I be?'

Brad opened the door wide, allowing Paolo and CC to pass.

'I can't think of any reason,' Brad said, 'but you've turned up outside where I work, so I wondered, that's all.'

155

'We've come to speak to the manager, but as you're here maybe you wouldn't mind answering a few questions.'

'About that girl you mentioned at the gym?' Brad asked, leading the way into the club.

Paolo looked around and decided he'd rather camp in a cemetery than spend the night there. There was no natural light and the walls looked almost as if they were running with damp. When he looked closer, he saw it was a paint effect. Around the outskirts of the room were a few dingy-looking armchairs and sofas, but apart from those, there was nothing offering anything in the way of comfort.

'We're not here about Sasha Carmichael, but I have recently discovered she used to come here with a couple of her friends. One of them is missing. Maybe you know her.'

Paolo pulled Marissa's photo from his pocket and showed it to Brad.

He shrugged. 'Not bad looking, but I can't say I remember her.'

'Really?' Paolo said. 'Have another look. I would have thought she might stick in your mind, a pretty girl like that.'

Brad held the photo up to the light. 'Nope, don't remember her at all.'

Paolo took the photo and slipped it back in his pocket. 'Maybe your memory is a bit better when it comes to trouble outside. One of my officers was badly beaten not far from here on Saturday. He's in hospital in a coma. Do you know anything about that?'

Brad laughed. 'Unless it happened right outside the club, how could I possibly have seen anything? I have my hands full keeping the punters in line.'

There was such an innocent expression on the bouncer's face Paolo was sure Brad knew more than he was letting on. He was definitely one to watch.

'Let's try a different question. Who's bringing the drugs into the club?'

Brad's expression moved from innocent to angelic. 'There are no drugs in this club. We have a strict exclusion policy for anyone found in possession of any narcotic substances.'

156

Paolo laughed. 'You said that very well. How many times did you have to practise it before you were word perfect?'

Brad shrugged. 'Only once. You wanted to see the manager? I'll take you through to his office. Maybe he has the answers you need.'

He led the way to the back of the club and along a corridor. When he reached what looked like a dead-end he opened a door that Paolo wouldn't have known was there. Brad had reached up and pressed somewhere above what was clearly a secret entrance. As the door swung open, the décor changed from seedy to upmarket chic. This was somewhere the average clubgoer wouldn't know about.

'What goes on here?' Paolo asked.

'This is where the money clubbers hang out. They don't want to mix with the dregs, so they pay a membership fee and get shown how to access this room.'

Paolo caught the expression on CC's face and realised she was thinking along the same lines as him. What made some people think they were so far above the rest of the world they deserved special treatment? He knew the answer, but it didn't make it any more palatable. Those with money would always get more from life than those without.

'That way,' Brad said, pointing to two doors side by side at the back of the room. 'The manager's office is the door on the right.'

As he said the words he turned to go back the way they'd come in.

'Are you not going to tell the manager we're here?' Paolo called out.

'No need. You've been on CCTV since the moment you stepped inside the club. He'll be expecting you. When you're ready to leave, go through the door next to the manager's office and you'll find yourself in the alleyway at the side of the club. Our VIPs use it when they are, let's say, a bit the worse for wear and don't want the press to catch them looking like shit.'

He laughed and disappeared through the opening leading back into the main part of the club.

'What do you make of Brad?' Paolo asked.

'I wouldn't trust a word he says,' CC answered.

'My feelings exactly. Let's see what the manager's made of, shall we?'

As they walked across the room Paolo couldn't help comparing this room with the one the general public got to see and wondered what the point was in being a member of a club that you didn't want to be seen in. He shrugged. The ways of the rich were beyond him.

He tapped on the door and opened it without waiting for an invitation. If the manager knew they were on their way, why wait?

Seated at a desk facing the door was a man in desperate need of a diet and some exercise. Paolo thought he looked like a heart attack waiting to happen.

'Come in. I'm Andrew Carstairs, what can I do for you?'

The man hauled himself up with difficulty and waved a podgy hand towards the seats opposite his desk. Paolo wondered how much Carstairs weighed and if the chair had been reinforced to take his weight. Seeming to have expended too much energy in standing, he fell back into the chair. It screeched under the strain.

Paolo showed his warrant card and then sat down. 'We're here as part of an investigation into two crimes we believe may be connected with this club in some way. The first is that it has come to our attention someone is dealing drugs on the premises.'

'Not possible!' Carstairs said. 'I'd know if that were the case.'

Although he was speaking to Paolo, his eyes never left CC. He was almost salivating. Paolo knew she could handle herself, but still wanted to shake the man.

'Hey, would you mind looking this way when you're speaking to me,' Paolo said.

Carstairs looked in Paolo's direction, but couldn't seem to stop himself from flicking glances at CC every few seconds.

'How often do you go out into the club?' Paolo asked. 'There could be all sorts of deals going down without your knowledge.'

Carstairs shook his head and managed to look away from CC as he pointed to the wall behind Paolo. 'I see everything from here.'

Paolo turned. The entire wall was covered in screens showing every aspect of both rooms of the club.

'Impressive, but that doesn't mean you see everything.'

'No, I have Brad and the other bouncers for that. I can assure you there is nothing that goes on here that Brad doesn't know about. Now what was the other thing you wanted to ask about?'

'One of my officers was badly beaten near here. He'd been watching The Pipe, looking for the dealers I just mentioned, when he was set on. Do you know anything about that?'

'How would I? It's nothing to do with The Pipe if someone gets mugged off the premises.'

'Who owns the club?' Paolo asked.

'Why do you want to know? We've done nothing wrong here.'

'Just curious, that's all.'

'In that case, I don't see any reason why I should tell you.'

Paolo stood. He was sure there was a connection between Brad Cooper and Greg Mallory, but he wasn't going to find out anything from this man.

'We'll be on our way, but may well be back to visit again.'

Carstairs smiled. 'You're welcome any time, but not in the VIP room unless you come armed with a warrant. We don't like our celebs hassled.'

Paolo waited until they were out of his office before speaking to CC. As he opened the door into the alleyway behind the club he heard her mutter.

'What did you say?' he asked.

'I said what a creep. Did you see the way he kept leering at me?'

'I did. He looked as though he wanted to eat you.'

She laughed. 'He looks as though he's eaten a few before me.'

They walked to the opening into the street before Paolo realised how close this alley was to the one where he'd found Jack. They had come out behind the club. Across the road, almost diagonally opposite, was the place where Jack had been beaten.

Chapter Thirty

Paolo had just done up the car seat belt when his phone rang. Straining to reach his pocket without undoing the seat belt proved to be impossible.

'Don't pull away yet, CC,' he said, unclipping the belt and retrieving the phone. He saw Andrea's name on the display. 'Sterling.'

'Sir, you might want to go to Tom Sidcup's address. We've just had a call in from one of his neighbours. She swears he was peering into her bathroom while she was in the shower.'

'How can that be? Have you checked with the surveillance team?'

'I did, sir. The officers there are adamant he never left the property, but we know he did once before without them spotting him, so maybe he did it again.'

'What's the neighbour's address? I'll go there first.'

Paolo put his phone on speaker so that CC could key the address in to the SatNav.

'The neighbour is a Mrs Kenney. She lives at 144 Cheshire Grove. I believe it's the road behind Sidcup's house,' Andrea said.

'Thanks. Before you go, I want you to look into something for me. Find out who owns The Pipe. The manager didn't seem to want to share that information. There may be nothing in it, but let's check it out.'

He ended the call and slipped the phone back into his pocket.

'Okay, let's visit Mrs Kenney and find out why she's so convinced Sidcup is a peeping Tom. If she's right then we need to pay a visit to Tom Sidcup and find out how he is managing to evade surveillance.'

*

CC pulled into the open driveway of the Kenney house. 'How do you want to play this, sir? She's going to be surprised to find someone of your rank investigating a peeping Tom incident.'

'Quite right, CC. I think let's just say we were in the neighbourhood when the call came in.'

Paolo got out of the car and looked around. The area was well established with plenty of trees and nicely maintained gardens. Mrs Kenney's house looked as if it got regular licks of paint. This was definitely one of the nicer parts of Bradchester. Not somewhere you'd expect a peeping Tom to hang out – unless, of course, he happened to be one of your neighbours.

They walked up the short driveway. Paolo put a hand out to ring the bell, but the door opened before he could reach it.

'Are you the police? They said they'd send someone.'

Paolo nodded. 'Mrs Kenney? I'm DCI Paolo Sterling. This is DS Cathy Connors. May we come in?'

She nodded and stood back to allow them to pass. 'Please go through to the lounge. I'm so pleased you people are taking this seriously!'

'We take all complaints seriously,' Paolo said, sitting down and trying to find a comfortable position on an over-stuffed armchair.

He smiled. 'Could you, perhaps, take us through the events from the beginning?'

She nodded. 'I was in the shower this morning when I suddenly had such a strong feeling of being watched. It made me feel really uneasy. I glanced towards the window and there was a man's face looking in at me.'

He looked over at CC, seated diagonally opposite in what looked to be an equally uncomfortable chair. She was busy taking notes.

'Naturally, I screamed and the face disappeared.'

'You don't have a blind or curtaining at the window?' Paolo asked.

'No, there's never been any need. There's a tree right outside the window. No one can see in unless they climb the tree.'

'I see,' Paolo said. 'What happened next?'

Mrs Kenney looked confused. 'What do you mean? I got dressed and called the police.'

161

'I realise that, but what I meant was how did you know who to accuse?'

She smiled. 'Ah, I see. I recognised his face. I have frequently been on a bus where he was driving. A friend of mine's daughter had a nasty experience with him. I believe flashing is the correct term. Anyway, that's how I knew it was him. He's not at all liked around here.'

'Forgive me for asking, but are you certain it was Mr Sidcup? You don't think you might have jumped to that conclusion because you know something of his history?'

She glared at Paolo and then turned to CC. 'Isn't it always the way with men? They can't simply take a woman's word for something. You have to give them cast-iron proof.' She turned back to Paolo, a look of triumph on her face. 'You'll probably find he has some sort of injury, or scratches at the very least. He fell out of the tree when I screamed.'

Paolo stood up and handed her his card. 'My apologies for doubting you, but it was a question I had to ask.'

She nodded, giving Paolo the impression he'd been forgiven by the queen, but might still be hauled off to the Tower if he said anything else out of place.

'Will I need to appear in court?' she asked CC, clearly not wanting to engage with Paolo.

'Possibly,' CC said. 'It depends on what happens when we interview Mr Sidcup.'

'I'll trust *you* to keep me informed,' she said.

'I'll do my best,' CC promised.

Paolo would have been happy to bet his pension CC was close to choking on the mirth she was holding back. They managed to make it out of the house and into the car before she let rip on a gurgle of laughter.

'Oh my God, sir. I don't think she liked you at all. What a typical man you are, not taking a woman's word for something.'

'When you've quite finished making fun of me, CC, do you think you could stop laughing long enough to drive to West Castle Street?'

She wiped a tear from her cheek, but was still grinning. 'I'll do my best, sir.'

If anything, Paolo thought, West Castle Street was even more upmarket than Cheshire Grove. The houses were slightly larger, the gardens definitely bigger and the drives just a bit longer.

CC stopped the car in the street. 'Want me to conduct the interview again, like last time?'

Paolo unclipped his seat belt. 'No, I think I'll do it this time. I might come on a bit heavy. See if I can shake him up.'

They approached the gate and pressed the buzzer.

'Yes, who is it?'

'Mr Sidcup, it's DCI Sterling and DS Connors. May we come in?'

'Why? What do you want?'

'It might be better for you if we discuss this inside. Or, if you prefer, you could come with us to the station.'

'No, come in, but I haven't done anything, so I don't know why you're even here.'

The gate slid open and they walked up to the front door. Paolo rapped on it and waited. It didn't take long before he heard footsteps. Tom Sidcup opened the door and it was obvious he'd been in an accident of some kind. His face was covered in scratches and he had a makeshift bandage on his right hand. Blood was seeping through the gauze, but it didn't look too serious.

Paolo walked ahead into the room where they had conducted the previous interview. CC followed Sidcup and Paolo smiled. If having CC behind him didn't make the man feel intimidated, nothing would. When he reached the centre of the room, he turned suddenly so that Sidcup stopped walking. CC stood directly behind him.

'Now, Mr Sidcup, I have a few questions for you. Let's start with how you got those scratches and cut your hand, then move on to what makes you think you have the right to spy on your neighbours while they are in a state of undress.'

'I don't know what you mean. I didn't. Who said I did? She's lying.'

Paolo smiled. 'I never mentioned it was a woman. Why would you assume that it was?'

Sidcup shrugged. 'It was obvious. Some pervert has been peering through a bathroom window, so it must be a woman inside.'

Paolo sat down. This was going to be easier than he'd thought.

'I didn't mention a bathroom window, Tom. Do you mind if I call you Tom? Mr Sidcup is very formal and we're just having a little chat.'

Sidcup nodded. 'Tom's fine,' he said, sinking onto the sofa.

Paolo could see beads of sweat forming under his hairline. It was time to ramp up the pressure.

'You were seen, Tom. Your neighbour recognised you.'

'She couldn't have, the window was . . .' He stopped as if he'd tasted something sour.

Paolo watched his face contorting. Probably trying to think of a way out of the corner he'd painted himself into.

'The window was what, Tom? Steamed up? But you could still see her, couldn't you?'

'Like getting your jollies up a tree, do you?' CC said.

Tom spun towards her, almost as if he'd forgotten she was in the room. Paolo left her to finish the job he'd started. She moved away from the doorway where she'd been standing and walked over to Sidcup.

'Do you sneak out along your garden and climb over the wall at the end? That would put you in your neighbour's garden. It's an easy trip then to the tree so you can get up to the right height. You like looking at naked women when they don't know you're there, don't you, Tom?'

Paolo saw Sidcup visibly shrink back from CC. The man looked as if he'd like to crawl away and hide.

'What else do you like, Tom?' CC asked. 'Do you like abducting young women? Want to have them under your control?'

Tom's head shot up. 'No! I've never done anything like that.' He looked over at Paolo, almost pleading with him to understand, man to man. 'I just like to look, that's all.'

CC stepped back, allowing Paolo to take over. He stood up.

164

'Maybe you'd let us have a little look around, just to make sure you're telling the truth.'

Tom shook his head. 'No, I don't have to let you.'

Paolo sighed. 'You're quite right, Tom. You don't have to let us do anything, but I'll be back later with a warrant, so you might just as well say yes now.'

'What? Why? I haven't done anything.'

'Oh, but you have, Tom. You exposed yourself to young women on the bus and now we find you're a common peeping Tom.'

CC laughed. 'Your parents named you well.'

Paolo choked. 'What's it to be, Tom? A friendly look around with your permission, or a stringent search with a warrant?'

Sidcup shook his head. 'My solicitor told me about people like you pretending to be all friendly. Then you come in and start planting evidence to stitch people up. Go get your warrant. You're not looking around here without one.'

'That sounds like you've got something to hide, Tom.'

'Get out. I want you to get out now.'

Paolo nodded to CC. 'Let's go. We'll see you again soon, Tom.'

As they walked back to the car Paolo wondered if Tom was really capable of abducting someone. Most peepers never went beyond creeping around and looking in windows to get their thrills. On the other hand, Sidcup had exposed himself on the bus, so maybe he was escalating.

'What do you think, CC? Is he our man?'

She clicked the remote to open the car doors before answering. 'To be honest, sir, I don't know. The man's a creep, for sure, but I don't know about the rest.'

Paolo pulled open the passenger door and climbed in. As CC took her place next to him, he realised they hadn't checked to see what car might be tucked away in Sidcup's garage. He pulled out his phone and hit speed dial. It was answered on the second ring.

'Andrea, I want you to get DC Merton onto the database to find out what type of car Tom Sidcup drives.'

'I can do that for you, sir,' she said.

'No, I've got another job for you. I want you to get a head start on the paperwork we need to obtain a warrant on Sidcup's place. Make sure it covers the entire house and grounds. We're heading back to the station now. If we can get it sorted today, so much the better.'

'Okay, sir. By the way, I haven't had much success finding out the real owner of The Pipe. I've traced ownership through various companies, but can only get as far as the shell company.'

'Now why would a simple nightclub in Bradchester need to hide behind a shell company?'

'No idea, sir.'

Paolo laughed. 'It was a rhetorical question, Andrea. Leave that for now and concentrate on the Sidcup warrant. At the very least the man is a pervert, but maybe he's our killer as well.'

Chapter Thirty-one

Paolo and CC, flanked by a contingent of uniformed officers, waited for Tom Sidcup to open the door. Paolo was ready with the warrant should he refuse them entry, which was just as well because the person who opened the door clearly wasn't Sidcup. An attractive young woman, dressed conservatively in a dark grey suit, greeted Paolo with a scowl.

'I'm Jennifer Sanderson. My client said you might be back; I'm here to safeguard his interests. Your name and rank, please?'

'I'm Detective Chief Inspector Sterling and this is Detective Sergeant Connors. We have a warrant to search this property.'

'Before you come in I'd like to check its scope so that I can monitor what you can and can't do.'

She held out her hand and Paolo passed the warrant over. He watched her face as she read; trying to get a feeling for how difficult she intended to make the situation.

'This seems to be in order,' she said, handing the papers back. 'I will be remaining here with my client while you conduct the search. I expect him to be treated with respect. He will not be answering any questions unless I am present, but I should warn you that I have advised him to say nothing to you until we have ascertained exactly what crime it is you think he might have committed.'

Paolo nodded. 'Fair enough. If you'd stand back, my people are ready to get started.'

She stood aside and Paolo waved everyone forward. As he followed in their wake a tantalising aroma wafted across the hallway.

'Someone's a good cook,' he said to CC. 'The smell is reminding my stomach I haven't had chance to eat a damn thing so far today.'

She nodded. 'That makes two of us. I'm ravenous.'

They followed Jennifer Sanderson into the lounge. Tom was standing in the middle of the room looking at the officers filing into the house, a look of horror etched on his face.

'What are they going to do? Why are there so many of them? I don't want them trampling all over my home.'

Before Paolo could answer, the solicitor waved her hand dismissively.

'They are going to search for evidence of a missing woman. I advise you once again, Tom, not to say anything at all – not even in response to seemingly innocuous questions. We will wait here until they have finished.' She turned to Paolo. 'I expect my client's home to be left in a state similar to that in which you found it. There are not likely to be people of any age or gender hiding inside sofas or mattresses, so I advise you not to take liberties and insist on ripping them open. Your warrant does not entitle you to damage his property.'

'We have no intention of causing any damage, but I would remind you we are looking for a young woman who may be in considerable danger. Please don't think I will allow you, or anyone else, to impede our search for her.'

He turned to CC and saw in her face the exact emotion he was feeling. Why did solicitors always feel their dodgy clients had more rights than the people they hurt? If Jennifer Sanderson could make them go away without conducting the search, she would do it and not give a thought to a fellow human being who could be terrified and in danger of losing her life to a madman. Paolo managed to draw in his anger. There was no point in lashing out at the solicitor. They needed to find Marissa. He could only pray she hadn't already met the same fate as Sasha.

'CC, go and make sure all the doors can be opened, including the garage.' He glanced over at Jennifer. 'If we find any locked doors we want the keys, or we will break them down. *That* is within the parameters of the warrant. I hope that's understood.'

She nodded. 'Perfectly.'

Paolo took a step towards Sidcup. 'Those scratches on your face look even more inflamed than they did earlier. Have you been tree-climbing again?'

Tom opened his mouth to answer, but Jennifer moved in front of him.

'As I said to you just now, DCI Sterling, my client will not be answering any questions, in particular those intended to inflame. Now, I'm sure you have things to do, or are you going to leave everything to your underlings?'

Two hours later they had little to show for their efforts other than a laptop which Paolo would send to IT to see what delights were in the encrypted files. Even the car in the garage wasn't much help as Andrea had already discovered Sidcup owned a Ford Fiesta, but the colour was too light to match the one in the CCTV.

Dispirited and concerned for Marissa, it took all Paolo's will-power to stop himself from shaking Sidcup to get at the truth. If the man wasn't their killer, he needed to know so that they could concentrate their efforts elsewhere.

He could barely contain his irritation when Jennifer Sanderson insisted on looking through every room to ensure her precious client's rights hadn't been violated. The same pervert who, at the very least, was guilty of spying on naked women and flashing his penis at unsuspecting females.

'Just as a matter of interest, Tom,' Paolo said. 'You have a beautiful home. How could you afford this on a bus driver's salary?'

'I inherited it,' Sidcup began, but stopped when Sanderson raised her hand.

'Mr Sidcup will not be answering any questions, Detective, unless they are pertinent to the case you are investigating. Would you like to tell me why you need to know how my client came to be the owner of this property?'

Paolo shook his head. 'Not directly pertinent, but all background information is valuable in our investigations.'

'Then I suggest you restrain yourself from asking irrelevant questions. My client has nothing more to say at this juncture. Good day to you.'

Paolo nodded and signalled to CC it was time to leave. He managed to hold his temper in check until they were in the car.

'How come slime like that has someone to protect him?'

CC shrugged. 'I take it that's a rhetorical question?'

'It is. I want Mike to look at the laptop as a priority. If he has Marissa hidden away somewhere, I wouldn't mind betting he's set up some sort of video feed so he can watch her.'

'Have you ruled out the three guys from the gym? Sasha and Marissa sometimes went there together. If they knew Sasha then they would at least be aware of Marissa, even if they didn't speak to her.'

Paolo shook his head. 'It's more than likely that Brad recognised her from the gym, if not from the club, and I haven't ruled anyone out, but none of them have done anything we can act on.'

'Where to now, sir?'

'Back to the station so I can speak to Mike in IT, then we are going to see Angelica Macduff. The poor girl doesn't yet know another of her friends is in trouble.'

Chapter Thirty-two

As Paolo walked into his office, he felt his phone vibrate just before it rang. He pulled it from his pocket and glanced at the screen as he sat down. He didn't recognise the number, but it was an international call.

'Sterling,' he said, praying it wasn't bad news about Katy.

The connection was terrible. All he could hear was a voice breaking up against howling static.

'I can't hear you,' he said. 'If you can hear me, please call again.'

The line went dead. Less than a minute later, it rang again. The same international number.

'Sterling.'

'Dad, it's me.'

'Katy! We've been so worried about you. Are you okay?'

'Listen, Dad, I can't stay on too long because the charity are paying for this call. Did Danny tell you we've broken up?'

'He told your mum. Why didn't you come home with him?'

'I didn't want to. I'm really happy out here, Dad. After the fight with Danny I came to help out in one of the rural schools. They so desperately need teachers here. I know I'm not qualified, but I'm staying on for a bit until they can get a proper teacher. Can you tell Mum I'm fine? Tell her there's no 4G where I am, which is why I've had to come into town to call you. I guessed you might be worried.'

Worried? Paolo thought, we were beyond worry, but he didn't say those words.

'Don't worry, Katy, I'll call your mum right now.'

'Okay. Thanks, Dad. Got to go. Love you!'

Paolo sat for a while staring at the phone. His little girl had grown up. He was so proud of her, so why did he feel like crying? Shaking himself, he scrolled through his contacts until he found Lydia's number. He touched the screen to call her, wondering how she'd react to seeing his name on her phone. The last time they'd spoken he'd promised to call her back and hadn't had chance to do so.

'Well, this is nice. I thought you were dead and no one had bothered to tell me.'

Paolo laughed. 'Lydia, I promise, if necessary, I'll come myself as a ghost so you can be certain I've died. Listen, I've just had a very short call from Katy.'

'Why hasn't she answered any of my WhatsApp messages? Is she in trouble?'

'No, nothing like that.'

He explained about the lack of internet connection and what Katy wanted to do.

'Paolo, why didn't you tell her to come home? She's too young to be out in the African bush all on her own.'

'Lydia, she's old enough to make her own decisions. Besides, she's not alone. She's with other charity workers. We have to let her find her own way.'

She sniffed. 'I know. You're right, but that doesn't mean I like it.'

For the first time since he and Lydia had both been teenagers, Paolo didn't know how to end the call. Should he suggest they meet up? Just say goodbye as if they hadn't spent the night together? Silence on Lydia's part made him wonder if she was thinking along similar lines.

'Do you . . .'

'Would you . . .'

Paolo laughed. 'You first,' he said.

'Do you want to come over tonight for something to eat?' Lydia said.

Paolo remembered how hungry he'd felt in Sidcup's house. He still hadn't eaten, but the hunger had faded. Thinking of Lydia's cooking brought it back with a vengeance.

'I'd love to, but I can't guarantee what time I'll get there.'

'When did you ever? I'll make something that can keep, just in case you're really late. If you're not going to get here before nine, let me know and I'll stick it in the freezer for another time.'

Paolo ended the call wondering exactly where he and Lydia were headed. They'd been down this road so many times and it always ended in disaster.

Paolo was about to go in search of CC to visit Angelica Macduff when his phone rang. The display showed Chief Willows' name and Paolo felt his gut contract. Now what?

'Sterling.'

'Paolo, this is Chief Willows. I've been in contact with the hospital and it appears Jack has surfaced from his coma. The doctors are cautiously optimistic he will make a full recovery, but that remains to be seen.'

'That is excellent news, sir.'

'It certainly is. I'll keep you updated on his progress. What's happening with the missing person case?'

'I'm going with CC to interview one of her friends who might be able to point us in the right direction. Apparently Sasha Carmichael and Marissa Piper shared a few activities.'

'Look, Paolo, you know as well as I do the papers are full of rubbish saying we're not doing our job. We have a drug death unsolved, a murder unsolved and now a missing woman to add to the list. We need a break on this one, Paolo. Don't let me down.'

'Doing my best, sir.'

Paolo ended the call and breathed a sigh of relief. Thank God Jack was on the mend. Did his enormous sense of relief make him a hypocrite? He hoped not. Paolo didn't like the man, not one iota, but he didn't want him to suffer either.

He stood up and grabbed his keys from the desk. If they didn't get a move on Angelica Macduff would have left work. He toyed with the idea of calling ahead, but didn't want to tell her over the phone that her friend might have been snatched by the same person who'd murdered Sasha.

★

173

CC pulled into the car park at Holistic Healing and drove into a space next to the entrance gates. They were almost directly opposite the main entrance.

'We should easily see her from here when she comes out, sir.'

'I'd like you to approach her, CC. I think that would be less intimidating. Don't mention Marissa. Just say we need to talk to her about Sasha's possible movements prior to her murder. Mention Sasha's belief she was being watched and tell her we want to find out exactly what Sasha had said.'

'Right you are, sir,' CC said, unbuckling her seat belt. 'Shall I bring her over to the car, or suggest we chat in the pub back there on the corner?'

'Suggest the pub. If she agrees, give me the nod and I'll head over to grab a table.'

Paolo watched as CC walked across the car park to take up a position to the side of the massive glass doors. Holistic Healing was clearly a money-making enterprise. Paolo found it interesting that all the so-called natural ways of living and healing seemed to be so expensive to follow. He laughed as he imagined Katy telling him not to be such a cynic, but it was hard to avoid making that comparison when sitting outside a business that seemed to be making a fortune.

In the distance Paolo saw CC move from her spot against the wall and walk towards the entrance. The two women exchanged a few words before CC waved towards the pub and Angelica nodded. Paolo climbed out of the car and locked it. Would he ever get used to not having Dave with him on these interviews? Probably not, but there was no point in dwelling on the past.

He walked the short distance to the corner and entered the Fox and Hounds. It was many decades since the area would have been rural, but the pub had clearly been standing since the time this would have been a country village. Now it was part of the sprawling conglomeration of modern Bradchester.

Paolo went through the heavy oak door and headed for a table next to an inglenook. Before sitting down, he read the inscription on the wall. *This hostelry opened for custom June 1705 during the reign of her most Sovereign Majesty Queen Anne.* None of the companies nearby would have even existed when the pub was built as a place to rest during travels back then.

He'd only just sat down when CC and Angelica came in, followed by a crowd of workers, presumably from the surrounding businesses. He waved to CC and she brought Angelica to the table.

'CC, can you get us something to drink? Miss Macduff, what would you like?'

'Call me Angelica. Just lemonade for me. I have to drive home.'

'I see they have a coffee machine behind the bar. A lemonade for Angelica, a black coffee for me and whatever you're having,' Paolo said, passing CC a twenty-pound note.

'Please, sit down, Angelica.'

'Can you tell me what this is about? Have you found out who killed Sasha?'

'Would you mind if we waited until my colleague returns with the drinks? I need her to take notes, just in case something occurs to us later that we need to follow up on.'

Paolo, not the best of small-talkers, tried to interest Angelica in the weather, but she smiled and shook her head.

'Please don't feel you need to be polite. I'm already on edge wondering what you have to tell me.'

'Sorry,' Paolo said. 'You won't have to wait much longer. It looks as though our drinks are about to arrive.'

He waited until CC had unloaded two coffees and a lemonade and returned the tray to the bar before turning to Angelica.

'As you know, we're looking for the murderer of Sasha, but I'm sorry to say it seems another of your friends might be in danger.'

Angelica nodded. 'Marissa?'

'Yes.'

'I guessed as much. I haven't been able to get hold of her, but hoped against hope she was still away on business.'

'She never made it back to her apartment or office. We believe she was abducted as she made her way home. I'm sorry.'

She pushed her drink away as if the sight of it made her ill. 'What can I do? How can I help?'

'We need to know where Sasha and Marissa's lives overlapped. There must be a common connection and that's what we have to find. We know they attended the same gym and went to The Pipe.'

'Well, that's a good place to start,' Angelica said. 'That bouncer always gives me the creeps.'

'Brad Cooper?'

She nodded. 'That's the one. I'm convinced he was trying to get Sasha onto ecstasy.'

'What makes you say that?'

'Because he deals in them. I've seen him and so has my boyfriend. And the pizza guy. Both of them are at it.'

Paolo glanced at CC who was furiously scribbling. 'You say you and your boyfriend have actually seen them dealing?'

'Brad lets the girls in ahead of the guys to make sure there are always more of us than the men. When we're inside, Brad seems to know who to approach. Many of the girls are so out of it it's a wonder they can function.'

'And the pizza guy you mentioned?'

'Yeah, he concentrates on the guys waiting to get in. My boyfriend's been approached loads of times by others in the queue, but he says it's the pizza guy who supplies the ones offering tabs.'

'Would you be prepared to come to the station and make a statement to that effect? It would help in our hunt for Marissa because we could then get a warrant to search the club and the homes of the two men.'

Angelica nodded. 'I'll do anything I can to help.'

'Do you think your boyfriend would do the same regarding the pizza delivery guy?'

Angelica nodded again. 'I'm sure he would. We could both come this evening, if that's any good? The only thing is we don't know who the pizza guy is. He turns up on his delivery bike, hands over the tablets to Brad, or one of the men in the queue, then drives off.'

Paolo smiled. 'Don't worry about his name. We know exactly who that is.'

'You do?'

He nodded. 'Yes, he's on our radar. Is there anything else you can tell us about The Pipe? Anyone you feel is worth our while investigating?'

Angelica shook her head. 'Not really. If I think of anything, I'll let you know.'

Paolo nodded. 'Okay, so we know they went to the same gym. Are you also a member?'

'I am, but I rarely go. You've seen what time I leave work. By the time I get home I'm in no mood to go out again. Well, I don't mind going out, but not to kill myself on some evil machine.' She shrugged. 'Sasha and Marissa, though, they went quite often. At least a couple of times a week. Did you know that bouncer guy was also Sasha's personal trainer?'

'We did,' said Paolo, 'and we're looking into that. Do you know if Marissa was also one of his clients?'

'I don't think she was. She wasn't into the whole keep fit thing in the same way as Sasha, but she liked to work out. From what I can remember she lifted weights. She looks like a light breeze would blow her over, but she's incredibly strong.'

'How do you mean?'

'We were walking through the park on our way home from a night out when we heard someone calling out. There was a homeless guy under a tree who was trapped by an enormous branch. I suppose it must have fallen on him while he was sleeping. Before I knew what she was going to do, she'd run over and heaved the thing off him.'

Paolo smiled. 'That must have been some sight, but maybe it was a rotten branch and so not too heavy.'

Angelica shook her head. 'You're wrong. Apparently the homeless guy had been trying to get out from under it for ages. I tried to lift it and it weighed a ton. Marissa is really, really strong, so how come whoever took her was able to overpower her? She wouldn't have gone without a fight. So that's good, isn't it? She'll be fighting to get free.'

Paolo nodded, but kept to himself the thought that fighting back could already have caused Marissa's captor to kill her.

177

Chapter Thirty-three

As CC pulled away from the Holistic Healing car park, Paolo's phone rang. When he saw Chief Willows' name on the screen he felt like rejecting the call. The man never rang with good news. Fearful that Jack might have had a relapse, Paolo braced himself for whatever Willows had to say.

'Sterling.'

'Paolo, I want you back at the station immediately.'

'Sir, I intended to –'

'I don't give a damn what you intended to do. I want you in my office the second you get here.'

Paolo took the phone from his ear and stared at it. 'What the hell?'

'I couldn't help but hear that, sir. Any idea what it's about?'

He shrugged. 'Not a clue. Drop me at the station and then you can pick up your car and head on home. If it's something we need to follow up on tonight, I'll call you. Tomorrow will be busy. We need to search Marissa's home, just in case there is something there that could point us in the right direction. Then we'll go to pay another call on Brad Cooper.'

'And the creepy pizza guy?'

'Oh yes,' said Paolo, 'Greg Mallory will definitely be getting a visit from us.'

Paolo tapped on Willows' door and opened it when he heard a growl from inside. He stuck his head round the door, unsure if he should enter or not.

'You wanted to see me?'

'Come in and sit down. I've been at the hospital talking to Jack. He has a long way to go for a full recovery, but he was able to fill in the missing details from the night he was attacked.'

Paolo felt a massive sense of relief. He'd been fearful Willows' news was going to be the opposite of positive, but if that was the case, why did Willows look as if he'd swallowed a lemon?

Willows picked up a piece of paper, stared at it, then put it down again. Paolo waited. What the hell was going on? This wasn't like Willows at all. He normally went straight to the point.

'Paolo, I've known you a long time. I've always believed you were a man of integrity. Not someone who would lie or shift blame onto others.'

Feeling as though he was under attack, but not knowing why, Paolo nodded.

'I'd like to think that's true, sir.'

Willows shrugged. 'So would I, Paolo, so would I, but I've been given good reason to doubt it.'

Paolo sat forward. 'I'm sorry, I'm not following you. What exactly are you saying?'

'I told you I went to visit Jack. He tells me it was entirely your idea that he went alone to confront Brad Cooper and Greg Mallory that night.'

Paolo shook his head. 'That is not true. Not at all. I intended to go myself, but Jack insisted on going. When I said I would go with him, he was adamant it would be better if he went alone. He said he knew all the hiding places around the club and none of them were big enough for two.'

'That's not what Jack told me today.'

Paolo knew he had to keep his temper in check. 'I told him if he went alone, it was for observation of Greg Mallory only. In fact, I stressed that he shouldn't approach the man at any cost.'

'If that were the case, Paolo, what were you doing there?'

'I decided to give Jack some backup.'

'Without telling him? Didn't you think that might have put him in danger?'

Paolo felt as if he was walking through treacle. 'I did tell him.'

'When? You just told me he was going alone with your blessing.'

'It wasn't with my blessing. I didn't want him there on his own, so I called him and told him I was coming out. He tried to refuse, but I insisted. Look, sir, I have good reason to believe Jack knew what was going on at The Pipe and withheld information from me and the team. He certainly was well aware of Brad and Greg because he'd been watching The Pipe, but when we interviewed both men at the gym Jack held back that information.'

Willows sighed. 'If nothing else, Paolo, it seems you've lost control of your team. Jack told me it was Brad Cooper who beat him. Apparently the man is an expert in one of the martial arts. Which, to my mind, is all the more reason not to send an officer alone on surveillance.'

Paolo stood up. 'As I said, I didn't send him, he volunteered. He also refused assistance and tried to prevent me from going out to join him that night. I can only assume he wanted to make the arrest and get the glory.'

'That is an offensive thing to say, Paolo. I don't expect outbursts like that from you.'

'Really, sir? My reputation is being ripped to shreds and you don't think I'm going to get angry?'

'Paolo, sit down. *Sit down!*'

Paolo fell back onto the seat, but every fibre of his being wanted to be out of the office and shaking Jack until he told the truth.

'Obviously there will have to be an inquiry. It will be even-handed and impartial. If it is found that Jack withheld information, he will be dealt with. However, your conduct will also be under the spotlight. I am not favouring either account, Paolo, so don't think I am.'

'Is that all, sir?'

Willows nodded. 'For the time being, yes.'

'Good, in that case, I have a job to do. We have reliable information Greg Mallory and Brad Cooper are dealing at the club. Whether or not the manager is involved remains to be seen. Now, however,

180

we have another reason to pick up Cooper. As we know from Jack's testimony, the man is guilty of an attack on a police officer.'

Paolo managed to leave the room without exploding, but it took all his self-control. He needed to get back to his office and call CC. They would search Marissa's apartment and then later head out to The Pipe. There was no point in waiting to pick up Brad and Greg. They'd do it tonight in full view of all those waiting in line at the club. It was time to get the message across that drug dealers and those who attacked police officers were not above the law.

What a difference between the estate agent holding the keys to Sasha Carmichael's flat and the concerned landlady at Marissa's apartment. The moment Paolo had explained who they were and why they were there, Ellie Simpson couldn't have been more helpful.

'I knew there was something wrong when Marissa didn't show up,' she said. 'I've been feeding her cat and she is as reliable as clock-work about coming home on the day she says she will.' She handed Paolo the keys. 'You will find her, won't you?'

'We are doing our best,' he said. Turning to CC, he pointed to the stairs. 'Second floor, first door on the left.'

He nodded to Ellie Simpson. 'We will return the keys to you as soon as we've finished looking around.'

Following CC up the stairs he thought about how much easier their job would be if everyone was as helpful. CC already had the door open by the time he reached the second floor.

Marissa's apartment was as unlike Sasha's as it was possible to be. Where Sasha's had been tidy, Marissa's was cluttered. Sasha's flat was filled with quality furniture, but Marissa's looked as if she picked up a number of pieces from second-hand shops and built the rest from flat-pack stores. Even so, Paolo thought Marissa's was homelier. It looked lived in, rather than just a place to sleep.

There were only two tiny rooms in addition to the kitchen and bathroom. Paolo pointed to the bedroom.

'You start in there and I'll take the lounge.'

There wasn't much to search. A bookcase with only a few books, most of the space was taken up with knickknacks and photos. He picked up one of three women wearing sarongs on a sun-filled beach. Sasha, Marissa and Angelica all looked as if they hadn't a care in the world.

It only took him a few minutes to realise there was little that would help the investigation in the lounge and was about to go to help CC when she appeared in the doorway holding a large book.

'What have you got there, CC?'

'A journal, sir. There's a stack of them in the bottom of the wardrobe, but this one was at the side of the bed. It looks as though she kept a regular record of her life. I've read a few of the entries and I'd say this was a form of therapy for her.'

'Anything of use to us?' Paolo asked.

CC nodded. 'Marissa took Sasha's concerns more seriously than Angelica did. She made a list of everyone she'd seen eyeing up Sasha in ways that might be construed as creepy. Top of the list was Greg Mallory, closely followed by Brad Cooper.'

'Does she give reasons?'

CC shook her head. 'No, sir, look!' she said, turning the journal towards Paolo.

'The entry opens with Sasha's name and then Marissa talks about how worried she was and lists those two men by name. But look who else she put.'

Paolo leaned forward and saw the words: *creepy bus guy!* He was beginning to wonder whether Marissa had been taken because she knew too much.

Chapter Thirty-four

Paolo and CC stood on the corner opposite The Pipe. The rest of the team were deployed ready to back them up and, if necessary, prevent any civil disorder. For the time being the manager was in the clear, but maybe Brad would be prepared to throw his boss under the bus to help himself.

CC touched his arm. 'Look there, sir. Isn't that Darius Nelson in the queue? The other guy you interviewed with Jack?'

Paolo looked over to where CC was pointing. 'So it is. He's fallen under the radar, but maybe we need to keep an eye on him. He didn't mention knowing Sasha from The Pipe.'

CC shrugged. 'They might not have crossed paths, sir. Look at the numbers waiting to get in. I would imagine you could come here many times and not spot people you know from elsewhere. It must be packed solid in there.'

Paolo had his phone on silent, but the vibration alerted him to the call he'd been waiting for.

'Sterling,' he whispered.

'We've got him in custody, sir. We flagged him down as he was leaving the pizza place and discovered a load of pills in a secret pocket in the delivery bag.'

'Well done. Put him in one of the interview rooms and leave him to stew. I'll be back shortly.'

Paolo smiled and ended the call. 'We can go, CC. That was Colin Merton. They've picked up Greg Mallory. Let's go grab Brad Cooper and head back to the station.'

As they strolled across the street Brad glanced over. He looked completely unfazed by the fact he was being approached by two police officers. In fact, Paolo thought, the bastard looked as if he was in control of this situation. He was going to enjoy showing Brad the error of his ways.

'I'm afraid I can't let you in, officer. You're not the right type of clientele.' He grinned at CC. 'You, on the other hand, would fit right in. Free entry for one night only.'

'Very funny, Brad,' Paolo said, 'but I'm afraid you're going to have to find someone else to mind the door.'

'Really? Why's that then?'

'Because we'd like you to come to the station for a little chat.'

Brad laughed. 'I don't think so. Have you seen all these people waiting to enjoy themselves? You don't want to let them down, now do you?'

Paolo took a step closer to Brad. 'I'm trying to do this with the least disruption, but if you persist in being a wise guy, I am quite happy to arrest you with as much noise and attention as I can manage.'

'On what charge? I'm not doing anything wrong.'

'You are under arrest for grievous bodily harm and attacking a police officer. Now, why don't you do the sensible thing and get someone to take your place here?'

Brad's grin stretched even more, reminding Paolo of Alice's Cheshire Cat.

'I'll call John to take my place,' Brad said. 'Would you like to search me? Gorgeous here is welcome to put her hands on my body.'

'If my officer laid hands on you, believe me, you would not enjoy it. Now, make the call and let's get going.'

A few minutes later a man Paolo thought must have a serious steroid problem came out to relieve Brad. Paolo had never seen anyone with biceps that large.

'You going to be long?' Muscles asked. 'Only it's heaving in there and Del can't watch 'em all on his own.'

'Not sure how long I'll be, Mick,' Brad said. 'These nice police officers want a word with me down at the nick.'

184

Paolo saw a flicker of emotion cross John's face as he registered the warning Brad had clearly given him.

'Okay, let's go,' Brad said. He turned to the people at the front of the queue. 'Nothing to worry about, peeps. I'm off to help the police with their enquiries,' he said, laughing. 'The sooner I can get this mix-up sorted, the sooner I'll be back on the door. In the meantime, John will be taking care of you. Have a good time.'

He waved and then held his hands out to CC. 'What? No handcuffs? Where's your sense of fun? I thought you'd be up for the dominatrix role.'

'Don't push your luck, Brad,' CC said. 'You're not my type, but I'd like nothing better than to hand you over to the real hard men in prison. They'd love a bit of fresh meat like you. Still, maybe my wish will come true one day.'

Paolo laughed. In any exchange of words he knew CC would come out on top. Brad would learn that too if he kept trying to push her buttons.

'Brad, give it up. You're not going to get a rise out of Detective Sergeant Connors, no matter how hard you try. Come on, this way. You've just told everyone, the sooner we get to the station, the sooner you can get back on duty – believe me, that isn't going to happen.'

They walked either side of Brad to the car where two uniformed officers were waiting.

'In you get,' Paolo said, signalling Brad to take the middle seat so that he'd have no access to the doors without climbing over an officer.

Paolo closed the door on the interview room where Brad Cooper had been less than helpful. Apart from repeating over and over that he wanted his solicitor, he'd given them nothing to work with.

'Any news on the warrants to search the Cooper and Mallory residences?' Paolo asked DC Merton as they passed in the corridor.

'Not yet, sir, but I'm on it. I take it you're heading to interview Mallory?'

Paolo nodded.

'As soon as the warrants come through, I'll come to get you.'

'Good stuff, Colin. Okay, CC, are you ready for this one? He has his solicitor with him, I believe, so we might not get much out of him.'

CC opened the door to the interview room, giving Paolo a clear view of the occupants. Bloody hell, he thought, not her again!

'Harassing another of my clients, DCI Sterling?' Jennifer Sanderson said.

'Not harassing, Ms Sanderson. The term is interviewing. And may I say what an interesting clientele you appear to have.'

Jennifer's perfectly shaped eyebrows shot upwards. 'Meaning?'

Paolo sat down opposite Mallory as CC took the seat across from the solicitor.

'Nothing sinister intended by my remark,' Paolo said. 'It's just that our earlier meeting was over another unsavoury individual.'

'I'd thank you not to refer to my clients in that way, DCI Sterling. That person has nothing to do with why I am here, so I would ask you to be a little more professional. Now tell me, why has my client been dragged from his place of work and brought here? Is he being charged with a crime?'

'Not yet, but we do need to ask him a few questions.'

She nodded. 'My client will be answering no comment to all questions until we are able to determine the direction of this investigation. Unless you are prepared to charge my client, you have precisely twenty-four hours and then I will be demanding his release. Have I made myself clear?'

'Perfectly.'

Paolo switched on the recorder and gave details of the date and time, who was in the room and who was being questioned.

'Mr Mallory, we have a reliable witness, actually two witnesses, who say they have seen you dealing drugs outside The Pipe over a considerable period of time.'

'No comment.'

'In addition to this, when you were apprehended by DS Merton you were found to be in possession of tablets which are currently being examined by our forensic department. Would you like to save us the trouble of waiting for the analysis and tell us about those tablets?'

This time Mallory looked towards his solicitor before answering. Paolo was annoyed to see her give a nod of reassurance.

'No comment.'

The silence was shattered by a loud ringing tone and Jennifer Sanderson reached forward to pull a phone from the briefcase in front of her.

'I'm sorry,' she said, looking at the phone display. 'I'm afraid I have to take this call. Would you excuse me for a moment?'

Paolo nodded. 'Interview paused at 21:06.'

Jennifer Sanderson waited to make sure the recording had stopped, then stood up and left the room. It seemed to Paolo that only a minute had passed before she returned. He looked at his watch. Sure enough she had only been out of the room for about thirty seconds.

He waited for her to settle once again next to her client before reaching forward to restart the recording.

'Interview resumed at 21:08. Tell me, Greg, what is your association with Brad Cooper?'

'He –' Greg began.

Jennifer Sanderson coughed and Greg's lips closed momentarily.

'No comment,' he said, looking ever more uncomfortable, Paolo was pleased to see.

'Who is your supplier?'

This time Greg looked at Jennifer Sanderson with something like pleading in his eyes.

'You know, Ms Sanderson, it looks to me like your client wants to talk to us. Perhaps you'd like to reconsider your advice to him?'

Before she could answer there was a tap on the door. It opened and Colin Merton looked in to give Paolo a thumbs up. Paolo stood up and CC did the same.

'I'll give you time to chat to your client, Ms Sanderson, but he might want to know that we have a warrant to search his apartment and garage space, so if there is anything incriminating there, it could help his case if he tells us about it, rather than my people finding whatever he has concealed.'

'Yes,' Greg said. 'I want to talk.'

'Mr Mallory, I really think you should follow my advice and not comment.'

'Yes, but –'

She held up her hand. 'Before my client speaks to you I'd like to have a word with him. Please turn off that recording device.'

Paolo reached forward. 'Interview terminated at 21:14,' he said before touching the button. 'I'll give you and your clients five minutes' grace before we leave to execute the warrant.'

As he and CC moved to the door Paolo saw the look of panic on Greg's face. They left the room and closed the door.

'He's ready to roll over,' CC said.

'I agree, but I'm not sure he's that far up the food chain. He looks terrified enough to spill his guts, but I wonder how much he knows. Brad, on the other hand, I wouldn't mind betting is involved in this up to his eyeballs. I think we'll keep our pal Brad Cooper waiting until after we've searched Greg's place and his. Maybe we'll have a bit more ammunition to use.'

CC nodded. 'Good idea. While we're waiting for Sanderson to try to stop Greg from talking, shall I go and see if Cooper's legal counsel has arrived?'

'Yes. Let's hope his solicitor is less on the ball than the charming Ms Sanderson.'

CC laughed and headed for the interview room housing Brad Cooper. Paolo watched as she had a word with the uniformed officer on the door, who shook his head. CC shrugged and came back to Paolo.

'Apparently Brad Cooper is fuming because his solicitor is tied up with another client and he has to wait.'

A thought occurred to Paolo. 'I wonder if the client is none other than Greg Mallory.'

CC's mouth formed a perfect circle. 'It will be interesting to see how she handles the conflict of interest if that's the case.'

They soon had their answer. The door opened and Jennifer Sanderson came out.

'Mr Mallory is no longer my client as we have agreed to part company. I have recommended to him that he not answer any further questions until such time as he is able to gain legal representation. Now I would like you to escort me to Brad Cooper, who, I can assure you, will not be making any comment.'

Paolo left Greg to fester while waiting for the duty solicitor to arrive. As he climbed into the car he turned to CC.

'At least the drug case is finally coming together. I wish we could say the same about that poor missing woman.'

She started the car and reversed from the parking space before answering.

'You don't think they are connected in some way?'

Paolo shrugged. 'I honestly don't know. I thought our peeping Tom might be the one, but apart from watching him, there's not much more we can do. I just hope she is still alive. If Brad or Greg are holding Marissa in their homes this is our best chance of finding her.'

CC nodded and flicked the indicator to turn left into George Street.

'I think we'll soon wrap up the drugs situation. I get the feeling Greg can't wait to tell us whatever we need to know. I'm not so sure about Brad Cooper with Jennifer Sanderson at his side.'

'Let's just hope we find enough evidence that we don't need to worry about the not so charming Ms Sanderson.'

CC slowed to take the roundabout for the dual carriageway turn-off. 'It's a pity we couldn't get a warrant for The Pipe, but apparently we don't have enough to get that one.'

Paolo nodded. 'If we find anything at all in Brad's place, I don't think we'll have any trouble at all getting a warrant issued.'

'Okay, listen up, everyone. I want this place torn apart,' Paolo said, standing in the entrance hall of Greg's apartment. 'We are not only looking for drugs; we are also looking for secret doors. Marissa Piper is still missing and it's possible, albeit unlikely, that Greg Mallory is connected to her disappearance. Give it all you've got and report directly to DS Connors.'

He turned to CC. 'I want you to stay here and oversee this search.

I'm going to take Andrea with me to Brad Cooper's place. Let me know the second anything, or anyone, turns up.'

She nodded. 'Will do, sir.'

He watched as she pulled on gloves and gave him a thumbs up before moving towards Andrea waiting by the front door.

'Ready to go, sir?' she asked.

'You drive,' he said and handed over his car keys. 'I believe CC has already put Cooper's address into the SatNav. There's a team on the way there now.'

As they travelled down in the lift Paolo felt the detective constable's attention on him.

'Do you have a problem, Andrea?'

She coloured up, but shook her head. 'No, sir, it's just I didn't think you liked anyone driving you other than CC.'

'What makes you think that?'

'Jack was complaining that you wouldn't let him drive when the two of you went anywhere.'

Paolo smiled, but it was hard. 'That had little to do with not wanting anyone to drive me and far too much to do with how I felt about losing Dave.'

Andrea shook her head and muttered something that Paolo couldn't quite hear properly, but it sounded very derogatory about Jack. Knowing he really shouldn't ignore whatever she'd said and would have to discipline her if he admitted to hearing anything, he was relieved the lift doors chose that moment to open. It seemed Andrea was yet another solid cop Jack had managed to antagonise.

'Let's go,' he said. 'I have a good feeling about this search.'

The drive to Cooper's house was a quiet one. Paolo guessed Andrea was nervous about saying anything out of turn. He understood that, but missed CC's more irreverent comments. He missed Dave's companionship even more and wondered if he'd ever get beyond feeling like there was an empty space in his working life.

As the SatNav announced they had reached their destination, Paolo was pleased to see several police cars were already in position. What surprised him somewhat was the size of Cooper's house. Set in grounds of probably nearly an acre, the three-storey Georgian mansion wasn't at all what anyone on a bouncer's salary would be expected to own – not even when his income was supplemented by personal-trainer activities.

'You know, Andrea, I have a feeling our Mr Cooper is either living wildly beyond his means, or has a source of income the revenue office knows nothing about.'

He climbed out of the car and walked over to the uniformed officers.

'We start at the top of the house and work our way down. I want every wardrobe checked for false backs and every carpet lifted to search for trapdoors. We are here primarily to search for drugs, but it's very possible a young woman is being held here. If that is the case, we have to find her.'

He looked at each officer in turn, hoping his fear that they might already be too late to save her didn't show on his face. 'I don't want to hear months from now that a secret door was found leading to a dungeon where a young woman starved to death because her kidnapper was locked up in our cells. Do I make myself clear?'

A sea of earnest faces nodded in unison. He walked up the steps to the portico with Andrea. 'I might as well try the doorbell first. There could be someone inside who can let us in.'

He rang and listened. Not a sound came from inside the house. He took a step back and signalled to the men holding the battering ram.

'Okay, men, break it down. Let's get in there.'

Chapter Thirty-five

Paolo watched as two officers rammed the door. A satisfying splintering sound signalled the moment they made the breakthrough. He waited until the way was clear, then entered the house, amazed at the tastefully furnished interior. Who would have guessed Brad Cooper was not only an art lover, but also a collector of fine porcelain. The wall of the lounge was full of delicate figurines and miniature dogs of all shapes and breeds.

The world really is full of unusual people, Paolo thought, looking around in wonder at the silk curtains and leather furniture. Each of the four sofas would probably have cost more than Paolo had spent on all the furnishings combined in his home.

'Andrea, I want you to go through every drawer in that desk,' he said, pointing to something that looked like it belonged in the palace of Versailles.

'Any idea what I'm looking for, sir?'

He shook his head. 'Not a clue, but considering the size of this place, Brad Cooper must have a lot to hide. The carpets alone must have cost a fortune. I'm going upstairs to see if he has a room set aside as a study. I can't imagine there won't be a laptop at the very least hidden away somewhere.'

As he walked up the marble stairs his phone rang. CC's name appeared on the screen.

'CC, you should see Brad's home.'

'Not what you expected, sir?'

'Not at all. Anyway, never mind that. What have you got for me?'

'We've found a stash of tabs, most likely ecstasy, but I'll get them over to the lab for testing. Nothing more at this stage. No sign of Marissa Piper ever having been here, but we're still looking.'

'Good work, CC. The tabs alone should be enough to make Greg Mallory tell us whatever he knows. Unfortunately, looking at the difference in lifestyle between Mallory and Cooper, I doubt Mallory has much to tell.'

He ended the call and continued to the first floor. Several officers were in the first room to the left at the top of the stairs. Paolo looked in. It was another palatial example of home design on steroids. The opulence made Paolo feel ill. This wasn't a home, it was a show house, but who was Brad looking to impress?

'Sir!'

He came out onto the landing to see Andrea climbing the stairs.

'There's nothing in that desk, sir. It's for show, rather than for use. I only found a few stationery items, but none that had been used.'

'In that case, Andrea, there must be somewhere Brad uses as an office.'

'Unless he uses the club, sir,' she said.

Paolo shrugged. 'That's possible, I suppose, but the only office I saw when I was there was the one the manager used.'

They glanced into three other bedrooms, but none of them had a computer or looked as if they were used as an office, but then Paolo found what he'd been looking for. One room was fitted out with shelves of books, a wraparound desk housing a laptop attached to two screens and several filing cabinets.

'We've hit pay dirt here, Andrea. You take the desk; I'll start on the filing cabinet.'

She had just sat down when there was a shout from down the hall.

'Keep at this, Andrea,' Paolo said. 'I'll go and see what they've found.'

Following the sound, he ran back to the first bedroom he'd looked into. The bed was covered in clothes which were being thoroughly searched by two officers. A third officer was standing next to a massive walk-in wardrobe, now completely empty of its former contents.

'There is definitely a false panel here, sir. I thought you'd like to be present when we break through.'

Paolo nodded. 'Thank you. Take it easy when you break it down. There might be a woman trapped behind there.'

'I'll go as gently as I can, sir,' the officer said, picking up a claw wrench and beginning to lever in the join at the back of the wardrobe.

The sound of wood splintering was followed by a crash as the entire back section came away. Paolo and the officer lifted it clear of the wardrobe and placed it next to the adjoining wall. When Paolo stepped back to look, an involuntary whistle escaped.

'Bloody hell. Call up the photographer from down below. No one is to touch a thing until it's all been recorded.'

Paolo was so in awe at the sight before him that he jumped when the photographer touched his arm.

'Sorry, DCI Sterling. I didn't mean to startle you.'

'No, no, of course you didn't. Sorry, I was stunned by that.'

The photographer looked in the direction of Paolo's pointing finger.

'I can understand why, sir. I don't think I've ever seen so many packs of drugs in one place. I take it they are drugs of some kind?'

Paolo nodded. 'Almost certainly. Probably packs of cocaine, but until the lab gets to analyse the stuff, we won't know for sure.'

He stepped to one side to give the photographer room to work and began counting. There were four panels, each with six shelves. On every shelf there were at least ten rectangular packs wrapped in plastic. If it was cocaine or heroin, the street value had to be astronomical. The problem now was finding out if Brad was the shark at the top of the food chain, or one of the minnows swimming blind. If he wasn't the big boss, was the owner of The Pipe the one they needed to hit next?

He heard Andrea's footsteps approaching and turned to see her enter the room and stop as her eyes took in the contents of the wardrobe.

'Good God! There must be a fortune in there.'

'There is, but I'm thinking more of the misery it would bring on the street to the poor sods who take the shit.'

She nodded. 'You're right. I hate drugs, but I hate the bastards who supply the stuff even more. Sorry, sir, I know I should keep my thoughts to myself.'

'Not on this subject, Andrea. Say what you feel. Anyway, you came to tell me something, I think.'

'I did. I think you should come and see what I've found. I thought it explained how Brad Cooper could afford this house, but now I've seen that,' she said, pointing to the drugs, 'maybe what I've discovered isn't such a shock.'

Paolo followed her back to the office to find papers spread all over the desk and filing cabinets.

'You know you wanted me to find out who owned The Pipe,' she said, 'and I explained I couldn't get beyond the holding companies of various enterprises? Look, sir, I've found links to Brad Cooper in each of those companies. It's going to take a bit more research, but I'm almost certain Cooper owns The Pipe.'

'Excellent work, Andrea. That alone should be enough to secure a warrant to search the club.'

Paolo went back to the bedroom and waited until the drug packets had been removed and sent off to the lab before going in search of Andrea who was back in the office looking for more information on Brad's business dealings.

'Found anything else interesting?'

She looked up from the laptop. 'No, sir. I think there might be some hidden files on this, so it would be a good idea to send it to IT.'

'I agree. Bag it and seal it. We'll take it with us. It's time to get back to the station and see what Greg Mallory has to say before we hit Cooper with the news that his bedroom secret has been uncovered.'

As they went down to the ground floor, passing the bedrooms still being searched, Paolo called out to the senior officer.

'I'm heading off. I want you to continue here until you are absolutely certain there is nothing more to find. What still has to be done?'

'We've just about finished in here, but the garage and shed still need to be searched.'

'Okay, call me if you find anything at all. The drug haul is great, but my main concern now is Marissa Piper.'

'I've got your direct number. You'll hear from me if we find her.'

Paolo nodded his thanks and turned to Andrea. 'Let's go and have a chat with Greg.'

'Are you sure you don't want to wait for the duty solicitor to get here?' Paolo said for the third time since re-entering the interview room.

Greg shook his head.

Paolo pointed to the table. 'Please speak for the benefit of the recording.'

'No, I don't want to wait. Fat lot of good my last solicitor did for me.'

'Okay, you say you want to tell us everything, so what do you know about the packets of heroin, or possibly cocaine, we found in your colleague's home?'

'What colleague? What are you on about? I don't know anything about hard drugs.'

'Fair enough,' Paolo said. 'Let's talk instead about the pills we found at your place. What have you got to say about those?'

Greg shrugged. 'They're just some ecstasy. Nothing bad. Just some good-time pills.'

'Good-time pills that killed someone,' Paolo said.

Greg shook his head. 'Nah, no way. They don't kill.'

'What about Sally Mendip? Did you supply her? According to her father, you two were an item.'

'Yeah, we spent some time together, but I never gave her any tabs.'

'Why not? You were supplying everyone else. Why not Sally? Did you know the tabs were bad?'

'They weren't! They aren't . . . I mean, the bloke who makes them said they were good and he should know what he's doing.'

'Who did you get them from?'

'If I tell you, will I get off a bit lighter?'

Paolo shrugged. 'Maybe. I can't make any promises.'

'It was Darius Nelson. He works at the hospital. We were in the

196

gym one day and he said he could get some stuff, would I take it to The Pipe and pass it on to Brad, so I did.'

'What about the tablets at your place?'

'They're the latest from Darius. I was going to drop them off later tonight.'

'And what about the other drugs? How do you fit into that set up?'

'I don't!'

Paolo laughed. 'From here it looks like you're in it up to the hilt. That's not going to go well for you when the CPS hear about it.'

'I'm telling you,' Greg Mallory yelled. 'I don't know anything about cocaine or heroin. I'll admit to the pills, but that's it.'

'You'd better hope the pills you've been passing on aren't the same composition as those that killed Sally Mendip, or you'll be facing a manslaughter charge at the very least.'

Paolo watched as his words hit home.

'Where is Marissa?'

'Huh? What?'

'Marissa Piper, where is she?'

'I don't know. She's nothing to do with me. I fancied her friend, not her.'

'Her friend Sasha? The one you claimed not to know when we told you she was dead? Did you kill her?'

Greg's face crumpled and he began to sob.

'No! I didn't kill Sasha. I didn't! I've changed my mind. I want a solicitor.'

Paolo reached forward and placed his finger on the switch to end the recording. 'Interview terminated at 23:16.' He pressed the button and stood up. 'As soon as the duty solicitor gets here I'll make sure he comes to you.'

The moment he was outside, he turned to Andrea. 'Get Darius Nelson picked up immediately and then sort out a warrant to search his home and place of work at the hospital.' He looked along the corridor to see CC walking towards him.

'Nothing more at Greg's?' Paolo asked.

She shook her head. 'Nope. No sign of Marissa, unfortunately.'

'I'm still waiting to hear from the officers at Cooper's house.' He filled her in on Brad's financial situation and ownership of The Pipe. 'Let's go in to chat to Brad Cooper and the annoying Ms Sanderson. He has some explaining to do, but I doubt she'll allow him to talk.'

They walked along to the interview room. Jennifer Sanderson stood up as they entered.

'It's about time. I've waited long enough. My client and I are leaving.'

'I'm afraid not,' Paolo said. He slid photographs of the drug packets across the table. 'We'd like to hear what your client has to say about the drugs found secreted in his home.'

'He has no comment to make until we have conferred. I would like time to do that now.'

Paolo nodded. 'Of course, that's his right. By the way, Brad, why didn't you tell me you owned The Pipe?'

Jennifer Sanderson put up her hand, but Brad ignored her.

'Because it was none of your business.'

'Why would you play at being a bouncer when you own the place? Oh, hang on,' Paolo said, 'was it because that gave you access to the clubgoers? Made it easy to sell your wares?'

Brad laughed. 'It gave me a buzz to decide who came in and who got left out.'

'And did it give you a buzz to beat a police officer almost to the point of death?'

'That's quite enough,' Jennifer said. 'My client has nothing more to say until we have consulted.'

Paolo and CC left the room. He was no sooner outside than his phone rang.

'Sterling.'

'We've searched every inch of this place. There's no sign of Marissa Piper.'

Paolo thanked the officer and ended the call. His heart sank. The chances of finding her alive seemed to be shrinking by the hour.

Chapter Thirty-six

Paolo woke and stretched out a hand to grab his phone to check the time. Only five in the morning. They hadn't left the station until well after midnight. He could try to get back to sleep, but he knew the chances of that were minimal. He might just as well get up and shower.

He thought of Jack, no longer fighting for his life, but apparently fighting to get Paolo sacked. Not that Willows had actually said that, but why else would Jack lie about what had really happened that night?

As the water cascaded over him, he ran through the conversations he'd had with Jack that day and evening. He shook his head, this was ridiculous, he was now doubting himself. If even he couldn't accept without hesitation that he'd acted correctly, how was Willows meant to believe him?

He switched off the water and stepped out to grab a towel, mentally planning his day as he rubbed the water off. Catch up on paperwork until about nine, then get started on the interviews. With a bit of luck, by then, the warrants to search The Pipe and Darius Nelson's various haunts would be through. Feeling better than he'd imagined possible just minutes earlier, Paolo hung up the towel and went to get dressed.

Paolo had just signed yet another report on how much money needed to be allocated to meet government budget requirements when CC knocked on his open door.

He looked up. 'You look like someone with good news, CC.'

She waved papers at him. 'Warrants to search The Pipe, Darius Nelson's home and place of work.'

Paolo stood up. 'Great. Let's get going.'

'The only downside,' CC said, 'is that Nelson works at the hospital, so we cannot touch anything that might impact on patient confidentiality.'

'Sounds fair,' Paolo said. 'I doubt he's using patient records to manufacture his pills.'

'Where do we start?'

'I want you with me today. Andrea and Colin can lead the search at Nelson's home and move on to the hospital from there. We'll go with the other team to tear apart The Pipe. If Cooper is involved in Marissa's abduction, that's somewhere he might have her incarcerated.'

Paolo hammered on the door of The Pipe until the muscle-bound guy who'd stood in as bouncer for Brad opened the door.

'What the fuck?' he said, looking at Paolo's massed rank of officers.

'It's Mick, isn't it?' Paolo said. 'I've got a warrant here to search this place. Is the manager around?'

Mick shook his head. 'It's just me and the cleaners until later. I can't just let you in. The manager will go apeshit.'

Paolo smiled and waved the search warrant. 'One, we have the right to enter. Two, you've got more to worry about if I go apeshit than if your boss does. Three, if you try to stop us from carrying out the search you will be arrested. Clear enough for you?'

As Mick nodded, Paolo called over to one of the officers. 'I'd like you to keep an eye on our friend Mick. Make sure he doesn't call anyone.'

'Yes, sir. Come with me,' he said to Mick, leading him inside the club.

Paolo turned to the rest of his team. 'I want this place searched from top to bottom. If there's a rug on the floor, I want it taken up. Cupboards against walls to be moved. Anything that could conceal a secret entrance has to be investigated. I don't care how long it takes, if Marissa is here, we need to find her.'

He looked at the earnest faces of his officers and knew every one of them felt as he did.

'CC, I want you to take charge of the private area and the manager's office. If the door's locked, make Mick the bouncer open it up for you. The rest of you, come with me. We'll tackle the main club.'

Paolo watched CC lead her fellow officers towards the section the average club user probably didn't even know existed.

'Right, here's how we're going to tackle this. I want you working in pairs. Each of you to go over wherever the other has searched, just in case there is a chance something gets missed the first time of looking. Okay, let's get going.'

Three hours later Paolo and CC watched as the cars pulled away, ferrying the dispirited officers back to the station.

'I can't believe we have torn this place apart and there's not a sign Marissa was ever here,' CC said. 'What's your thought, sir?'

Paolo could feel the lack of sleep clogging his brain. If three of the four obvious suspects, Sidcup, Mallory and Cooper weren't holding Marissa, that just left Darius Nelson. Of them all, to Paolo, Nelson seemed the least likely suspect. He pulled his phone out and called Andrea.

'How's it going? Any sign of our missing woman?'

'No, sir, but we have found Nelson's pill-manufacturing set-up in his spare room. It looks like he's been stealing drugs from the hospital and creating his own version of ecstasy. We've sent the tabs for analysis.'

'Good work, Andrea. How much longer do you need to finish up there?'

'We're just about ready to head to the hospital. I think we'll get a better reception when we show what Nelson's been up to than we would otherwise have done.'

'I think you're right. Keep me posted on any new developments.'

'Will do, sir.'

Paolo ended the call and relayed to CC what Andrea had told him.

'So what's our next move, sir? Do we go back to the station and interview Nelson now, or wait for Andrea and Colin to report back from the hospital?'

'I think we should go back to the station and see what Nelson has to say for himself. Whether or not there is anything to find at the hospital, he's caught red-handed on the tab manufacture.'

Back at the station, Paolo was desperate for coffee, but knew time was against them. They had to keep going while things were working for them. He led CC across the main office and headed for the interview rooms.

'Let's start with Greg,' Paolo said. 'He's definitely the weakest link and is ready to throw Darius to the wolves.'

CC laughed. 'He certainly isn't cut out to be a big-time drug lord, that's for sure.'

As they entered the interview room, a skinny and dishevelled-looking young man stood up and held out his hand.

'I'm Steven Jones, duty solicitor. My client wishes to make a statement.'

Paolo sat down next to CC and switched on the recorder. He gave the time and details of who was in the room.

'Now, would you like to say that again, Mr Jones?' Paolo asked, thinking Steven Jones didn't look old enough to have left school, far less studied for enough years to gain a law degree.

'My client, Greg Mallory, wishes to make a statement.'

Greg nodded vigorously. 'I do. I did it.'

Paolo held up a hand. 'Let's take this one step at a time, Greg. What exactly are you admitting to? Do you know where Marissa Piper is being held?'

'What? No! I already told you I had nothing to do with her. All I did was sell ecstasy tablets for people to take at The Pipe. I handed them over to Brad Cooper. I don't know what he did with them.'

'You acknowledge supplying Brad Cooper with ecstasy tablets?'

Greg nodded.

'Please speak in answer.'

'I do. I did.'

'You did this knowing that such an act was against the law?'

Again Greg nodded, but words spilled out at the same time. 'I knew, but everyone knows they're just a bit of harmless fun.'

'They weren't harmless to Sally Mendip. She lost her life after taking some.'

'I swear I didn't know they were bad. I thought Sally was lovely. I'd never have done anything to hurt her.'

'But you must have realised it was your stuff that killed her. Why didn't you come forward? More to the point, why didn't you stop dishing them out? You knew they were bad.'

Greg shook his head. 'No, I didn't. He said she must have taken something else because his stuff was clean.'

'Who said that? Where did you get your supply?'

'I already told you! I got them from Darius Nelson. He's a theatre nurse at the hospital and gets the stuff. I thought they must be okay. He said it was all okay, you know?'

Paolo looked at Steven Jones. 'Would your client like to make a written statement?'

Greg nodded before Steven could answer. 'Yes, I want to do that. I'm so sorry. I really didn't know the tabs were bad.'

Paolo left Greg in the care of his solicitor to write his statement, overseen by a uniformed officer.

'That was easy,' CC said as soon as they were outside the interview room.

Paolo nodded. 'Let's chat to Darius next. Although, with the evidence of his pill-making factory, if he has any sense he'll own up and try to get stuck with a lesser charge.'

'They don't always have sense, though, do they, sir?'

'Unfortunately, no, but let's hope Darius Nelson is the exception that proves the rule.'

Paolo opened the door to the next interview room, ready to do battle with Nelson's solicitor, but when he looked in there wasn't one.

'Have you called for legal representation?'

Nelson shook his head. 'Nah, there's no point. I know what you guys have found, so why would I fork out a load of dosh when no one can help me?'

Paolo looked at CC. This was far too easy.

'I'm going to record our conversation,' he said as he sat down.

'Do what you like. I'm not likely to get more than a slap on the wrist whatever you charge me with.'

Paolo switched on the recorder and went through the protocol of stating time and occupants. Then he added: 'Mr Nelson, could you please confirm for the sake of the recording that you were advised of your rights and have refused legal counsel?'

'Yeah, whatever.'

'Please state your name for the record and that you have refused legal counsel.'

'Darius Nelson here and I don't want a solicitor. Happy now?'

'Mr Nelson, do you admit that you have been making ecstasy tablets and passing them to Greg Mallory to sell to Brad Cooper at The Pipe?'

'Well, yes to the first bit, but not to the rest.'

'You admit making the tablets?'

'Yeah, there's no point in denying it. You found all the equipment, didn't you?'

'We did. Did you sell the tablets to Greg Mallory to pass on to Brad Cooper at The Pipe?'

'I sold them to Greg. What he did with them after that is nothing to do with me. Like I said, the most I'm going to get for making a few tabs is a slap on the wrist and be told not to be such a naughty boy ever again.'

Paolo turned over the picture of Sally Mendip. 'Do you recognise her?'

Darius glanced at the photo. 'Nah, should I?'

Paolo leaned forward. 'You should because she is the reason you are going to get far more than a slap on the wrist. You will be going to prison for a good long time because of her.'

'What the fuck?'

'She died, Darius. She died after taking ecstasy supplied by someone in The Pipe.'

'Well, that don't mean anything. She could've got the stuff from anyone, couldn't she? You're not pinning that on me.'

'Greg Mallory says he spoke to you after Sally died. So you knew she'd died because of your tablets. Samples of your home-made drugs have been sent for analysis. I would be prepared to bet my pension the composition is going to be the same as that which killed Sally Mendip. You could face a charge of manslaughter at the very least.'

Paolo leaned forward. 'Tell me,' he said, changing tack, 'what was your connection to Sasha Carmichael? We know you were pestering her.'

'How? I mean, I wasn't.'

'And Marissa Piper? What have you done with her?'

'What are you on about? I didn't do anything with either of them. Fuck this! I've changed my mind. I want a solicitor. I'm saying nothing more until I get one. You're not pinning shit on me that I didn't do.'

Paolo reached forward. 'That is your right,' he said as he terminated the interview and switched off the recorder.

As they got outside Paolo shrugged. 'I knew that was going too well.'

'But we'll get him when the lab comes back with the analysis. Also, we have Greg's testimony. Do you really think he's holding Marissa?'

Paolo shook his head. 'No, I don't think he's got it in him. Time to deal with Brad. Ready?'

CC smiled. 'As I'll ever be.'

As Paolo expected, when they entered the interview room housing Brad Cooper, Jennifer Sanderson was sitting by his side. This one wasn't going to be easy.

He moved to the table and sat opposite Sanderson. After he'd started the recording and filled in the date, time and room occupants, he looked at Sanderson before addressing Brad.

'Hello once again, Ms Sanderson.'

'Shall we get on with this? My client has no comment to make. I suggest you make arrangements to let him go home. Unless, that is, you intend to charge him.'

Paolo smiled. 'We certainly do intend to charge him.'

'With?'

'Drug trafficking and the attempted murder of a police officer.'

Paolo watched, but not a flicker of emotion crossed Brad's face.

Brad grinned. 'No comment.'

'We have also been through your home. Nice place, by the way. What do you have to say to this?' Paolo asked, flicking photographs of the drug packets on the hidden shelving.

'No comment.'

'We also know you have been passing on ecstasy tablets at The Pipe.'

'No comment.'

'A young woman died as a result of taking those tablets. What do you have to say to that?'

'No comment.'

Paolo gathered up the photographs. 'Nothing at all to say, Brad?'

'No comment.'

'You saw Detective Constable Cummings trying to get into The Pipe via the alley entrance and attacked him. Then you dragged him across the road to a dead-end alley where no one was likely to find him for several days. You left him for dead.'

'No comment.'

'If I hadn't found him when I did, you'd be facing a murder charge.'

'No comment.'

'Did you kill Sasha Carmichael?'

For the first time a flicker of emotion crossed Brad's face.

'No comment.'

'Are you holding Marissa Piper?'

'What the fuck?'

His solicitor glared at Paolo as she reached out to touch Brad's arm and shake her head.

'My client has no comment to make.'

Chapter Thirty-seven

The next morning, feeling wearier that he'd thought possible, Paolo walked out from his office into the main room. All his team were hard at work, but they seemed to be no closer to finding out who had taken Marissa.

CC was on the phone as he approached her desk. After a few more words, she ended the call, but gestured for Paolo to wait. He watched as she made another call, shook her head and then looked up.

'This one is a bit weird, sir, but I think it might be important.'

'In what way?'

'Do you remember Sasha Carmichael's neighbour saying she thought she'd seen a gas fitter leaving the apartments on the night Sasha was murdered?'

Paolo nodded. 'I do, but we couldn't find a connection to any of the companies operating in the area.'

'The first call was from John Soames, the assistant manager at Fit to Go Gym. He was passed on to me because of the connection to the Sasha Carmichael case. He wanted to know why no one had been to the gym to follow up on a theft. One of the members had his locker broken into and everything taken, wallet, car keys and phone, but as far as we are concerned, sir, the really important thing is that whoever broke into the locker also took the man's gas fitter's uniform.'

'What? Why was this not picked up earlier?'

'That's the thing, sir. My second call was to records. There is no detail regarding the incident. Either it wasn't logged, or it was never reported.'

'Let's get going, CC, we need to follow up on this.'

CC pulled into the first available parking space at the gym.

'Lots of cars here today, sir.'

'It seems to be a popular place. I wonder how Brad's one-to-one clients will feel when news gets out about Brad Cooper's sideline in hard drugs.'

'It makes me wonder if he was peddling them here as well,' CC said.

'That thought occurred to me, too, but I don't think he would have done that. The Pipe is his domain where he can control what happens. Here, there are too many variables outside his control.'

Paolo heard the click as CC pressed the button and the central locking kicked in. Walking over to the entrance, he was glad it was CC with him most of the time now. They had settled into a good unit.

He opened the door and CC entered ahead of him. As Paolo followed her in, he saw John Soames talking to one of the members. He wished he'd worn sunglasses to shield his eyes from the glow of her gym clothes. How anyone could put neon lime green with such a vivid shade of pink and think it looked good was beyond him. He must be getting old. He should ask Katy the next time he spoke to her if it was normal to wear such garish colours.

John Soames looked up and quickly ended his conversation. The young woman seemed a bit aggrieved to Paolo's eyes. Maybe she had the hots for the assistant manager. He was certainly a good-looking man. Fit, too. Paolo wondered if he was also a personal trainer here. They were going to need to replace Brad Cooper, that was for sure. He smiled. Just for attacking a police officer, the entrepreneurial bouncer would have been looking at a long, long stretch behind bars. Add to that the drug charges and he was likely to be an old man before he saw the outside world again.

Paolo nodded hello as John came towards them.

'I believe you had a burglary here but no action has been taken. Would you like to fill me in on the details?'

'Damn right no action was taken. Our member is threatening to sue us and your lot have done nothing about it.'

Paolo noticed a few women had stopped just inside the doorway and were clearly listening to their conversation.

'Are you happy to discuss it here, or shall we go upstairs?' Paolo said, pointedly looking in the direction of the women.

Soames glanced over and then looked back at Paolo.

'Probably best if we talk elsewhere. Follow me.'

He led the way up to the manager's office. 'I realise our problem is small fry to you guys, but our members need to believe their belongings are safe in the lockers.'

Paolo gestured for CC to enter the office and then went in and sat at the manager's desk.

'Why don't you tell me about it from the beginning?'

Soames looked skyward and sighed. 'There isn't really a lot to tell. One of our members works for the gas board. He comes here straight from work and puts his belongings and uniform in a locker while he works out. When he's finished, he showers and gets dressed again. Except, the last time he was here his locker had been opened and everything stolen. Nothing was left inside.'

'You say the last time. Has he not been back since?'

'Not to work out, no. He's moved over to the gym on Bleacher Street. It's nowhere near as good as this one, but he says at least the staff there are trustworthy.'

'But he has been back?'

'Yes, to complain and demand a refund of his annual fees. Callum told him to take it up with the owner.'

'You sound as though you disapprove.'

Soames nodded. 'Stupid attitude to take. We should have just refunded his fees and paid whatever it cost for a replacement uniform. But no, Callum said that if we did that everyone would be pretending

209

they've had stuff stolen just to get their fees refunded. Instead of which, we now have someone bad-mouthing us all over the town and we're losing clients as a result.'

Paolo could see Soames' irritation screaming from every pore. 'When did you report this to the police?'

'I didn't. Callum did. We were all in this office when he made the call. Whoever he spoke to said someone would be out to take statements, but no one came.'

'I'm sorry to say that we have no record of the call. As far as we are concerned, the theft was never reported.' Paolo held up a hand to stop Soames from reacting. 'I'm not saying the call wasn't made. I'm saying nothing was logged. We'll look into that.'

Paolo looked at his watch. 'What time is Callum due in today? I'd like to find out if he can remember the name of the person who took the call.'

At that moment, CC got up and went to stand next to the plate-glass window overlooking the gym foyer. It wasn't like her to stop taking notes, so Paolo knew something must have caught her eye.

'Sir, sorry, I think I need to go downstairs to talk to someone. I'll be right back.'

'No problem, CC.' He turned to Soames. 'Would you mind waiting a moment before we go any further?'

'Fine by me as long as something gets done eventually.'

Within a matter of minutes, CC came back into the room. 'A word alone, sir?'

Soames stood up. 'I'll leave you to it. I'll be downstairs if you need me for anything.'

CC went over to the window and waited. 'Sorry, sir, I wanted to be sure he'd gone back downstairs before I showed you these.'

She held out her hand.

'Love heart sweets. Where did you get them?'

'While you were talking to Soames I glanced up at the CCTV screen showing the foyer and saw a couple of women laughing and showing each other the sweets. That's why I went to the window, to

210

make sure they were love hearts, just like the one found in Sasha's kitchen.'

'First the gas fitter's uniform, now the sweets. Did they say where they found them?'

CC nodded. 'Apparently there is always a bowl of them in the ladies' changing room.'

'I think we need to get Soames back up here.'

'On my way, sir.'

Paolo heard CC's footsteps running down and watched from above as she met up with the assistant manager and pointed up towards the office. Clearly the man got the message because he immediately headed towards the stairway.

CC bounded in ahead of Soames. 'Sir, I'm going to the ladies' changing room to bag up the bowl of sweets.'

'Good. In the meantime, Mr Soames, perhaps you could show me the various places the CCTV looks into.'

He pointed to the various screens. 'Only those you can see. We have cameras in all the public places. The cameras are on timers, so they will flick between various angles.'

'What about the changing rooms?'

Soames shook his head. 'Nope. We're not allowed to cover those areas. That's one of the reasons we had no idea who'd taken the gas fitter's uniform.'

Paolo stood up. 'Show me how you decide which screens to show.'

'I can't.'

'Why not?'

'Only Callum has access to the controls. I don't have his passwords.'

Paolo pulled out his phone. 'Mike,' he said as soon as the call was answered, 'I need you urgently at Fit to Go Gym. How soon can you get here?'

'I can come right now.'

'Great.' Paolo ended the call and turned to Soames. 'I need you to give me the owner's number.'

'But why?' Soames looked close to tears.

'I wasn't asking. I was telling you. Give me the owner's number.'

211

Soames rummaged in the desk until he came up with a book of numbers. 'I'm not authorised to call him.'

Paolo held out his hand for the book. 'I don't want you to call him. I'm going to do that. Please sit over there while I do so.'

Paolo keyed in the number and waited, hoping the owner wouldn't insist on a warrant to view the CCTV controls.

'James Baker's secretary. How can I help you?'

Paolo explained who he was and stressed the urgency of speaking directly to her boss.

'Certainly, detective, I'll see if I can put you through to him.'

Before Paolo could argue his case, the line went silent. Drumming his fingers on the desk, he forced himself to keep calm. As time seemed to stretch from seconds to minutes, he wondered if he'd been cut off. He was about to dial again when the woman's voice came back on.

'I'm sorry, detective, Mr Baker is in conference and doesn't wish to be disturbed at this time. Could I take your number and ask him to call you when he's free?'

'No, you may not. Please tell Mr Baker that if he doesn't take my call I will be arriving at your offices to speak to him in person, regardless of who else might be in the room.'

'I'll do my best,' she said and her voice disappeared again.

Within seconds, a man's tone replaced the softer sound of the secretary.

'There was no need to issue threats, detective. I'm a very busy man and –'

'I'm sure you are, Mr Baker, but are you too busy to help save a young woman's life?'

'What? How? I don't understand.'

'We have reason to believe one of your employees might have abused his position at Fit to Go Gym by viewing areas that shouldn't be covered by your CCTV cameras. I can get a warrant to access your computer system, but while waiting for that a young woman's life is in danger. The person holding her has already killed once. Would you give your consent to allowing our technician to override the passwords?'

'Yes, of course, I had no idea. If there is anything else you need, I'll tell my secretary to authorise it without delay.'

Baker's voice had switched from aggression to conciliation and Paolo realised he'd perhaps pushed too hard before explaining the situation, but he couldn't get the thought out of his head that they could already be too late to save Marissa.

'Thank you, sir. I appreciate your help.'

Now all he had to do was wait for Mike to arrive.

CC came back up with the bowl of sweets in a large sealed evidence bag. She put them on the desk next to Soames. Paolo watched the man's face but he simply looked stunned.

'Do you recognise these?' Paolo asked.

'No. Should I?'

CC stepped forward. 'They were in your ladies' changing room.'

Soames laughed, but to Paolo it sounded more like a choke.

'I never go in there. Why would I?'

'Who does have access to that room?' Paolo asked.

'The members and the cleaning staff. No men are allowed in there.'

'Not even management?'

Paolo thought if Soames shook his head any harder it would fall off.

'Absolutely not, unless there is an emergency plumbing or lighting problem, but that is always dealt with when the room is empty.'

'I'll need to check with the manager. I asked earlier what time he would be in, but we were interrupted before you could answer.'

Soames shrugged. 'I don't know when Callum will be back. He called in sick and I've had to cover for him. I'm already working more hours than I should, so I'm hoping he'll get over whatever it is that's wrong with him. He's a bit of a wimp when it comes to being sick. Can't handle any kind of weakness in himself.'

Paolo stood next to the window and looked down over the foyer, willing Mike to appear. It seemed like for ever before the door opened and he came in.

'CC, go down and let Mike know we're up here,' he said. 'Mr Soames, while you are here, I would like you to write down Callum

Jennens' address and phone numbers. Can you do that for me, please?'

Looking pleased at being able to do something so mundane, Soames pulled a notepad towards him and began writing, briefly looking up as the door opened.

'Ah, Mike,' Paolo said. 'Come in. We need your expertise. I have a strong feeling there are more cameras than Mr Soames here knows about. I have the owner's permission for you to override the password controls and see exactly where else is being recorded.'

Mike nodded and waited for Soames to vacate his seat. Paolo watched as Mike's fingers flew over the keyboard. In no time at all he looked up and smiled at Paolo.

'Easiest system ever. Whoever put the controls in place was an amateur. What do you want to see?'

'Can you take us through the various cameras one by one?'

Mike nodded. 'Sure thing.'

The first few shots were the same as the ones Paolo had seen each time he'd been in the office, but suddenly a different view altogether came onto the screen.

'That's the spot,' CC said. 'That's exactly where I found the bowl of love heart sweets.'

The image was focused on a small area in close up.

'Any other cameras in the ladies' locker room?'

Mike hit the keyboard and several other images came up, but none of them within the ladies' changing room.

'Go back to the camera showing where those sweets had been, please, Mike.'

The screen flickered briefly and then returned to the area.

'This would have shown the watcher clearly what was going on with regard to the sweets. I wonder what their significance is. Mike, is it okay if I leave you here to secure this evidence? I'll send someone over to assist as soon as I can.'

As Mike nodded, Paolo grabbed his phone and called Andrea. 'I need you to organise a warrant at this address.' He waited until she had repeated it back to him. 'It is a matter of the utmost urgency. I

214

think that is where Marissa Piper is being held. Arrange backup and then meet me there as soon as the warrant comes through. Can you also get an ambulance out to the address as well? We don't know what might have happened to Marissa. She could need medical attention. I also need a team to come to the Fit to Go Gym. Mike will wait here for them and explain what has to be bagged and tagged.'

As he was about to leave, he remembered Soames had looked relieved when he had confirmed Callum's alibi for the night Sasha was murdered. He turned back to the assistant manager.

'When I first spoke to you and asked for your whereabouts the night of the murder, you said you were downstairs and Callum was in the office. We now have reason to believe he left here early that night. Why did you not tell us that?'

Soames' face turned bright red. 'I didn't know!' he said.

'How could you not know? For god's sake, man, tell me. I don't have time for your histrionics.'

'Please don't tell my wife.'

'I bloody will if you don't answer me.'

'I was in the medical room with the door locked. I'm having an affair with one of our members. I don't know if Callum left that night.'

Resisting the urge to punch him, Paolo went to find CC. If John Soames hadn't lied just to cover his own tracks, Marissa might never have been put in danger. CC was already waiting by the door. Thank God he never needed to explain to her what needed to be done.

'Let's go, CC. I just hope we get there in time.'

Chapter Thirty-eight

As CC pulled the car to a screeching halt outside Callum Jennens' detached house, Paolo pointed to the driveway.

'Look at the car.'

CC nodded. 'It would certainly fit the model we saw on the CCTV footage the night Marissa was taken.'

Paolo was now more convinced than ever that Marissa was being held by Callum, whether inside this house, or somewhere else remained to be seen. He looked at his watch. It was only half an hour since he'd asked Andrea to secure the warrant. It felt like hours.

'CC, I don't think we should wait. Let's see if we can get Jennens to let us in. Just follow my lead on this. Okay?'

'I'm ready, sir.'

Paolo got out of the car and waited for CC to do the same and lock it. As they walked along the short drive Paolo thought he saw one of the downstairs net curtains move.

'Did you see that, CC?'

'The curtain?'

Paolo nodded. 'I think he's going to be on his guard. Let's keep it as friendly as possible until Andrea arrives with the warrant and backup.'

They reached the front door and Paolo rang the bell. It was answered almost immediately, but only opened as far as the security chain allowed. Callum Jennens peered through the gap. He looked dishevelled and had some nasty-looking cuts on his face.

Paolo smiled. 'Sorry to disturb you at home, Callum, but we

have a few questions to ask and your assistant manager said he didn't know when you would be back at work. Is it okay if we come in?'

Callum shook his head. 'Now isn't exactly a good time for me. Perhaps you could call back later, or I could come to the station. Yes, that would be best. I'll come to the station.'

As he said the words, he began to close the door. Paolo put his hand out to stop him.

'I wouldn't put you to so much trouble. We only have a couple of questions. It isn't worth making you come down to the station when I'm sure you could answer them now.'

'I'm not feeling very well at the moment,' Callum said. 'I need to go and lie down.'

Paolo put his foot in the doorway. 'Is that your car on the drive? Is it a nice little runner? I'm thinking of buying one for my daughter. She's in Africa at the moment. Would you recommend it for a young woman?'

Callum looked confused, but nodded. 'Yes, I suppose so. Look, I really need to go. Hang on, what's she doing?'

Paolo pretended he hadn't seen CC move to peer in through the window.

'Detective Sergeant Connors, come here this instant and apologise to Mr Jennens.' He turned to Callum. 'I must apologise for my colleague; I have no idea what she was doing.'

CC came back, giving Paolo an infinitesimal shake of the head. 'Sorry, sir. House interiors are my passion.'

Jennens looked anything but convinced and tried again to close the door. At that moment Paolo heard the sound he'd been waiting for. The sirens were faint, but getting louder. He had to keep Callum talking. Who knew what he might do to Marissa if he was able to close the door and get to her. Paolo was praying he wasn't too late. Whatever happened, he wasn't going to allow Jennens back into the house.

'What year is it?'

'What?'

'Your car. Did you buy it new or second-hand?'

'Why do you want to know?'

The sirens could now be heard coming ever closer. Callum tried once again to close the door.

'Please move your foot. I need to go.'

Paolo nodded as if he had every intention of complying. 'Yes, of course. Sorry, I can see you're feeling unwell. Tell me, how did you come by those terrible scratches on your face?'

'I . . . I fell . . . that's right . . . I fell over while I was gardening. I fell into a rose bush.'

Two squad cars pulled up in the street and Paolo was relieved to see Andrea get out of one brandishing the warrant. Paolo kept his foot in the door as she ran up to join him. As she handed over the warrant, the welcome siren of an ambulance getting ever closer added to the noise level.

'Mr Jennens,' Paolo said, raising his voice to make sure he was heard clearly, 'this is a warrant enabling us to search your home and outbuildings.'

'Why? I'm not hiding anyone.'

Paolo smiled. 'What makes you think we are looking for someone?'

'Because . . . I . . . because of . . . you were asking at the gym about Sasha.'

'We were, but you knew Sasha was dead. We spoke about her at the gym. How did you know we are now looking for someone else?'

'I didn't!'

'Step aside, please. We have the right to enter your premises. If you wish to call your solicitor, you may do so, but you cannot impede our search in any way. I suggest you either open the door, or move away as one of my men will force it open.'

Callum's face disappeared from view. Paolo heard the sound of his footsteps as he ran towards the back of the house. He signalled to one of the uniformed officers to come forward.

'Break the chain.'

In minutes the door was open and they could enter. The hallway was wide with doors leading off from either side. A central staircase led upstairs. At the far end was an open door, leading into what looked like the kitchen. Paolo pointed towards the back of the house.

'A young woman has been missing for several days. We have good reason to believe she is being held here. Tear the place apart if you have to, but we need to find her. You men, take the doors to the right. CC, you and I will tackle the doors on the left. Andrea, take four men and search upstairs, in case he headed up there.'

They split up.

The first door Paolo opened led into a spacious lounge, but it was dominated by heavy dark furniture that might have been popular when Victoria was on the throne. Paolo found it depressing, but he wasn't there to criticise Jennens' taste in home décor.

'Where do you think that door leads?' CC asked, pointing to the far side of the room.

'Good question. Let's have a look.'

CC opened the door and Callum Jennens leaped out of a shallow cupboard, brandishing a length of chain.

'You can't have her. She's mine. She loves me.'

Paolo and CC stepped back, out of range of the swinging chain.

'Now, Callum, you don't want to hurt me or my colleague, do you?' Paolo said, nodding his head as a signal to CC. Thankful that she'd picked up on his meaning, Paolo was pleased to see her move to Callum's left, making it harder for the man to keep both of them in range.

Paolo took half a step forward.

'Stay there,' Callum hissed.

Behind them, Paolo heard more officers coming into the room.

'Get out,' Callum screamed. 'Get out of Grammy's house. You're making it dirty. Grandpa gets mad at her if the house gets dirty.'

Paolo took a step to Callum's right.

'I'm going to sit in that nice comfortable chair.'

'No!' Callum yelled. 'That's Grandpa's chair. No one sits in that chair.'

'I'm going to sit there,' Paolo said, making sure he had Callum's full attention. 'And then I'm going to put my feet up on that nice clean table.'

Callum lunged at him, but as he did so, Paolo saw CC flick out her leg. Her foot connected with his body, and he crumpled. Paolo leaped forward and snatched the chain from his hand. He dragged Callum to his feet and pushed him towards a uniformed officer.

'Keep Mr Jennens company in here. He is not to leave this room under any circumstances unless accompanied. Understood?'

He watched as Callum was taken to a sofa and made to sit down. Two officers stood over him.

'It would go better for you if you tell me where Marissa Piper is. Certainly your home would suffer less damage.'

'She loves me.'

Paolo took a step forward. 'Sorry, what did you say?'

'She loves me. She wants to be with me.'

Paolo forced himself to remain calm. 'Fair enough, I'm sure it's a beautiful love affair, but where is she?'

Callum shook his head. 'If I tell you, you'll try to come between us and she wants us to be together.'

'If she wants to be with you, I promise I won't do anything to break up your relationship, but why don't you let me talk to her? She can tell me herself.'

Callum shook his head, tears flowing. 'You'll take her away from me. I know you will.'

He put his head on one side. It looked to Paolo as if he was listening to someone.

'No, Grammy, I had to do it.'

Realising Callum was answering a voice only he could hear, Paolo signalled to the uniformed officer that he should keep Callum in the room. He nodded towards the door and CC took the hint. As soon as they were both outside, Paolo shut the door, but could still hear Callum arguing.

'An act? Or a genuine madman?' CC asked.

'That's for the courts to decide, but he's not completely sane in my eyes.'

A shout from below interrupted them.

'Down here, sir. We've a locked door.'

220

Paolo hurried down the steps to the cellar. The door looked heavily reinforced. It wouldn't be easy to break it down.

'No sign of any key?'

'No, sir.'

'Wait here,' Paolo said.

He ran up the steps and entered the lounge. Callum was still involved in his one-sided conversation.

'I need the key to the cellar.'

'Grammy, I had to! I had to make her love me. She took the sweet.'

Paolo rushed across the room and shook Callum. 'Focus on me, Callum. Look at me! Where is the key?'

He didn't answer, but his hand went to his trouser pocket as if confirming something was still there.

'Do you have it on you?'

'Grammy, I love her.'

'Officer, hold his arms. I need to search his pocket.'

Callum put up no resistance when the officer held his arms behind his back, but struggled to get free the moment Paolo reached into the pocket he'd just touched.

'No! No! You can't go in there. She's mine.'

Paolo pulled the key free and ran downstairs. He didn't have time to argue with a nutcase. He put the key in the lock and felt an enormous sense of relief when the door swung open.

The stench of unwashed body odour hit him as he entered the small room. Feverishly, he felt for a light switch and flicked it. Although still gloomy, the light was enough for him to see the outline of a woman chained to a bed against the far wall. She wasn't moving.

'We need medics down here. Now!' he yelled as he ran over to the bed.

He knelt down and felt for a pulse. It was there, but faint.

'For fuck's sake, someone help this woman,' he shouted.

'It's okay. We're here,' a voice sounded by his ear. 'Please move away, sir, so that we can get to her.'

Paolo stood and turned to the second paramedic standing by the bed. 'I take it she'll be going straight to hospital when you've stabilised her?'

She nodded.

'CC, stay here and secure this scene when the paramedics have done their job. I'll be upstairs if you need me.'

He took the stairs two at a time, telling himself to calm down when all he wanted to do was strangle the bastard who'd locked up Marissa in that dungeon. By the time he reached the lounge he was sufficiently in control to be able to keep his hands to himself.

'Callum Jennens, I am arresting you for the kidnap and assault of Marissa Piper.'

'But she wanted to be with me.'

Paolo took a deep breath and continued with the caution, ignoring Callum's pleas of innocence.

'There will be a further charge of the murder of Sasha Carmichael.'

Callum shook his head. 'That was an accident.'

Paolo held up his hand. 'I strongly advise you to call on a solicitor before you say anything else.' The rage he'd had almost under control nearly consumed Paolo. He had to get Callum out of the room before he gave in to his desire to choke the man. He looked at the uniformed officers. 'Take him away and book him. I'll be back to the station shortly.'

As he was about to leave the lounge, the paramedics came past with Marissa on a stretcher.

'My love,' Callum shouted, trying to pull away from the officers holding him.

Paolo rushed forward and grabbed Callum's arms, dragging him back into the room.

'Leave her be,' he hissed in Callum's ear. 'You've done enough damage to that poor woman.'

'But she loves me,' Callum wailed. 'She loves me.'

Paolo and the two officers held on to Callum until they heard the siren signalling the ambulance was on its way to the hospital. He let go, feeling tainted just by coming into contact with the man.

'Get him out of my sight.'

'Yes, sir.'

Paolo watched as they half carried, half dragged Callum outside. While he was standing watching the scene, Andrea came down from the upper storey.

'There is some sort of shrine upstairs, sir,' she said.

'To one of the young women?'

She shook her head. 'No, sir, it's a bit weirder than that. It seems to be to a much older woman similar in looks to Callum Jennens. I think it might be a shrine to his grandmother.'

Paolo went with her to the next floor. The room she took him into was full of heavy dark furniture which was probably old-fashioned even when it was bought as new. The only bright place in the room was illuminated by several candles and a small jug holding a posy of roses. Above the makeshift altar was a shelf holding several pictures of the same woman. She looked careworn and fragile, but Andrea was right. There was a definite family resemblance. Paolo wondered if this was the 'Grammy' Callum had been listening to downstairs.

'I'll send up a photographer, although, if anything, photos of this are likely to help any defence strategy that pleads insanity.'

Andrea nodded. 'I know, but maybe he is insane. What he's done is not normal.'

Paolo sighed. 'To be honest, Andrea, I have no idea what normal is. All I do know is that I've dealt with so many sick minds over the last few years that nothing has the power to surprise me any more.'

'You sound down, sir.'

Thinking about Jack and Willows and all the crap he still had to face due to the lies Jack was telling, Paolo wondered if there was any point in trying to do his best. He gave himself a mental shake. He'd never been one to wallow in self-pity and he shouldn't start now, but his thoughts were gloomier than they'd ever been.

'Not really, Andrea. Just a bit off my game, that's all. I want you to go down and take over from CC in the cellar. Tell her to meet me at the car.'

She ran down the stairs. Paolo followed at a slower pace, thinking about his future in the force. Nothing had gone right since Dave's death. He'd even had a promotion forced on him that he'd have done anything to refuse. It was time for him to think about what he wanted from life. But first, he had a few cases to clear up.

Paolo checked the other rooms, confident all was being properly recorded, then left the house, surprised to see it was still light outside.

CC caught up with him just as he reached the car.

'Back to the station, sir?'

He nodded. 'Now that Marissa is safe, we can concentrate all our efforts on finding out where Brad is getting the drugs from. It's not enough to shut him down. When we get to the station, get in touch with financial crimes. See if they can find a trace back through his bank dealings to tie in with the supply. Also, I want all Brad's personal documents and computer analysed. In there somewhere will be the information we need about where the drugs originated.'

Chapter Thirty-nine

Paolo hoped everything they'd sent along to Interpol would be enough to shut down the operation. Obviously, he hadn't been able to share any information that might jeopardise their own case, but there was enough to point Interpol in the right direction. In the email he'd received in response, the sender said to expect a call about the evidence sharing. That was fine by him, but there wasn't really anything more they could send until all Brad's paperwork had been pored over by people more in tune with that side of law enforcement than Paolo would ever be.

When his phone rang he looked at the display. It was an international number. This must be the call from Interpol.

'Sterling.'

'This is Inspector Shepherd of Interpol. I just wanted to thank you for your assistance. We knew the drugs were going into your region, but weren't able to follow the route once the shipment left Spain. By closing down Brad Cooper's operation you've helped enormously.'

'No need for thanks,' Paolo said. 'We've passed along all the information we've found so far and will be happy to give you anything else that comes to light. I hope it will be enough to help shut down the North Africa to Spain operation.'

'I would hope so, too,' Inspector Shepherd said, 'but unfortunately, these gangs are like Hydra's head. We no sooner cut off one supply chain than another grows in its place.'

Paolo thought of the many smaller operations he'd shut down in Bradchester and acknowledged the truth in Shepherd's statement.

'At least they will have to regroup,' Paolo said. 'That will take time. Maybe that in itself might save a few lives.'

'I hope you're right. Like you, we do what we can to make it difficult for them to set up again,' Shepherd said. 'That's all we can do. Take care, DCI Sterling. Drug cartels like to punish those who interfere with their operations.'

Paolo smiled. 'They'll have to join a long queue of people who would like to see me pushed under a bus. Thanks for the call.'

'You're welcome.'

Paolo and CC followed the instructions given by the hospital reception and found Marissa's room. The emotion of finding Marissa alive was only just beginning to hit home and he felt drained, but if Marissa was up to making a statement, he wanted to get it down while events were fresh in her mind.

He tapped on the door and they went in. He was surprised to see Marissa sitting up. In the chair next to the bed was Angelica.

'Hello, ladies. Sorry to interrupt,' he said, 'but I'm afraid we need to ask Marissa some questions.'

Angelica stood up. 'I was just leaving anyway. Some of us have to work and can't lounge around in bed all day.'

She leaned forward and kissed Marissa's cheek.

'Thanks for coming,' Marissa said. Her voice was a bit croaky, but she sounded far more in control than Paolo had expected.

'Don't tire her out,' Angelica said as she left.

Paolo promised not to. He looked at CC who was ready to record their conversation.

'How are you?' he asked, taking the seat recently vacated by Angelica. CC pulled up a chair on the other side of the bed.

'Okay. Have you got that arsehole under lock and key?'

'We have. Don't worry; he won't be able to hurt you again.'

'Hurt me? If I get my hands on him I'll wring his miserable neck. If he hadn't taken me by surprise, there's no way he'd have been able to do what he did. Fucking arsehole. Excuse my French.'

226

CC laughed.

'That's the spirit,' she said. 'Look, I hope you don't mind me saying this, but even though you seem to be fully in control of your emotions, it might be a good idea to talk to someone about what you endured.'

Marissa smiled at CC and nodded. 'I have someone I can go to talk to. I was in therapy with her for a few years and she helped me get my life sorted by keeping journals. This is going to take more than a few pages.'

Paolo was pleased CC had raised that, but now they needed to get Marissa's account on record. 'Are you able to give a statement about what happened?'

She nodded.

'Before you start,' Paolo said, 'there is one thing that has been niggling at me. We know from Jennens' confession that he believed Sasha was in love with him because she took the love heart sweet and that is why he stalked and eventually killed her. From there, it seems you fell into the same trap. When did you take your sweet?'

She sighed. 'It must have been the night before I went on my last trip. I was in the changing room and chatting to one of the members. We were laughing about the fact that the sweets only ever had two choices, she loves me or she loves me not. I took a she loves me one and the other girl took she loves me not. It was just a joke. I can't believe he killed Sasha. He wasn't on my radar at all!'

'After you took the sweet, we believe he began to plan his abduction of you. He has confessed that he'd been listening in for some time to conversations in the changing room, which was how he knew which train you would be taking home that night.'

Marissa shrugged. 'You know, I can't even remember talking about it. I know Caroline, the girl I was with the night I took the sweet, was talking about getting a travelling rep's job. I was moaning about being away from home so much and often getting back late at night from some of my trips, so maybe I mentioned it then, but I honestly can't recall doing it.'

Back at the station, as he sat down at his desk, Paolo finally began to relax. The visit to the hospital had surprised him. Marissa, although far from a healthy state, had given a full and detailed statement. Mentally she was tough; she'd been able to fight back against Callum. Not many people, male or female, could have stayed so focused on getting free. Paolo admired her spirit.

As he felt some of the tension leaving his body, the quiet moment was interrupted by the strident tone of his phone.

'Sterling,' he said, barely able to summon the energy to answer the call.

'This is George Mendip. You left a message for me to call you back.'

'Ah, yes, Mr Mendip. I have some news for you. We have arrested the people who were responsible for supplying the ecstasy Sally took. It will be on the news later this evening, but I wanted you to hear from me rather than having it come up without any warning.'

Paolo heard Mendip sigh. 'Thank you.'

'I know it won't help you to deal with Sally's death, but I hope it gives you some comfort to know the men involved will be put away for a long time.'

'Not really. It's not going to bring my Sally back. My wife says you also lost a daughter some years ago. I'm sorry. I didn't know that when I said you could never understand how I feel. Does it ever stop hurting?'

Paolo took a moment before answering. 'Stop hurting? No. But it does get a little bit easier to cope with as the years pass. I'm sorry. I can't give you platitudes about time being a great healer or any of that crap. I still hurt every single day, but I'm much better at dealing with the pain.'

'Thank you for your honesty. I know you can't give me any details on the investigation, so I'll watch the news this evening with great interest.'

Paolo ended the call and thought about what he'd said to Mendip. Maybe he should have sugar-coated the truth, but he thought the MP genuinely wanted to know, from one grieving father to another.

Just as he was putting the phone back in his pocket it rang again.

Paolo looked at the display and was tempted to deny the call, but knew Chief Willows would simply keep calling until he answered.

'Paolo here, sir.'

'Could you please come up to my office, Paolo?'

'Is it urgent, sir? I am trying to get my reports finalised.'

'It is rather important. I would prefer to have the conversation sooner rather than later.'

Paolo could hear from Willows' voice this wasn't going to be a meeting to enjoy. Better to get it over with.

'I'm on my way up, sir.'

'Thank you.'

The phone went dead. Paolo stood up. So much for taking a moment to reflect, he thought. He went into the main office and made for CC's desk.

'I have to go upstairs for a chat. Afterwards we can go over the details of Marissa's statement. Not that we really need it after Jennens spilled his heart out, but it's as well to do a belt and braces job, just in case some clever barrister tries to make out he was coerced into a confession.'

CC nodded. 'Absolutely. I'll be ready for you when you come down.'

Paolo smiled and turned for the stairs.

Willows' door was open, so Paolo tapped on it and went in.

'Close the door and sit down, Paolo.'

Paolo flicked the door closed and wandered over to the desk. He sat down and waited. It seemed, having dragged him up here, that Willows didn't know how to say whatever it was that needed to be said.

'Paolo, I've given a great deal of thought to the situation in which Jack found himself. I have spoken to him extensively and he puts forward a persuasive case for being the victim of an unfair order, leading to his life being put in danger.'

He put up his hand as Paolo attempted to speak.

'Let me finish. I wasn't fully convinced by what he had to say, but obviously, there will have to be an inquiry into what actually transpired. I wanted you to know about it in advance.'

'When will it be?'

'Probably in a month or so. We need DC Cummings to be recovered sufficiently to be able to attend the hearing.'

Forcing himself to remain calm, Paolo took a deep breath. 'What happens between now and the inquiry's conclusion?'

'You are, from this moment, on administrative duties only.'

'And the cases I've been dealing with?'

'I will be calling Detective Sergeant Connors up to fill her in on this situation. She will take over until such time as either you are cleared to resume your duties, or someone else is drafted in to take your place.'

Barely able to breathe, let alone speak, Paolo nodded and headed for the door.

'Please ask DS Connors to come up.'

Paolo walked back down to the office in a daze. CC must have seen something in his face because she stood up and came towards him as he crossed the office.

'Paolo, what is it? What's happened?'

He laughed, but even to his own ears it sounded more like a hyena baying than anything human.

'I'm not sure, CC, but I think I'm close to being fired.'

'What? No! Why?'

'Willows wants you to go upstairs. He'll fill you in. I'm going home.'

'But what about going over Marissa's testimony to make sure of our case?'

'Go upstairs, CC. You'll understand everything then.'

She stood for a moment looking confused, then shook her head and turned for the stairs. Paolo watched her go. Administrative duties? Filing reports and doing menial tasks to pass the time? Screw that! He was owed several weeks' leave. Now was probably the right time to take it.

Chapter Forty

The hustle and bustle of traffic outside Heathrow departures was amazing at such an early hour of the morning. Paolo took both cases out of the taxi and smiled at Lydia.

'No regrets?' she asked, taking the handle of her suitcase.

Paolo laughed. 'Nothing to regret. My choice was hanging around the station getting in everyone's way, or going with you to visit our lovely daughter in Africa for a few weeks. What's there in that to regret?'

Lydia smiled. 'You'll be ready to fight your corner by the time we get back.'

'If I want to fight. I've only ever known being in the force. Maybe it's time to reconsider. See if there's something else I'd rather be doing.'

As they walked into the airport, Paolo thought about what he'd just said and smiled. He would put all thoughts of his work life on hold for a bit and enjoy a holiday. Who knew what the future would bring, especially for him and Lydia. They'd tried once before but failed to make a go of it after their acrimonious divorce. Maybe this time it would work out. Maybe it wouldn't. Work, romance, life: he'd worry about all three when he got back from Africa.

He looked at Lydia and smiled. They were all problems for another day. For today and the next few weeks all he wanted was to be with her and Katy. The future could take care of itself.